THE VINEYARD IN ALSACE

BOOK 1, DOMAINE DES MONTAGNES

JULIE STOCK

CLUED UP PUBLISHING

THE VINEYARD IN ALSACE

ISBN: 9780993213519

This is a work of fiction. All names, characters, businesses, places, events and incidents, other than those clearly in the public domain, are either the products of the author's imagination or used in a fictitious manner. Any resemblance to actual companies, actual persons, living or dead, or actual events or localities is purely coincidental and not intended by the author.

Cover Design: www.Lawstondesign.com
Editing: Helena Fairfax
Proofreading: To The Letter Proofreading

To my grand-dad, Charles Kirzdorf.
Thank you for teaching me the importance of language and its ability to transcend barriers.

CHAPTER ONE

Fran

'Here, you can have this back!' I wrenched my engagement ring from my finger and flung it in the general direction of their naked bodies, huddled together under the sheet on the bed. *Our* bed. 'I obviously won't be needing it any more.'

'What the hell, Fran?' The thunderous look on Paul's face as the ring pinged against the metal bed frame almost made me doubt myself. I closed my eyes briefly. *Don't let him control you. You are definitely not the guilty party!*

I took one last look at him and then I turned and ran. I kept on running, as far and as fast as my legs would take me, blood pounding in my ears, my long hair whipping around my face. The whole time my mind raced with thoughts of his double betrayal.

Eventually, my body couldn't take any more and I stopped on the pavement near an underground station, doubled over and panting from the effort. Once I'd got my breath back a bit, I gave Ellie a call. She picked up on the first ring.

'Hey, Fran, how are you?'

That question pushed me over the edge into full-blown sobbing and once I'd started, I couldn't stop.

'What's the matter? Where are you? Is Paul there? Talk to me, please!'

'Hold on a minute,' I managed to choke out, wiping my face on the sleeve of my t-shirt. 'I'm at the Tube station and I need a place to stay. Paul...Paul...well, there is no Paul and me any more.'

I heard her sharp intake of breath before she said, 'Of course you must come here. Will you be okay on your own or do you want me to come and get you?'

'No, I'll be okay. I should be about half an hour. Thanks, Ellie.' I rang off and made my way down into the depths of the Tube, grateful that I would have somewhere to stay so I didn't have to go back home tonight. Afterwards, I couldn't remember finding my way to the platform. I was so distracted by all that had happened and in such a short space of time but the next thing I knew, I was squashed into a seat on a crowded rush-hour carriage, trundling north on the Northern line.

No-one spared me a second glance on the train. It was oddly calming to be sitting among complete strangers in my misery and to know I didn't have to explain myself. I wrapped my arms protectively around my body. *Why on earth had Paul done this to me?* I wracked my brain as the train rattled on, but I could make no sense of it.

When I arrived at Ellie's, she scooped me into her arms at once for a hug, which only made me start crying again. She patted my back comfortingly, and eventually the tears subsided.

'Why don't I get us both a drink and then you can tell me everything that's happened?'

I nodded silently. While Ellie was gone, my phone buzzed with yet another text message. It was from Paul, no doubt trying to find me, but I deleted it along with all the others and set the phone down on the table in front of me. Ellie returned shortly afterwards with two cups of tea. I wouldn't have minded something stronger under the circumstances but it probably wasn't a good idea to get drunk just now. I'd need a clear head for whatever was going to come next.

'So, what the hell has happened?'

And I told her.

'I can't even begin to process it, Ellie. Why would he do that to me in the first place but even worse, why would he do it to me just after we'd got engaged?'

'I don't know what to say, apart from telling you that I never really liked Paul - I'm sorry - and he's proved what a bastard he is by doing this to you. There's no excuse for cheating and you'll never be able to trust him again now.'

I winced at her honesty and at her harsh judgment of Paul.

'In just that one second, my life's been turned upside down. Everything I was planning on - you know, getting married, settling down, starting a family - is now in doubt. I feel like my life is over.' I set down my cup and let the tears roll down my face. My phone buzzed once more with another text. This time, I read it first.

'Where are you? I just want to know that you're okay. I'm really sorry, I've been incredibly stupid.'

'Well, at least he realises that much,' said Ellie, her lips tight with anger as I read it out to her.

My fingers hovered over the keypad but in the end, I deleted the message and turned off the phone.

'I'm going to bed, Ellie. I'm exhausted, and I just can't think straight. Hopefully, things will be clearer in the morning.'

Once I'd climbed into the little single bed in Ellie's spare room, sleep just wouldn't come. I tossed and turned restlessly as images of Paul in bed with this other woman invaded my mind. I thought again about what Ellie had said about never really liking Paul. Had I been taken in by him all this time? I covered my eyes with my hands, embarrassed by my foolishness. I lay there for hours, railing against the injustice of the situation and wondering how I would explain all this to my parents. By the time I finally fell asleep the sun was coming up but I had the beginnings of an idea about what I was going to do next.

'Are you really sure about this? You're still shaken up by what's happened and it's a bit early to be making decisions.' Ellie's concern was written all over her face and I knew it would be hard to leave my best friend behind when the time came.

We were on the Tube again travelling south into London from Ellie's flat in High Barnet and discussing my options on the way. I felt uncomfortable wearing one of Ellie's suits but I didn't have any choice. At least it would only be for today.

'I need to get away from him, Ellie, and from here. I've wanted to go back home for a while but Paul would never have entertained the idea so I didn't even bother discussing it with him. Well, now I don't need to think about what Paul wants. I can do what I like and what I want to do is to hand in my notice, move back to France and find a new job.'

'What kind of job will you be able to do there? They're not going to have the same opportunities in corporate banking as there are in London. Wasn't that the reason you came here in the first place? And didn't you always want to get away from the small town you grew up in?'

I pulled a face, looking round at the sea of miserable Monday-morning expressions. 'I don't want this life any more. I've given it a good try but it hasn't worked out and I'm ready to go home. I saw a great job at a vineyard just outside Strasbourg a few days ago, which isn't that far from where my parents live, but I didn't apply because I knew Paul wouldn't like it.'

'I had no idea that he was holding you back from going back home. You could have talked it over with me, you know.'

'I know and I'm sorry I didn't. I think I was afraid to confront how I was really feeling. Now things have changed, I'm going to go for it. If I get it, the ad said that there's accommodation available for me at the vineyard, so I can afford to take a pay cut.'

'And what about if you don't get the job? What will you do then?'

'If I don't get it, well, I can do my translating work anywhere. I'd prefer not to have to move back in with my parents but I might have to for now while I wait and see what happens. Amandine - my friend from university - is getting married back at home next weekend anyway so I'll just stay with my parents a little longer after that if needs be.'

'I'm just worried that you're going to make a hasty decision without considering all the options first, and then you'll regret it when you get back home. Not only that but if you go back to France, when will I see you?' She smiled at me but I knew she was only half-joking.

We both stood up as our stop approached, swaying as we tried to get our balance when the train came to a halt. Once off the train, I gave her a quick hug before we made our way towards the escalators carrying the mass of commuters up to ground level, where daylight beckoned.

'You are my best friend and we will always be there for each other, I hope you know that.' I stepped onto the escalator and turned back to look at Ellie's face as she stood on the step below me. 'Even though I'll hate leaving you behind, I need to do this, Ellie, for me. I've spent far too long doing what other people want me to do and it's time that I did what I want to do for once. Besides,' I continued after a slight pause, 'Alsace isn't that far away. You can fly to Strasbourg or even take the train from London via Paris.'

'Ooh, now you mention it, that does sound fun! I've never been to Alsace and it would be great to explore a different part of France.' Ellie grinned at me, drawn in by my idea, but I could tell she was still worried about me.

Once we'd gone our separate ways, I turned my thoughts to what I was going to do next. I had nearly a month's leave stacked up and I was planning to hand in my resignation and use my holiday as my notice period.

Half an hour later, I was walking out of the skyscraper I had worked in for the past four years with only a small box of paltry possessions to my name. My proposal had been accepted and I was then escorted promptly from the premises, my ID and security cards taken from me along the way. I'd expected to feel bereft but apart from a slight irritation at being manhandled off the site, I felt a great sense of relief. I'd never enjoyed working there once the honeymoon period had worn off but I'd become trapped, especially as Paul worked at the same company. Whenever I'd mentioned looking for another job, he'd always talked me out of it, telling me he liked us being together. Now, I'd been set free to do what I wanted to do and I couldn't wait to get started. I hurried back towards the Tube to make my way home to Ellie's flat.

As soon as I got back, I changed out of Ellie's suit and back into my clothes from the previous day. They weren't terribly clean but at least they were comfortable. Then I found the job I'd seen advertised by the agency again, filled in their application form and sent it off to the vineyard along with my CV. The closing date for applications was a couple of days away, so now I would just have to wait.

Feeling strengthened by my new resolve, I switched my phone on again, ready to go into battle with Paul at last. There were fifteen new messages from him. I went through each one but they all said the same thing, '*Where are you? Please come back so we can talk.*'

I deleted them all, realising that I had nothing to say to him after all. He had cheated on me and thrown all our wedding plans into disarray. What could he possibly say to put that right?

I put Ellie in the picture over dinner that night and to her credit, she didn't try to put me off.

'If you get the job, how far away from your parents' house will you be?'

'My parents live in Colmar but the vineyard is north from there, nearer to Strasbourg, about forty-five minutes away. So, far enough away that they won't be on my doorstep but near enough for me to get home from time to time.'

Ellie frowned slightly. 'So, you'll be far away from me and not exactly close to your family. Are you sure you'll be all right with readjusting to life on your own again?'

'I will miss you, of course, but I'll be okay. I can still talk to you on the phone, and you can definitely come and visit as soon as I'm settled. Right now, though, I want to wait to hear about the job application first, and then I'll tell my mum and dad what's happened after that.'

Didier

I could hardly believe it to be true. I read the email again just to make sure. A woman called Françoise Schell had applied for our vacancy at the vineyard, according to the message from the agency. I blew out a long breath, pushed my chair away from the desk and swung my legs up on to the edge. It had to be her. How many women could there be with that name who also happened to be bilingual in French and English? It had been four years since we had seen each other and I didn't expect to see her back in Alsace again. I pondered this good news for a minute or two longer before regaining my focus, putting my legs down and pulling myself back towards my laptop. I sent back an immediate reply asking the agency to invite her for an interview. If it really was the Françoise Schell I knew, I just had to hope that she would be prepared to put the past behind us so that we could work together for the benefit of the vineyard.

The door opened and my office manager appeared, his cheery face lifting my spirits as always and forcing me out of my reverie.

'*Salut*, Henri,' I said, shaking his hand.

'You look like you've had some good news.' He took off his jacket and sat down at his desk.

'We've had an application for the marketing manager position,' I replied, with a smile.

'That's great news. I can't believe we've had to wait so long. Tell me more.'

'Well, I don't know for sure but I think it might be an old friend of mine and if it is, I'm really happy about that because she'd be perfect for the job.'

'When you say old friend, what do you mean exactly?' He studied me closely. I'd told Henri a little about Fran but not everything.

'I think it might be Fran.' I stood up to make some coffees at the machine in the corner of the office. It was one of my few luxury purchases but we got good use out of it.

'That would be amazing if it is. But wouldn't it be a bit awkward, given what happened between you before?'

'Definitely. But I would love to rebuild our friendship and if we could do that, any awkwardness would be worth it.' I pressed the button on the machine and watched as two coffees filtered out into the cups below. I stirred them and handed one to Henri, which he accepted with a grateful smile. 'I just hope she comes for the interview.'

After a quick coffee, I pulled my boots back on and wandered out into the courtyard to make my way down to the vineyard for my usual morning visit. As soon as I appeared outside my dog, Princesse, joined me for the walk. She looked like she'd been exploring already, her sleek, red coat dotted with flecks of mud and obvious debris from the undergrowth.

As we emerged through the archway, I looked upon the view of the estate and felt the familiar sense of pride I associated with the land my family had worked for several generations. Not for the first time, I wished my father were still here to give me the benefit of his advice as I approached only my fourth harvest on my own. I tried to enjoy the beauty of the view rather than thinking about the painful past and the constant struggle to balance the books. The light mist over the vineyards was such a wonderful sight, it lifted my spirits immediately.

People were working here and there along the rows of vines as I walked along, and I greeted them all by name, like members of my own family.

'*Bonjour,* Etienne. *Ça va?*' I shook the old man's extended hand before moving on. When I spotted my winemaker, Thierry, at the end of the next row of vines, I made my way towards him to see how he thought things were progressing with this year's vintage.

'*Salut,* Thierry. *Comment ça va ce matin?*' Thierry came out every day to check the vines, just as I did.

'*Ça va, oui.* It's still looking good for this year but it's a bit early to make any predictions, of course. We don't want to tempt fate.'

I watched as he crushed a grape between his fingers and tasted the juice, his frown confirming his comments. I'd worked with Thierry long enough to trust his judgment but I still felt anxious about the harvest every year. I knew only too well how much the future of the vineyard, and all the people working in it, depended on a successful harvest; this year was no exception.

I spent the rest of the morning in the office sorting out bills for payment but just before lunch, the phone rang. Henri answered it and immediately pulled a face. I tried to make out the name he was mouthing to me and when I did, my heart sank.

'Isabelle.' I had nothing else to say to her now, no pleasantries, no bitter exchanges. She had worn me down.

'I am calling to check that you are still able to look after Chlöe this weekend. I have an important photo shoot to attend in Paris.'

'Yes. You do not need to check this with me. When will you bring her over?' My jaw had tensed from the moment I answered the phone and I had to consciously force myself to keep calm.

'I'll bring her to you on Saturday morning. I can't travel to you on Friday evening because we will be returning very late to Strasbourg and I will be far too tired to bring her then.'

Of course you will. Never mind whether Chlöe is tired or not.

'Fine. I will see you there on Saturday morning at eleven. Is there anything else?' I'd tried hard not to sound bitter but I still hadn't got over the impact of our separation. As I replaced my phone on the desk, I thought about our beautiful daughter and how much I missed her. She was the only good thing about my partnership with Isabelle; I couldn't wait to see her again and spend time with her over the weekend.

CHAPTER TWO

Fran

The next day got off to a good start. I opened my laptop to find an email waiting for me from the vineyard and held my breath as I clicked to open it. Then I jumped up to let out a great big whoop of delight when I realised that they were offering me an interview. I sent off a text to Ellie to let her know and then I realised that I would have to meet up with Paul in order to pick up my stuff. My heart sank as I thought about how awkward that was going to be. I knew he'd have lots of questions about what I was doing - questions I didn't want to answer. I thought about clearing out my things while he was at work but that seemed underhand. In the end, I decided to meet and talk to him first, and collect my stuff later.

'I'm ready to meet with you this evening if you're free. I can come round at six.'

He replied almost instantly.

'Thank God. It's so good to hear from you. I'll see you then x'

Needless to say, his kiss was lost on me. I slumped down into a chair, knowing that this was it. I felt really sad suddenly and on the brink of tears. I had given nearly four years of my life to this relationship and now I was going to have nothing to show for it. I had loved him and thought that we would spend the rest of our lives together, but now all of that commitment had been threatened and I was facing life on my own again.

At six that evening, I arrived promptly at the flat we'd been renting in Highgate. I decided to ring the entry buzzer rather than use my own key, and as I waited for Paul to answer, all the strangeness of the situation hit me. This used to be my refuge and now I hated it. Paul buzzed me in and I made my way slowly up to the first floor. He was on the doorstep by the time I got there, hopping restlessly from one foot to the other. I took in his swarthy face and his close-cropped hair and wondered what I'd ever seen in him.

'Hi,' he gushed, as though I were a long-lost friend. He stood back awkwardly to let me in. I brushed past him in the narrow doorway, unable to avoid his little paunch that had been steadily increasing in size over the past year. He knew better at least than to reach out and touch me. I made my way down the hallway, past the two bedrooms and the bathroom and into the large, bright lounge that I used to love so much. I sat in the only armchair so he couldn't sit next to me.

'Would you like a glass of wine?' He held up a bottle of Merlot, gesturing at the two wine glasses on the table.

'No, thanks. This really isn't a social call.'

'Please don't be like that. I told you in my texts, it was a stupid mistake. It was just sex after too much to drink. I don't feel anything for her, not like I love you.' His face was pained but his light tone gave him away.

I snorted in disbelief. I didn't even know I had a snort in me but some occasions demand it and lo and behold, a snort appeared.

'How can you say you love me when you betrayed me by having sex with another woman? It doesn't make me feel any better about this whole damn mess that you feel it was a stupid, drunken mistake. You still did it and I don't know if I can ever forgive you.' I stood up and started pacing.

'You can't really mean that. What about the wedding and all our plans?' His mouth dropped open and for a moment, he was speechless.

'Oh, so did you conveniently forget our wedding plans when you were in bed with someone else?' I shook my head in an effort to calm down. His ridiculous comments were only fuelling my anger.

'Look, I know I've been a fool but I really don't want to jeopardise what we have together. I do still love you.' Despite his declaration, there was a calculating look in his expression that only served to convince me that he was lying.

'Relationships are built on trust, Paul. How could I ever trust you again after this, or expect you to respect me if I just take you back without a word? No, this has been a wake-up call for me.' I sank back down into the nearest chair, suddenly weary of all the arguing. I took a deep breath before continuing. 'To be honest, Paul, we've been growing apart for some time.' I held up my hand to stop him interrupting and watched as he collapsed on to the sofa, a wary look on his face. 'I've been trying to leave the bank for ages, to move on and get a better job but you always talk me out of it. In fact, you've never been happy with me having a life of my own, visiting friends or even going home to see my parents.' I sat up straighter as I warmed to my theme. 'I'll come round tomorrow to collect my things. I'm going home to France to attend my friend's wedding. Then I'll look for a new job. This so-called relationship is over.' I stood in front of him and folded my arms.

'What? You're moving out and going back to France, just like that?'

'Just like what? You surely didn't expect me to stay after you cheated on me?' I stared at him, daring him to argue but to my surprise, he did.

'I didn't expect you to over-react like this, no. But you've made yourself very clear. If you feel like that, maybe I'm better off without you.' He had such a smug look on his face as he said it that it was all I could do not to slap him.

'Well, thanks for all that, Paul.' I prepared to go and he came towards me then, arms outstretched, obviously regretting his little outburst. I put my hands up, warning him off.

'Don't you dare touch me.'

'Fran, please, I'm sorry, I didn't mean what I said. I'm just angry.'

'So am I, Paul, but I'm angry at myself for letting you control me for so long.'

With that, I turned abruptly towards the hall and marched off to the door. He followed me but he didn't say another word. I looked back as I reached the top of the staircase to the ground floor, taking in the flicker of anger on his face, and I hoped he had finally got the message.

Didier

That afternoon, the agency contacted us again to suggest that we schedule the interview for our marketing manager for Thursday because the candidate had quite a way to travel.

'This must be your lady then. I think you're right,' Henri said as soon as he'd put the phone down.

'I feel hopeful but I don't want to get ahead of myself, just in case it isn't her.'

Henri nodded before continuing. 'The agency will have told her the name of the estate, though, so if it is her, she'll know she's going to see you again.'

'No, I never told her the name of the estate and, because it's not named after our family name, she won't be able to work it out. It will probably be quite a surprise for her when she sees me again.'

I was looking forward to seeing Fran again, despite the way we had parted.

Henri and I worked steadily through the afternoon before calling it a day around five. I went back to the cottage with Princesse at my heels and once she was settled, I made my way upstairs to get ready for dinner with my mother.

'*Salut, Maman.*' I kissed her on both cheeks in greeting after coming in through the back garden of her cottage.

'*Ça va, chéri?*' She looked up from the pile of papers she was studying with a smile.

'Not bad, thanks. How about you? What's all that you're looking at?' I frowned to think of her working so late, even though I knew she liked to keep herself busy.

'Oh, just administrative stuff from the government about the new regional specifications for independent winegrowers.' She sighed, took off her glasses and rubbed her eyes. 'Let's not talk business for the moment. What would you like to drink? I thought we might go out for dinner tonight for a change.'

'Can I have a beer please, *Maman*?'

She put the opened bottle and a glass on the table in front of me and I picked the bottle up before relaxing back into my chair.

'Some habits die hard,' I told her with a grin, noticing how she had pursed her lips as I took the first pull straight from the bottle.

'So, how has your week been?'

She asked me this every week, but I had to think carefully about how to phrase my answer this time.

'Well, you know the marketing manager job we've advertised?' She nodded. 'We hadn't had any suitable applications before this week but now we've had one from a familiar name.' I paused to let her think about it.

'Well, go on, I can't stand the suspense!'

'Fran has applied for the job.' She looked blank. 'Françoise - the girl I met at university.'

I watched her face fall in disappointment.

'Hmm. Well, I'm not sure you want her working at the vineyard, after she abandoned you in your hour of need.'

'Don't be like that. You know I didn't tell her about *Papa*. It wouldn't have been fair.'

'Fair to who, Didier? If she had really loved you, she would have stayed with you.'

'Well, she might feel the same about me - that I abandoned her because I didn't go with her to London. I decided to stay because of *Papa* but she didn't know that and it wouldn't have been fair to push her to stay with me.' I shrugged. 'Time has moved on and things have changed for both of us. We need a marketing manager and Fran has the qualifications for the job.'

My mother stared at me with obvious concern in her hazel eyes. 'You know nothing of her big city life over the past few years and she knows nothing of yours here in Alsace. You have a child now and the responsibilities that go with that. You need to think very carefully before leaping into anything new.'

'I know that, *Maman*. This is work and I'm not planning on leaping into anything.' I threw my hands up and gave her a smile, making her laugh.

'Come on, it is time for some dinner and you can bring me up-to-date with everything that is happening with my little grand-daughter.'

Fran

I kissed Ellie goodbye the next day before she went off to work, promising to be in touch regularly, and then set off once more for the home I'd shared with Paul. It was a bright, sunny day, giving me the courage to get going with my plans for a fresh start. I used my key to enter the main building but when I walked upstairs to our front door, there was an older man there, changing the locks. The old suitcase I'd kept in the bedroom was standing outside the flat Paul and I had shared. What a miserable bastard Paul had turned out to be!

'Erm, excuse me, can I come in? He's not here, is he?' I asked the workman, hoping he'd take pity on me.

'No, he's not, but he told me not to let you in,' the man told me grimly. He glanced up at me with sympathy in his eyes, though, and I managed a weak smile. 'Look,' he continued, 'if you make it quick, you should be able to do what you need to before I'm finished here.'

I nodded at him gratefully and slipped past, taking my suitcase with me. I did a quick sweep of the living room, kitchen and bathroom, checking Paul hadn't kept anything of real value to me before opening the suitcase to see what was in it. It was filled with clothes and toiletries, nothing more. I paused for a moment, trying to remember anything else I wanted to take with me. Suddenly, I remembered my grandmother's music box and I went to the bedroom to look for it. Thankfully, it had escaped Paul's notice and I picked it up carefully, wrapped it in one of my t-shirts and stored it in my case. Apart from that, there were only a few small pieces of furniture that were mine and I couldn't do anything but leave those behind - like the life I'd had with Paul. I thanked the workman as I left the flat and walked away from my old life.

By half past ten, I was on my way again, but this time to London St. Pancras to catch my Eurostar train to Paris. I sat on the Tube with my suitcase containing all my worldly possessions, thinking of all the good memories I had and trying not to feel regret for what had been lost. I heaved a big sigh but I knew in my heart that I was ready to set off for the brave new world. Only this time, that meant going back to France.

It was early afternoon by the time I got to Paris. As soon as I stepped off the train and into the bustling Gare du Nord, I felt like I'd come home. The heavenly smells from the *boulangeries* combined with the industrial smell of the trains told me I was in France and I realised it was more than three years since I'd last been here. My connecting train left from the Gare de L'Est, which was within walking distance, and so I set off for a stroll along the Parisian streets I was once so familiar with. I smiled as I came out onto Rue d'Alsace just ten minutes later. I was looking forward to going home.

After a *baguette au jambon* and a quick *café* at the station, I made my way to the departures board to see which platform my TGV train to Strasbourg would be leaving from. Once on the train, I found my seat fairly quickly and sank my tired body into the chair for the two-hour journey that was to come. The train left right on time and I leaned my head back and watched the landscape change from city to suburbs to green fields in no time at all. When I next lifted my head, the light had changed a little and I realised that I must have fallen asleep for a while. Looking at my watch, I couldn't believe that I had actually slept for just over an hour and we were now travelling through the Meuse region towards Alsace-Lorraine. I sat up and stretched and then retrieved my phone from my bag. There was a message from Ellie.

'Bonjour, chérie! Are you nearly there yet? Take care and let me know how everything goes. Good luck!'

That made me smile because she was virtually allergic to any foreign language. My interview was scheduled for ten the next morning so I'd booked into one of the cheap hotel chains in Strasbourg for my overnight stay. I was planning to spend a pleasant evening reacquainting myself with the city where I had spent my university years, before getting an early night.

After unpacking my essentials, I had a quick shower and went off to find somewhere nice to eat. As I wandered alongside the River Ill, admiring all the colourful canal boats, I regretted not having come back sooner. I crossed over the river and made my way to the small island in the city known as Petite France. There were window boxes hanging from the rails all along the water's edge, bursting with bright red and pink geraniums. The cobbled streets of the old quarter made for an enjoyable wander and I soon found a bistro that looked inviting for dinner. As I sat outside, feeling the warmth of the evening sun on my skin, all the tension in my shoulders slowly eased. I glanced down at my ringless wedding finger and I knew that I had made the right decision to return home. I was optimistic about the job interview the next day and confident that it was going to be the first step towards my new life.

In the taxi the next morning, I began to feel a bit nervous about how the interview would go. I knew I had all the skills they required but it had been a while since I'd applied for a new job. They'd probably conduct the interview in French too and I worried that my spoken French might be a bit rusty at first. I twisted my fingers together, considering all the things that could go wrong. By the time the taxi arrived just ten minutes after leaving the city, my confidence of the previous evening had evaporated.

I paid the driver and climbed out of the car, anxiously patting my hair to check it was still neatly tied back and smoothing down my navy linen dress and jacket to help straighten out the creases caused by the short journey. I was standing in an old courtyard with buildings on all sides. There wasn't a soul to be seen. I saw an open door on the other side of the courtyard and made my way towards it. My heels clicked on the cobblestones - they were definitely not as easy to walk in as my flats had been in the city last night. I grimaced as I picked my way painstakingly towards the open door. I was almost there when a dog came bounding out of the building at breakneck speed, barking a joyous welcome at me before spinning round and round me in excitement. I smiled at the dog's enthusiasm and tried to reach out and pet it, only to find the dog jumping up at me. I turned away, not wanting to get my outfit dirty, and wobbled, sure I was going to lose my balance and fall. Suddenly, I felt a strong pair of arms go round my waist, halting my tumble and saving me from embarrassment. I glanced down to see the muscled, tanned arms that were holding me, just before they set me upright again. I gathered myself together and turned round to face the man who had saved me from disaster. My mouth dropped open in surprise.

'Didier? *C'est toi?*' I felt my cheeks redden as I recognised the man in front of me.

'*Oui,* Fran, *c'est moi.*' He grinned at me, holding tight to the dog's collar, which he had managed to grab before it tackled me again. 'You have come for the interview, yes?'

Now I was thrown. 'How do you know about that? Do you work here?'

'*Certainement*. I'm the *Domaine* manager. Your interview is with me.' He disappeared back inside the building, re-emerging a few minutes later *sans chien* and beckoned me across the courtyard to another building.

I had no choice but to follow him, my mind whirring. Could this self-assured man be the same Didier I had known in my student days? The one I had left behind when I went to London? I really wanted this job but could I handle working alongside Didier, after all that had happened between us in the past? I decided to carry on as if we didn't know each other and to be as professional as I would have been without him there. He led me into a small office and gestured for me to take a seat. He pulled a swivel chair out from behind the other side of the desk and wheeled it nearer, sitting down very close to me in the confined space. His closeness unnerved me and all thoughts of professionalism suddenly went out the window.

'*Alors*, it's a pleasure to see you again. Is it really just four years since we were at university together?'

I nodded, incapable of speech. I took a deep breath and tried to control my pounding heart. He studied my CV for a minute, giving me time to look at him. His dark, curly hair was longer than I remembered and kept flopping in front of his eyes. His skin was a golden brown, no doubt from working outside in the vineyard, and his body looked toned and fit, even in a slightly crumpled t-shirt and jeans. He'd put on a pair of black, square glasses to read the paperwork, which only seemed to add to his allure. He looked up then, staring right at me with his mesmerising green eyes and I knew that it would be easy to fall under his spell once more.

'Let me tell you more about the job. It is for a marketing manager for the *Domaine* who must be able to speak English and French fluently. You can still speak French, yes, after being in England so long?' His eyes twinkled and I noticed his lips turning up at the corners. I suddenly remembered what those lips tasted like and the thought warmed my whole body this time. He was waiting for a reply.

'Yes, of course. I was working as a bilingual translator in the marketing department of a large bank in London.'

'And what is it that has persuaded you to come back here after so long? You were very happy to be leaving Alsace when I last saw you.' He glanced away as he said this and I recalled how upset he was when I told him I was leaving to take up the job in London.

'I...I felt it was time to come home, that's all. I had no idea you worked here, otherwise I wouldn't have wasted your time.' I stood up and so did he, bringing our bodies very close together.

He gazed deep into my eyes, trying to find the answers I wasn't prepared to reveal.

'It is not a waste of my time to be with you, Fran. It never has been and I think you would be a good person for this job. Please sit down and let me tell you more about it.' He took a step back towards the desk waiting to see what I would do. I hesitated for several seconds. Then, slowly, I sat down again.

CHAPTER THREE

Later that morning, I kicked off my shoes with relief and flopped onto the bed in my hotel room, just as my phone buzzed with a text.

'How's your first day of freedom been and how did the interview go?'

Bless Ellie for thinking of me.

'Freedom has been great. Interview was interesting, lots to tell you. I'll call you later.'

'Ooh, sounds intriguing. You'd better call me back. I want to know how soon I can come and stay!'

After a lazy lunch and another afternoon of sightseeing around Strasbourg, including some time wandering around the magnificent Gothic cathedral, I decided it was time to call Ellie for some advice. Leaving the pink hues of the minster behind me, I made my way back to my hotel wondering how exactly I would explain my feelings about the job to her. All day I had been wrestling with the common sense my head was telling me on the one hand, as opposed to what my heart was telling me on the other.

'Hey you, how was your day?' I asked when she picked up,

knowing how much she disliked her job at one of the investment banks in the City.

'Oh, the same old crap, you know, flak from the people calling in and from the staff you're trying to put them through to. You can't bloody win on reception. I still hate it as much as ever. I need a proper job. Anyway, enough of all that, what happened at the interview?'

So I told her all about it.

'Let me get this straight, then. You had your interview with the Didier you went out with when you were both at university - the same Didier you split up with when you came over here to work at the bank?'

'Yes, that's right. I haven't really told you the full story before, I'm sorry. It was all so painful and I just wanted to forget about it and move on. Anyway, I wanted him to come with me at the time but he said he couldn't move away from his family, and on top of that, if he wanted to get a job on a vineyard, he would have to train in France. I understood all his reasons but I couldn't forgive him for not coming with me so we didn't part on good terms.'

'Hmm. He offered you the job, though, and you obviously want the job, from what you've said about it.'

'I do! You should have seen the plans they've drawn up for the new Visitors' Centre and I'd be overseeing the setting up, the building works, the hiring of staff and the promotion. It would be such a wonderful opportunity for me.'

'So, why are you stalling?'

'If I took the job, I would have to work side by side with Didier every day, and I wouldn't even be able to get away from him in the evenings either. Given our history and everything that's happened with Paul, I just don't know if it would be the greatest idea to be this close to Didier again. Just sitting opposite him at the interview, I felt myself drawn in by him again, but so much has changed since we last saw each other. We need to keep a professional distance.'

'But what if he's in a relationship with someone else. Do you know?'

'I don't know. I did hear that he started seeing someone else after I left so I assumed that was the end of that. He could be married for all I know.'

'Exactly. You just don't know and I don't think you should let your past relationship get in the way of this wonderful job. You should put yourself first. You want the job. He said it's yours, so take it.'

'Well, when you put it like that, you make it all sound so easy! I think you're right. I'd regret it if I didn't take it.'

'Excellent. Can I come and visit for a weekend then? It's not too far out in the sticks, is it?' She laughed her rich, throaty laugh and I knew it would be lovely to see her.

'Let me accept the job first, and see what the accommodation is like, but you know I'd love to have your company for a whole weekend.'

That night, I lay in bed in the semi-darkness of the hotel room going over my conversation with Ellie and I knew she was right. Time had moved on for both Didier and me. I owed it to myself to take this job and to leave the past behind where it belonged.

Didier

'What do you want me to do then?' Henri asked me the next morning. 'About the job, I mean.'

'I want to know what Fran decides as soon as possible. Maybe we should ask her to come back to see the cottage? If she's unsure, that will definitely help her make up her mind. Could you give her a call this morning and invite her please?' I glanced at my watch and saw that it was still early. 'Wait till nine before calling, though. She might be enjoying a lie-in.'

My mind started to drift then, as I recalled how Fran had been every bit as beautiful as I'd remembered, with her long, dark hair framing her face, and her body had felt every bit as good too. I coughed awkwardly, hoping that my face wasn't giving my thoughts away, and tried hard to refocus on the work I had to do. In the end, I decided to go for a wander in the vineyard, hoping the fresh air would clear my mind for me, and I left Henri to the job of calling Fran.

I took the route across the grass and past the little cottage I had called home for the past two years. I realised I would have to move out if Fran did decide to take the job and I began to wonder how on earth I was going to make the château habitable both for myself and for Chlöe when she came to stay. I was inspecting some vines towards the bottom end of the estate when my mobile buzzed with a text.

'You might want to head back to the cottage to make sure it's tidy :)'

I chuckled at the warning from Henri, stood up and started the climb back up the hill.

I spent the next hour tidying the cottage as Henri had suggested. I had no idea I was so messy because normally, my housekeeper came in every day when I was at work and sorted everything out for me. Still, it was high time I got round to doing some of these things for myself. I worked my way steadily round the compact living room and the adjoining kitchen, picking up magazines, books and toys, throwing away empty cartons and the like, as well as doing the small amount of washing-up left over from breakfast.

I sat down on the single bedframe in Chlöe's room and looked around, realising with a pang of sadness that there were hardly any of her toys or clothes here. I decided I would talk to her over the weekend about how we might make her visits more homely for her. I put her few toys back in the basket we kept under the bed, straightened the duvet and crossed the tiny landing. I gave my room a quick glance, taking in the made bed and mostly tidy surfaces, decided it would do and ran back downstairs again. I shooed Princesse back outside and shut the doors so that I could give the floors a quick sweep.

When I'd finished, the cottage looked much more presentable and I was pleased with my efforts. The cottage was going to be the pièce de résistance in my plan to get Fran to accept the job, with its idyllic setting in the middle of a beautiful garden, as well as its views across the vineyard slopes from its typical blue shuttered windows. I was hoping she would fall in love with it and that it would be the final push she needed to say yes. I'd sensed she was nervous about working alongside me because of our history, so I needed to step up my game if I was going to persuade her to stay.

I left the cottage just before eleven and made my way back to the office to wait for Fran to arrive. I wanted to be there when she stepped out of the taxi this time, so that I could take her straight down to see the cottage. I had a feeling it would be as high on her list of priorities as it was on mine. It wasn't long before I heard the crunch of gravel in the courtyard and I went outside to meet her once again.

Fran

Didier opened the car door and put his hand out towards me, obliging me to take it. His rough, calloused hands spoke of the hours he must have already spent working the vines on the estate and I found them reassuring. He let go of my hand and I realised we were standing very close to each other once again. I went to take a step backwards, but he anticipated my move and took a gentle hold of my elbow so I couldn't distance myself.

'It is good to see you again,' he said softly, leaning in to kiss me on each cheek, as old friends would do in France.

The brush of his lips and his curly hair against my skin brought back long-buried memories of the intimate time we had spent together in the past. I shook my head, trying to regain my composure, and this time I did step back.

'And you. I would like to talk more with you about the position here, and to see the vineyard and the accommodation before I finally make my decision. Would that be convenient today?' I deliberately kept my tone business-like.

He grinned at me and I felt my cheeks heat slightly. 'Yes, of course,' he said. 'Let me show you the accommodation first of all. I think you will love it and you will see it is so much more than that. Henri can give you a tour of the vineyard later. Please, this way.' He took my elbow once again, guiding me through the archway that led on to the estate. I'd learned my lesson from the previous day and was wearing my flat shoes this time as we crossed an open expanse of grass on the other side of the archway. Little by little, a sweet, almost fairy-tale cottage came into view, with roses growing up a trellis outside the painted, wooden door and the typical pale blue shutters at the window that I loved. I could hardly speak for delight. The smell of the flowers all around was heavenly and, as I breathed it in, I felt dizzy with the beauty of it all. I turned to find Didier watching me, enjoying my reaction.

'I take it you approve of the cottage?'

'Oh, I love it. It's magical. Does this cottage really come with the job?' I'd let my guard down now and I knew I would find it hard to hold out much longer.

'It really does, yes.' He laughed. 'Shall we go inside?' He pushed open the door, revealing a cosy lounge in front of us, with an enormous sofa and a well-used fireplace. A small kitchen was off to one side and there was a rickety-looking wooden staircase winding up to the left. The cottage was full of someone else's things, though, which confused me: coats, boots, bags, newspapers and magazines, and a hefty pile of books on the coffee table in front of the sofa. It seemed someone else already lived there.

'Would you like something to drink?' he asked. 'I have some home-made lemonade if you'd like it.'

I nodded on my way towards the back door and the garden, which I could see calling to me outside. The view from the back garden was of the whole estate and I could see the vineyard in the distance, as well as the main house in the foreground. It was a modest château but it had obviously been a while since it had been cared for in the way it deserved. The gardens in front of it were a bit overgrown too. Didier joined me a moment later and passed me my glass.

'What a beautiful place! Is someone else living here at the moment though?' I tilted my head to one side.

'Yes, I live here at the moment, so I get to see these wonderful views every day. I find it easier to manage my time by living here, as it's between the office and the vineyard. I will move out of course, if you decide to accept the job.' He looked at me and his eyes twinkled knowingly. He had chosen to show me the cottage on purpose, sure that once I'd seen it, my mind would be made up. I took a long sip of my drink while I pondered what to say next. I turned round instead, heading for the staircase so that I could go up and see the bedrooms. At the top of the stairs there were two rooms, one of which I guessed must belong to Didier, and perhaps his partner, if he had one. I glanced left and right, taking in the simple double room on one side and the smaller guest room on the other. I had a quick look in both rooms, finding them unnaturally tidy, with no clues to offer about their inhabitants. I took in a deep breath before descending the staircase to talk to Didier once again.

'What did you think of the bedrooms? It's a bit squashed, I know, but for one person it's probably enough.'

'It's lovely, Didier, but where will you live if you have to move out of the cottage?' I frowned, not wanting to displace him.

'I will move back to the château, there's plenty of room there.' He paused for a moment to take a sip of his drink but he didn't take long to get back on track. 'Now, what else did you want to talk to me about?'

I bit my lip as I wondered how to begin. 'A lot has happened to me since we were together and I'm sure it is the same for you. So I need your promise that we will simply be work colleagues and nothing else.' He raised his eyebrows at that but didn't say anything.

'Our lives have moved on and I want to look forward. I really want this job and I don't want to let the past get in the way of that.' I blew out a breath at the end of my little speech.

'As you say, our lives have moved on and there is no point living in the past. I know that only too well, Fran. There is a big job to do here and I need someone I can rely on. I believe that person could be you.' Despite his positive response, a shutter seemed to come down over his eyes. He took my now empty glass, moving back towards the kitchen before I could reply. After putting the glasses in the sink, he turned to me again. 'So, would you like the job?'

'I would but I think it might be best for it to be on a temporary basis. Perhaps a one year contract while we see if we can work together?'

He looked surprised but I held firm.

'As you wish,' he said finally.

CHAPTER FOUR

I followed Didier back to the courtyard in silence, feeling deflated after what had passed between us in the cottage, despite the fact that he had offered me the job. Didier strode ahead and disappeared inside the office, re-emerging a minute later with another man behind him.

'Fran, this is Henri, my office manager.' I reached out to shake Henri's hand. 'He's going to give you a short tour of the vineyard and I will speak to you again before you leave.' He turned away without even waiting for a reply from me.

'*Mademoiselle*, shall we?' Henri pointed in the direction of the archway that led to the cottage and I fell in step beside him.

'Have you worked here long, Henri?'

'Yes, for a few years.' I recognised his clipped accent from the phone call to my hotel earlier in the day. 'This building is where we make all our wines,' he went on, 'and where we plan to build the Visitors' Centre.' He pointed to a large, old barn on the left. As we passed alongside the building, I noticed how ramshackle it looked with bricks missing here and there, and crumbled pieces of cement lying on the ground. I was curious to see the inside, as I couldn't imagine it being fit for the purpose of making wine at all. We continued along the gravel path to the end of the barn and then past another, smaller barn. The doors of this one were shut tight.

'What happens in there?' I asked.

'Oh, that's where we hold our wine tastings at the moment. It's a bit cramped in there when we have a lot of visitors, which is one of the reasons why we want to build a new space.' He gave me an encouraging smile.

'How many visitors do you get a day?'

'It varies. In the summer, probably between twenty and thirty people come every day but in the winter, there aren't so many. We don't have visitors in the autumn because we're too busy with the harvest and we just don't have spare staff.'

We finally arrived at the end of the buildings and I could see the vineyard spread out below us, where rows and rows of flourishing vines were all being tended by hand. The heat of the day was rising now, making it even harder work for those people to be caring for the vines in such conditions. I knew that hand-picked grapes led to better quality wines and understood that it must have been a conscious decision by the vineyard owner to choose this method of vineyard management.

'Have you seen the château?' Henri interrupted my thoughts, pointing to the slightly shabby looking house I had seen from the back door of the cottage.

'Yes, I saw it earlier. It looks like it needs some work doing to it.'

'It does need work, you're right, but it would require a lot of money to bring it up to standard.'

'But Didier told me he's going to move in there when I move in to the cottage.' I felt even worse about that now.

'I'm sure it will be fine, *mademoiselle*. It's time we were getting back, I think.' He had a guarded look on his face now and I assumed that was because he didn't want to give away any of Didier's secrets.

Henri turned and led the way back up the hill to the courtyard and I fell silent, trying to reconcile all the thoughts buzzing round my head. Didier was waiting for us when we got back and, after a brief goodbye, Henri disappeared inside once again.

'Did you enjoy the tour?' Didier appeared calmer now and closer to his usual easy-going self.

'Yes, very much. I'm looking forward to starting work next week.'

'Will you be staying in Strasbourg over the weekend?'

'No, I'm going home to see my parents and I also have a wedding of one of my university friends to attend so the timing has all worked out well.'

'That wouldn't be Amandine's wedding, would it?' He smiled at my expression of surprise.

'Do you know her too?'

'No, I've never actually met her. I've been friends with her fiancé, Laurent since before university and we took the same business course together in Strasbourg.'

'We'll see each other there then.'

'I'll look forward to it.'

My return taxi arrived just then, saving me from having to say any more, and soon, I was on my way back to Strasbourg with a new job but also with more on my mind than when I had set off from the city that morning.

As I was packing up my things in preparation for leaving the hotel, my mind drifted back to Didier and the way his face had closed down after I'd made my speech suggesting the temporary contract. I didn't regret what I'd said, I just wished I'd managed to phrase it better. I released a sigh and then jumped as my phone buzzed, jolting me out of my thoughts. I was expecting it to be Ellie asking about the job, so I was shocked to see my mum's name pop up on the screen.

'Chérie, it's Maman. Where are you? I haven't heard from you for a few days and I'm just worried that everything's okay. Please call me, darling, and let me know you're safe x'

I rang my mum back there and then.

'Mum, hi it's me,' I began. 'I'm sorry I haven't been in touch.'

'Oh, Fran, *mon dieu*, I've been so worried about you!' I could imagine her with her hand over her eyes in typical dramatic fashion and I had to smile. 'Is everything all right with you?'

'I didn't mean to frighten you, Mum, I'm sorry. It's just that a lot has happened to me in the last couple of days.'

'Like what, sweetheart? What has happened?'

'Mum, I've split up with Paul. I walked in on him in bed with someone else so I left him.'

'*Oh, non, c'est pas possible*. I'm so sorry he did that to you. What are you going to do? And what about the wedding?'

'Well, the wedding's definitely off. I can't trust him again after this so I've moved out of the flat and I've just got myself a great new job.'

'A new job? Where?'

'It's in Alsace, *Maman*.' I held my breath, waiting for her reaction.

'Oh, I wish you'd let us know but still, that's great news. I can't wait to hear all about it.'

'Mum, I'm really sorry, there just wasn't time to let you know before the interview. But I'm in Strasbourg now and I'm still coming home for the weekend for Amandine's wedding. Then I start my new job on Monday. Can you or dad collect me from the train station later please?'

'Yes, of course, *chérie*. It will be so lovely to see you. It has been a long time since we were all together as a family.'

'Is Lottie home then?' It had been ages since I'd seen my sister and I longed to catch up with her too.

'Yes, she came home today quite out of the blue. It's so wonderful to see her again after all this time.'

'I'll call you later then when I know what time I'll be arriving. *A bientôt*.'

'*A bientôt, chérie*.' And with that she rang off. I realised how wonderful it would be to see my family again and I felt guilty then for not contacting my mum sooner to tell her what had happened. Paul had been so against coming back to France each time I'd suggested it that my visits home had become less and less frequent. I couldn't even remember the last time I had called home. I blew out a long breath and determined that things would be different now.

Ellie texted me shortly afterwards and I called her straight back to tell her about the job and the cottage.

'That sounds wonderful,' she said when I'd finished giving her all the details.

Then I told her about the phone call with my mum.

'Well, I hope you have a wonderful family get-together and I hope the wedding goes well too, and that Monday brings the fresh start you're looking for.'

'Thank you and I promise we will sort out a date for you to come over and stay as soon as possible!'

'You'd better!' She was still laughing as we said goodbye.

Didier

I'd been thrown by Fran's comment about putting the past behind us and I was even more disconcerted by her insistence on a temporary contract. I trudged back to the office feeling decidedly more downbeat than I ought to have, considering that she had accepted the job.

'I take it she said no then,' Henri said when I went in and slumped down in my chair.

'She said yes actually, but she put me firmly in my place about putting the past behind us in order to work together again now, so I feel upset about that even though I can't really blame her in all honesty.'

'Perhaps it will be easier when she starts working here and you get to know each other again. You need to give her time, I think.'

'I know you're right and I am trying to think about it from her point of view.' I heaved a big sigh.

'Look, why don't we go for a drink at the bar tonight and we can maybe talk more about it then?'

We left work at six after what felt like a very long afternoon and walked down to the village to our usual bar. We sat on stools at the counter and asked for two glasses of Pastis. As the alcohol slipped down, I could feel the tension from my earlier meeting with Fran slipping away.

'Better?' asked Henri, knowingly.

I nodded.

'I realise now that Fran must have been more hurt by my behaviour than I'd appreciated when she went to London. I didn't want to beg her to stay but now, looking back, I almost wish I had. I could have really done with Fran's support to see me through those difficult times.'

'I remember it all happening so quickly, much more quickly than any of us had expected, including the doctors.' Henri rolled his eyes then because the doctors had given my dad six months to live but in the end, he had only managed three. It had been a shock for all of us. 'You should have told her, Didier. If she had known your dad had cancer, she would have stayed with you, I'm sure of that.'

'I know she would but I didn't want her to stay with me out of pity and I didn't think it was fair to stop her following her dreams. Anyway, she felt stifled by life here so it was best for her to explore what city life might hold for her.' I shrugged, remembering how difficult it had been to make that decision at the time.

'And then you might never have met the lovely Isabelle.' Henri pulled a face and ordered two more glasses of Pastis as if he needed something to help block out the memory of Isabelle's arrival on the scene.

'I was a wreck after my dad died, you know that - trying to keep the estate going, while looking after my mum as well. Isabelle came along at my lowest point. I really needed someone and I was flattered by the attention she paid me. I had no idea how much she would change my life.'

'And not for the better either, with the exception of Chlöe of course.' His face lit up and that made me smile too.

'Well, you're not doing a very good job of cheering me up, are you?'

'How can you say that? I haven't even mentioned how your mum and Isabelle hated each other on sight! I've been very gentle with you if you ask me.'

'Hmm. Well, it's easy for you to criticise when you're not involved with anyone. Maybe we should talk about the terrible state of your love life instead.'

'I just haven't found the right woman yet but it doesn't mean I'm not having fun looking.'

'You're getting on a bit now, though. Time's running out. Look at me, off to another wedding tomorrow. All my friends will be married off soon.'

'Well, at least you'll have Chlöe to keep you company and you won't need to talk to Isabelle at all.'

'That is definitely a plus point. It will be Chlöe's first wedding and I expect she'll love it.' I chuckled at the thought of my little girl attending a wedding. 'Right, come on then, I'd better get home and sort myself out before the morning. I don't want to be hung over.'

Fran

The journey by train from Strasbourg to Colmar was beautiful, passing through luscious, green vineyards in the shadow of the pine-clad Vosges mountains and alongside gurgling rivers and streams, bringing me deep into the heart of the Alsace wine region. I had about five more minutes to go before reaching Colmar when my phone buzzed. I was surprised to see Paul's name on the display and I berated myself for not having blocked his number yet.

'Hi, Fran, how are you getting on? I miss you so much. I'm really sorry about what I said before. I'd like to meet and talk if you'd be up for that?'

What could I say to that? He had a nerve after the way he'd behaved in leaving my things outside the flat and changing the locks. I didn't want to talk to him again so I took the British way out and didn't reply at all. I made sure to block his number straight after reading his text.

A few minutes later, I grabbed my suitcase and my bag and descended from the train onto the platform at Colmar. There were window boxes all along the platform railings, overflowing with tumbling red, white and pink geraniums, and I smiled as I remembered that Colmar had been awarded the title of *ville fleurie* for many years and clearly still took that award very seriously. I loved to see and smell all the flowers and it felt good to be home again. I came out of the station building into the car park and looked around for my parents.

'Fran!' My dad was waving at me from the car. I smiled broadly at him before making my way over.

'*Ah, chérie. Que c'est bon de te revoir!* I missed you.' He kissed me firmly on both cheeks and then again and gave me an all-enveloping hug.

'Hey, Dad, I've missed you too.' I passed him my case and went round to the other side of the car to get in.

'So, we are speaking English, are we now?' he asked as he put his seat belt on.

'Well, I thought you might need the practice, Dad, after all this time.' I loved the banter between my dad and me, and we'd both slipped straight back into it as if I'd never been away.

'How long is it since we've seen you? Was it last Christmas, really?' he asked, glancing briefly over at me.

'I think it was, yes. Ages ago, I'm sorry. So, what's new?'

'Not a lot, really. We're both working hard, as always. Did I tell you I work one day a week from home nowadays?' I shook my head, not really remembering if he'd told me or not. 'It's good to be at home more. I wish your mum would do the same.'

My dad worked as an accountant for a large restaurant chain in the region and, although he enjoyed it, I knew it was a lot of work for him as he got older. My mum worked part-time as a waitress in one of their restaurants in Colmar.

'And is Lottie home for good from her travels, did she say?'

'She's already gone again. Just a flying visit, she said, on her way up to Strasbourg to meet up with her latest boyfriend. I hardly even had the chance to speak to her. She sent you her love and said she'd be back again soon.' He sighed. I didn't say anything but I felt worried about my little sister. I made a mental note to text her over the weekend so we could meet up now we were both back in France.

As we got closer to home, my dad focused on the twists and turns of the road. My parents' home was on the outskirts of town, almost back out in the countryside, and it had a nice bit of land with it too. As we turned into the drive, my eyes lit up at the sight of the farmhouse once again. My mum poked her head out of the window to give us a quick wave before coming out to greet us.

CHAPTER FIVE

'Come on in, darling, it's so good to see you.'

I gave Mum a long hug, realising just how much I'd missed her. 'I wish Lottie was here as well but it can't be helped, I suppose,' she continued. 'Dinner will be ready soon and you can tell us both all your news while we eat. We've missed you. We really shouldn't leave it so long between get-togethers,' she said, gesturing at me to sit at the table as she removed her apron. She put a tall, green, flute-shaped bottle of Alsace Pinot Blanc on the table and I smiled at the familiarity of it all.

'I know, *Maman*, but now I can do what I want without Paul holding me back, we will see each other more often, especially since I've got this new job near Strasbourg.'

I went on to tell them how I'd seen the job a few weeks previously but only had the courage to apply for it when everything went wrong with Paul.

'You'll never guess who the vineyard manager is,' I said, looking from one parent to the other. They waited patiently while I kept them in suspense. 'It's Didier. Do you remember?'

My mum gasped. 'Ooh, I bet that was a surprise! What did you say?'

My dad stood up to open the wine and poured it into some Alsace goblets while I told them the story.

'He was definitely the last person I was expecting to see there but the interview went well and he told me that same day that he wanted to offer me the job.'

'Have you accepted it?' my dad asked.

'I went back yesterday to confirm whether I'd take it or not. I knew I wanted the job but I didn't want the relationship we'd had before to get in the way in the future, so I made that clear before I accepted. I also asked him for a temporary contract for now.'

My mum winced as I finished speaking. 'How did he take all that?'

'I think he was a bit surprised to be honest but so was I when I found him there waiting to interview me.' Even as I told my mum though, I wondered if I had offended Didier with what I'd said.

The oven beeped, breaking into the momentary silence, and my mum went over to take out the *flammekueche* she'd made for dinner. Although it wasn't a wood-fired oven, the tart always tasted delicious and my mum had been perfecting it over many years. It was our favourite dinner, a bit like a thin pizza, smothered with crème fraîche, onions and bacon lardons, and topped off with gruyère cheese. The smell filled the whole kitchen as my mum removed the tray from the oven and it felt really good to be back home.

'Ooh, *Maman, merci!*' I beamed at her as she brought the tray to the table.

'I know it's your favourite, *chérie,* and I thought you deserved a treat after all the horrible times you've been having. Is it definitely over between you and Paul?'

'He cheated on me, *Maman,* and I caught them at it in our bed. Despite the love I used to have for him, I don't think I could ever get past that.' I popped a string of gooey melted cheese in my mouth and closed my eyes to savour the flavour.

'No, of course, I understand that. I can't believe how stupid Paul was to treat you that way.'

'There's a lot you don't know about Paul, to be honest.' I glanced at them both before taking the plunge. 'I didn't want to tell you before because I knew you'd worry but Paul was very controlling. He never wanted me to come home to visit and he hated me doing things without him. If we'd stayed together, all that would only have become worse. I think I've had a lucky escape.'

For a few minutes, we tucked in to the lovely dinner Mum had made without further discussion. After we'd eaten, I stood up and walked outside into the darkening back garden, trying to clear my head of all thoughts of Paul.

My dad joined me shortly afterwards and came over to give me a hug, perhaps sensing my misery. I began to cry then, all the tears I should have already cried for me and Paul that I hadn't had the strength to do as yet. My dad held me tight and I wiped my eyes.

'I'm so sorry for what happened between you and Paul,' he said gently.

'Thanks, Dad. Right now, it stinks and I just need some time to get over it.'

'I know, and it will get better in time, honestly. Anyway, maybe it's for the best for you to split up if he can't be faithful before you even get married.'

I didn't know what to say to that but deep down, I couldn't help thinking he was right. He gave me one last hug and we turned to go back inside.

'Are you okay?' my mum asked.

'I'm fine,' I lied and she knew it.

'At least you have the wedding to look forward to tomorrow,' she said and then, realising her mistake, she gasped and blushed furiously. 'Oh, what am I saying?'

'Don't worry, I know what you meant. I am looking forward to it. It will be lovely to see Amandine and some of my other university friends again. It will be a good distraction.'

We all went off for an early night but I lay awake for a long time, still thinking about Paul to some extent but also about Didier.

Didier

After my usual early morning inspection of the vines and a chat with the workers on shift, I took a leisurely drive down towards Hunawihr, remembering at the last minute to put the car seat in for Chlöe. It would be good to spend the weekend with her. I had plans to sort out her room in the château and to ask her what toys she'd like to bring over to keep at my place.

I felt slightly awkward in my suit as I now spent most of my days in t-shirts and jeans, adding a jumper and a jacket only when the weather changed with the seasons. I'd hung my suit jacket in the back of the car before I set off in the hope I would feel more comfortable driving without it. The shirt and tie were already beginning to annoy me though, and I had to force myself not to roll up my sleeves and undo the top button. I wanted to look smart for once, for the wedding, and I didn't want to ruin the effect.

It was a lovely sunny morning as I drove south along the wine route and I enjoyed looking at the rows and rows of vines, now heavy with fruit, swaying gently in the breeze. The bunches of grapes were ripening to maturity as the season drew to an end, and winemakers everywhere would be checking sugar levels obsessively. It was always a dilemma deciding when to start the harvest because it depended so much on the weather: too early and there wouldn't be enough sugar in the grapes, and too late might mean the grapes were hit by early autumn frosts. Still, I was excited about the harvest, even though it was the most frantic time of the year for the estate and would be stressful while it was happening. If everything went well, there would be some wonderful celebrations afterwards and that always felt good.

I felt myself unwind as I got closer and closer to the village and I wondered if this day away from my own worries was all I needed. I knew Laurent and his new wife-to-be were having the civil ceremony beforehand for very close family and that the rest of the guests were gathering at the church afterwards. As I approached the village, I could see the ancient church perched up on its hill overlooking things and the unusual fortified cemetery surrounding it. It was picture postcard perfect. I found somewhere to park and, realising I'd arrived a bit early, I did a tour of the village to get my bearings. I found the *Salle des Fêtes* where the reception would be held, and then it was time to go and find my seat in the church.

Inside the slightly darkened building, I was surprised to note just how many guests were already there. I glanced round to see if Isabelle had arrived with Chlöe but there was no sign of her. She was always on the late side so I hadn't really expected to see her. I found myself a seat along a wooden pew and left a place for Chlöe next to me. I explained to the older lady on the other side so she would know I wasn't being rude and then we chatted for a few minutes about how we both knew Laurent. She was one of his mother's friends, in fact, and had known him since he was a little boy. After a natural break in the conversation, I glanced round again to look for Chlöe and Isabelle but instead of them, I saw Fran entering the church, searching for somewhere to sit.

Fran

The sun was already shining when my dad dropped me off at the church for Amandine's wedding ceremony. I was glad I'd chosen to wear a short-sleeved wrap dress for the day ahead, although I had brought along a jacket as well just in case it turned chilly later on. As I passed through the gates towards the 15th century stone building, I was struck by how I'd never seen another church quite like it. It was situated on a small hillside, overlooking the village and surrounded by vineyards, and its steeple was just like a turret on a romantic castle.

The church building surrounded the steeple in a circular shape and the grounds were surrounded by an outer wall, to protect it from attack in days gone by. The charming setting appealed to the romantic in me. I stopped still for a moment, enjoying the peace and the beautiful view of the vineyards all around. I wondered whether there still was a romantic in me after all that had happened in the last few days but, even as I processed that thought, I knew that my natural optimism had already begun to bounce back and that I would get past it all with time. I came out of my reverie and started walking towards the door of the ancient church once again.

As soon as I stepped inside, the cooler air enveloped me and I had to wait for my eyes to adjust to the dim light. I walked down the nave looking in each pew for a suitable seat. I was hoping to see someone I knew from my university days so I could feel a bit more at ease among all these strangers. Then I heard someone call my name. I glanced round quickly and spotted Didier sitting on one of the pews halfway down the church.

'You arrived early, then,' I said, sitting down next to him.

'Yes, I had an easy journey down here this morning.' He gave me one of his intoxicating smiles. 'How's your weekend going so far?'

'Fine, thank you.' I noticed there was an empty space on his other side and I really wanted to ask him about it but didn't have the courage. Besides, I knew it wasn't really any of my business. He caught me looking there before I could pretend otherwise but he didn't say anything. Feeling awkward, I wished I'd followed etiquette and sat on the other side of the church since I was for the bride but I didn't want to seem rude by moving. Instead, I edged a bit further away along the pew, noticing just how closely I'd been sitting next to him.

As I looked around the church, three older people walked in and sat on opposite sides of the front row. I assumed they were the bride's mother and the groom's parents. Then Laurent, Amandine's fiancé, arrived looking very handsome in his navy suit but also a bit nervous, fiddling with his tie as he talked with his parents and best man. I'd only met Laurent a few times but it was obvious how much he loved Amandine and I hoped that they would be very happy together. Out of the corner of my eye, I noticed a little girl walking along the row towards me. I turned to look at her. An attractive woman, dressed in a bright-red leather jacket, black pencil skirt and a killer pair of heels stood at the end of the row watching the little girl as she walked along. She didn't follow her. When the little girl reached my side, I stood up to let her pass and the next thing I knew, she had thrown herself on to Didier's lap and was covering his face with kisses.

'*Comment ça va, mignonne?*' he whispered in her ear. As I watched, transfixed by this sight, I saw Didier glance at the woman and nod. To my surprise, she turned to leave without saying a word. I snapped my head back to Didier, my mind full of queries but, before I could say anything, an organ started to play announcing Amandine's arrival. I had no chance to ask the questions that were almost bursting from my lips.

Amandine looked gorgeous in a simple satin off-the-shoulder wedding dress. Her father looked as proud as a parent could possibly be as he walked slowly at her side towards Laurent, who was beaming at his bride. I heard the little girl gasp and when I looked over, she was straining from her vantage point in Didier's arms to see Amandine in her beautiful dress.

'*La dame est très belle, Papa, n'est-ce pas? Elle est comme une princesse!*'

I had to smile at her excited little voice. Didier's face was the picture of happiness and unconditional love for his young daughter. Things really had changed for Didier while I had been away. I wasn't sure whether I was more stunned by his gorgeous wife, or by the fact that he was a father.

Didier

The wedding ceremony passed smoothly. Soon, Laurent and his

bride were walking back down the aisle as husband and wife. I noticed Amandine glance over at Fran on the way and give her a little wave, as well as a proud smile, as if she couldn't believe her good fortune. I was pleased for them both.

Fran made her way to the end of the pew to join the other guests as they left the church. I picked Chlöe up and followed, answering all her questions about the ceremony. I was relieved to be back in the fresh air and to feel some sunshine on my skin. I knew Chlöe would love it too. Once outside, I set her down gently on the ground, took her hand and made my way over to a grassy patch to let her have a run around. She looked adorable in her pale blue dress as she toddled across the grass, stopping to study each and every thing she spotted. Once I was sure she was okay, I turned round to search for Fran. She seemed to be trying to find people she knew on the other side of the churchyard. She saw me looking and I gave her a smile that I hoped would melt her reserve and persuade her to join us. I knew she had her barriers up after the conversation we'd had the day before, not to mention the fact that she now knew I was married with a child. The smile must have worked because she gave in and came over to join me at the edge of the grass.

'I imagine you have a lot of questions for me,' I said as she came level with me.

'I do but I also know that it's none of my business to ask, especially after what I said yesterday about keeping our relationship on a professional footing.' I appreciated her honesty.

I cleared my throat. 'I was married, Fran, but my wife left me last year and she took our daughter, Chlöe, with her when she went. Chlöe lives with her mum but we have an informal agreement that she spends time with me whenever we can arrange it. Things are obviously not that good between my wife and me, which makes everything difficult.' I sighed and rubbed the heels of my hands over my face.

'How old is Chlöe?'

'She's nearly three.'

There was a long pause while Fran processed what I'd told her. I waited for her to take it all in and wondered if she would ask any more questions. I was so weary of all the games Isabelle had been playing since she'd left but I tried hard not to let Fran see that. When she stretched out her arm and took my hand in hers to give it a squeeze, I couldn't have been more surprised. She released my hand after a moment and looped her arm through mine. Her gesture was enough to show me she sympathised with my situation and for that, I was grateful.

'I'm sorry you've had an awful time. Relationships are much harder than we all realise. You do have a beautiful daughter, though, and that must alleviate some of the pain.'

'She is beautiful, you're right, and she means everything to me. I wish I could be with her all of the time but...' I tightened my jaw but said nothing more. It would be a while before I could tell Fran all that had happened between us. Chlöe broke the tension by running over to show us some daisies she had picked. I scooped her up into my arms.

'Chlöe, this is my good friend, Fran,' I said. She peeked out from under her mass of blonde curls to smile shyly at Fran. Then she extended her little hand towards her and Fran responded, grasping her hand in return.

'*Enchantée*!' Chlöe chimed and we laughed at her formality, making her giggle. The photographer began to gather everyone together for a group photo. Standing next to Fran, with my daughter in my arms, I felt happy for the first time in a long while. I was looking forward to the rest of the day in their company.

After the photographer had finished, we followed the rest of the guests out of the churchyard and made our way down the hill to the *Salle des Fêtes* to join the line of people congratulating the bride and groom.

'*Oh, Amandine, que tu es belle!* You look stunning. Congratulations to you both.' Fran kissed her friend on both cheeks and hugged her, before moving off to collect a glass of pink champagne.

Chlöe admired Amandine's dress while I congratulated Laurent, shaking his hand and then pulling him in for a quick hug and much backslapping.

Fran was sipping her champagne and people-watching when we approached her.

'I'm sorry to ask,' I said hesitantly, 'but could you watch Chlöe for me while I go to the toilet, please?' I guessed Fran probably understood how difficult it was for me on my own at an event with a little girl.

'Of course, if you think she'll be okay about staying with me.'

I bent down to my daughter to tell her and she reached out her hand to Fran. She took it gladly and went towards the grass again, knowing Chlöe liked to play.

When I returned, Chlöe was standing next to Fran watching the other children there from a distance. Fran had crouched down to her level and they were looking at the garden together. As I watched, Fran whispered something to her and then Chlöe's little hand flew to her mouth in excitement and her eyes lit up. I made my way towards them and crouched down on Chlöe's other side. She turned to me, putting her finger to her lips and it was all I could do not to laugh. She pointed to the robin they had spotted on the branch of a tree.

'Look at the bird, *Papa*. It's got a red tummy.'

'It's called *un rouge-gorge*. They all have red tummies.' I watched as her eyes grew round in surprise. It always made me happy to be with her. I smiled at Fran and the look she gave me in return made me feel that we were ready to move on from the awkward conversation we'd had the previous day.

Shortly afterwards, we stood again to begin making our way inside for the reception dinner. I almost couldn't bring myself to look at the seating plan in case this was the last we would see of Fran for the day.

CHAPTER SIX

Fran

Didier moved ahead of us and as Chlöe was still holding my hand, I ambled along at her pace. I watched Didier's handsome profile as he studied the plan and then turned to me with a big smile on his face. I returned it with a grin of my own, happy to know I was going to be on the same table as the two of them. Didier swept Chlöe up into his arms as we went into the main room and I was delighted to spot a group of my university friends already sitting at our table. We made our way over and I spent the next few minutes squealing and hugging them all. Most of them remembered Didier from our university days so there was no need for introductions. I sat down next to my good friend Marie, with Didier sitting on my other side.

'*Chérie*, it has been so long since I last saw you,' Marie began, hugging me to her. 'You must tell me all about your fiancé.' She grabbed my left hand, looking for my ring. I felt my cheeks heat and I heard the group fall silent all around. I didn't dare look at Didier. I didn't want him to know about my personal troubles just yet but now it seemed I had no choice but to say something.

I cleared my throat and lifted my head to look at her, knowing that everyone was listening. 'Erm, we split up so there is no fiancé to tell you about, I'm sorry.' I gave a little shrug and gradually everyone started talking again. I risked a quick glance at Didier hoping I wouldn't see pity on his face, which I didn't, but the intensity of his gaze surprised me and I swallowed nervously.

'I'm so sorry to hear that,' Marie said. 'What happened, Fran?'

'Um, he cheated on me.'

'The *salop*. You are better off without him!' I loved Marie for being so forthright.

'I know. You're absolutely right. I've moved back home, and on Monday I'm starting a new job near Strasbourg. I've been wanting to come home for a while and this gave me the push I needed.'

'Well, maybe it's a *gold lining*. Is that the right expression?' She nibbled at her lip as she searched the depths of her brain for her schoolgirl English.

'It's silver lining but not to worry, I knew what you meant.' We laughed together.

A waiter appeared with another tray full of glasses of champagne. I was grateful for the glass he offered me, taking a gulp for courage but then savouring the delicate taste as I swallowed. I looked over at Didier to find his chair empty. I glanced round and saw him laying Chlöe on a cushioned bench a few feet from our table. In all the excitement, she had fallen asleep. I smiled as I watched him take off his jacket and cover her with it. He kissed her gently on the forehead before walking back towards me. He gave me another intense look and I had to lick my lips, which had suddenly become dry.

'Your fiancé was mad to let you slip through his fingers,' he whispered in my ear as he sat back down again. His lips brushed my earlobe and his manly scent invaded my senses, sending a glorious sensation through my whole body. It was all I could do to stop myself from leaning into him. I sat back in my chair, thankful I hadn't given in to my instincts. He winked at me and picked up his glass of champagne. We clinked glasses and suddenly, my life looked quite a bit rosier.

Didier

While Chlöe slept, Fran and I caught up with her friends over lunch. It felt good to be among them and especially to be with Fran. I was about to ask her more about what had happened back in London when Chlöe woke up. I jumped up to go and tend to her, bringing her back to the table a few minutes later. I sat back down with her on my lap. She rubbed at her eyes with her hands and promptly popped a thumb in her mouth. With her flushed cheeks and her blonde curls massed around her face, she looked like a little cherub. I had put a plate of food aside for her to eat when she woke up and I offered it to her now. She reached out for some bread and I tore a piece off for her. As she nibbled on it, she began to wake up and I even got a smile a few minutes later. Soon she was wandering round the table, making friends with all the different guests. Once I knew she wasn't upset at being in a strange situation, I relaxed.

We all stood shortly after to allow the tables to be cleared away for some music and dancing. We went to get a drink while the *Salle* was transformed and wandered outside into the sunshine once again. This time, Chlöe was more confident and approached some other children who were playing on the grass.

'Is that why you came back home, to escape your fiancé?' I asked as we stood watching the children.

'Yes, in a way. I couldn't stay with him, obviously, after what had happened. I actually caught him in bed with the other woman.' She glanced across at me and caught me wincing in sympathy. 'But I'd been wanting to come home for a while now and Paul just wouldn't have agreed to it. I saw your job as soon as you advertised it and I knew it would be the perfect job for me - so perhaps it was fate when I found out Paul had been cheating.'

'Well, I can't wait to get started on our project at the vineyard. I really believe you'll be able to help us make it happen. We've been talking about it for so long but we need someone organised to manage it.'

'I'm definitely organised and I'm excited about doing something new. Just being here today, spending time with old friends and with my family this weekend, has made me feel so much better.'

'So, am I one of the "old friends" now or am I still just a work colleague?' I hoped she could see the twinkle in my eyes even as I made my point. She blushed and looked down, making me feel a bit guilty for teasing her.

'I'm sorry if I was blunt yesterday but I didn't know where I stood. I'd heard you had got together with someone else after I left so I assumed we had both moved on. Now we know we have both been through such a lot, keeping a professional distance is probably for the best, don't you think?'

I recognised her need to protect herself from any more hurt. 'I understand what you're saying but I hope we can work together as friends now. It's good to see you again and I want to make the most of that.' I took another sip of champagne and waited for her response. When she didn't say anything for a couple of minutes, I began to feel worried but eventually she spoke.

'It's been a hard time for me, Didier.' She paused, staring down at her hands as she twisted them together before her. 'I don't regret going to London, but the fact is the job wasn't anywhere near as good as I'd hoped and now I know my relationship with Paul was based on nothing but lies.'

She looked up at me then, her eyes shining with unshed tears.

'Nothing you do or experience is ever wasted, even though you don't feel like that right now. My marriage to Isabelle was nothing like I expected it to be but at least I have Chlöe, so that makes it all worth it. I'm now managing a vineyard, which is what I always wanted to do, so I have a lot to be thankful for. And so do you, I'm sure.'

'The best thing about going to London was that I met my friend, Ellie. Her friendship is something I'm really thankful for.'

A lone tear slipped down her cheek but she swiped it quickly away before giving me a watery smile. Then the sound of an accordion filled the air and everyone started to pile back inside for the evening entertainment. After scooping Chlöe up once again, I led the way back inside.

Fran

The accordion player, an older man with skin the colour of aged leather, was sitting right in front of the stage surrounded by a very attentive group of children, their eyes focused on his nimble fingers as he played. Chlöe pulled on Didier's hand, indicating she wanted to go and see the music man as well. He followed her, with an apologetic backwards glance at me, picking her up on the way so that she could see. Soon, she was clapping her hands in time to the music and smiling broadly at the lovely sound. Didier put her down so that she could join in dancing with the other children and started walking back towards me but Chlöe had other plans. She grabbed his hand. Seeing that she wanted him to dance too, he lifted her little body so that her feet rested on top of his and they moved round slowly together. It was a glorious sight and I couldn't help but laugh at the pair of them.

'Didier has changed a lot since we last saw him, *n'est-ce pas*?' Marie said as she came up alongside me.

'Yes, marriage and becoming a father are both fairly hefty life events.'

'Where is the wife, then?'

I looked at Marie, trying to gauge whether she was being nosy or if she was genuinely interested. 'Ah, they recently separated. Chlöe lives with her mum and visits her dad when she can.'

'Oh, what a shame. You should have married him when you had the chance, *chérie*.' With that nugget of wisdom she disappeared, leaving me with my mouth open at her cheeky comment. Didier had never asked me to marry him so I'd never "had the chance" to even consider what my answer would have been.

Once the accordion player had finished his latest tune, he moved off to loud applause, making way for the band that would play for the rest of the evening. I found a table to sit at and Didier joined me there shortly afterwards, leaving Chlöe with me while he went to get us all drinks. As Amandine and Laurent appeared in the middle of the dance floor for their traditional first dance, the lights dimmed and Chlöe released a loud gasp. She clasped her little hands together and watched, entranced, as they started to dance. Others soon joined them as the music changed into pop covers that we all recognised and loved. After half a dozen such songs, it was starting to get late, and I saw Chlöe yawn widely.

'I'm so sorry, but I think I'd better take Chlöe home now. She looks exhausted. How are you getting home?' A slight frown crossed Didier's brow.

'My dad will come and pick me up, don't worry.'

'I could always give you a lift if you're happy to leave now?'

The wedding reception would be much less interesting without Didier and Chlöe to keep me company. My university friends had broken away to mix with their own friends, and the only other person I knew was the bride herself.

'That would be great, if you're sure you don't mind.' He rolled his eyes a little before guiding me towards Amandine to say goodbye and good luck. A few minutes later, after settling Chlöe in her car seat, we set off towards my parents' home. Chlöe was asleep before the *Salle des Fêtes* was even out of sight.

We didn't talk much on the way back, except for the odd direction or two that I needed to give. He'd never been to my house while we were dating but he knew the way to Colmar well enough. All too soon, he pulled on to the drive and turned off the engine.

'Thanks for a lovely day today. It was a nice surprise to find out you were going to be there.' Didier gave me a smile that warmed my heart.

'Yes, I had a great day too, thank you. Give Chlöe a hug goodbye from me, won't you?'

'I'm sure you'll see each other again soon.' He paused for a moment as if he was going to say something else but then thought better of it. 'Well, safe journey home and I'll see you tomorrow evening.'

I made to get out of the car and he jumped out and ran round to my door. He offered me his hand and I took it. He leaned in to kiss me on each cheek and the combination of the sensation of his lips on my skin together with the smell of the warm night air was captivating.

'*A demain,* Fran.' He watched as I made my way to the door and once I'd opened it and was standing inside, he got back in the car. I waved as he reversed into the darkness. Then I closed the door gently behind me.

Didier

I drove away from Fran's house feeling a mixture of emotions. I'd really wanted to kiss her but I knew that would have frightened her off. If I was being honest with myself, I'd been a bit scared of taking that next step too, after everything she'd said. After all, it was only yesterday she'd told me she just wanted to be work colleagues, and she'd reinforced that again today. I was still attracted to her though, and it was going to be hard to keep a professional distance under those circumstances.

It was getting on for midnight when I arrived back at the vineyard. I lifted Chlöe out of her seat as carefully as I could, trying not to wake her, and carried her quietly back to the cottage through the darkness. This was the last time she would sleep there. We would have a busy day tomorrow moving our things over to the château so that Fran could move into the cottage. I went upstairs to Chlöe's little bedroom and laid her on the bed, before gently easing off her coat and rolling her first one way and then the other so that she was tucked under the covers. I kissed her on the forehead, dimmed the lights and, leaving the door ajar, I crossed the small landing towards my own room. I stripped down to my boxers and fell into bed, exhausted after a long but happy day. My last few thoughts were of Fran before I fell into a deep, satisfying sleep.

As always, Chlöe was up at the crack of dawn and raring to go, which was probably a good thing today and I was used to the early mornings anyway.

'*Qu'est-ce que tu veux manger ce matin, ma petite?*' I asked her. She was playing with Princesse, rolling around on the floor like she was a dog. I'd left Princesse with Henri yesterday so unless he'd brought her back up here, she must have run all the way back from the village this morning, finding her own way. I hoped Henri had brought her because I hated to think of her running along the path on her own, even though I knew she had a good sense of direction.

I nudged Chlöe gently with my foot trying to prompt an answer to my question about breakfast.

'*Des pains au chocolat!*' she cried. I lifted her up from the floor and threw her over my shoulder to carry her back upstairs and she giggled all the way. We both put on some old clothes and hurried back downstairs again to walk to the *boulangerie* to pick up some breakfast. I whistled to Princesse and she followed us out. It only took a few minutes for me to get down to the village on my own but with a toddler in tow, it always took much longer. I let her take her time until she complained of being hungry and then I hoisted her up on my shoulders for the rest of the way.

'*Bonjour*, Didier *et* Chlöe. *Ça fait si longtemps! Que tu es grande maintenant.*' Liliane was an old friend of the family and she had four children of her own so she knew a thing or two about toddlers. The delicious smells coming from the bakery were enough to make Chlöe's tummy rumble loudly and she laughed at the sound. We were in and out in a matter of minutes and we ate our breakfast on the way back, passing morsels to the dog.

After breakfast, I explained to Chlöe that today was our moving day and that it was going to be a big adventure. Her eyes lit up. We were only moving our clothes and things, not any furniture, so I was hopeful we could get it done by lunchtime. I packed a bag with our clothes and Chlöe packed a small bag of toys, and then we set off for the château. We met Henri on the way, so he pitched in too.

'What are you doing here this morning? You're not working on a Sunday, are you?' I scolded him.

'I brought Princesse up first thing to stop her running up here by herself. Then I just checked on a few things and before I knew it, it was nearly lunchtime.'

We put our things in the bedrooms and went back to collect the last remaining items from the cottage. I checked the fridge when we got back because I'd remembered I had asked the housekeeper to drop in some supplies for Fran the day before. I was grateful to see that she'd done as I asked and had also given the cottage a final clean for me. After we'd taken things over to the château for the last time, I went up to Chlöe's new room with her. It looked very forlorn and she wasn't smiling when she stood looking at it.

'By the next time you come, I will have made it beautiful for you,' I reassured her. 'Will you bring some more of your toys with you then?' I asked. She nodded. I took her hand and we went downstairs to where Henri was waiting.

'Time for some lunch?'

'*Absolument*,' I agreed, and we set off for the village once again.

CHAPTER SEVEN

Fran

'Françoise! *Bonjour, ma chérie,*' my father boomed at me as I appeared in the kitchen for breakfast the following morning. I frowned at him slightly. He knew perfectly well I hated being called by my full name.

'*Bonjour, Papa.*' I ignored his jibe. If I mentioned it, he would only keep it up. I sat down at the table and helped myself to a buttery croissant and some juice. My mum poured me a coffee, smiling kindly at me.

'How did the wedding go yesterday?'

'Oh, it was lovely, *Maman*. Amandine looked absolutely beautiful and so happy. A few of my other university friends were there, as well.'

'How did you get home? Did one of them drop you off?' my father broke in.

'Er, no.' I paused, wiping the croissant flakes from my hands and mouth with my napkin and wondering whether to elaborate. When I looked up, my dad was staring at me, still waiting for my explanation. 'Didier dropped me off, actually. He was there as well.' My mum raised her eyebrows. It was only a slight movement but I still noticed, and I had to smile.

'Well, that was very kind of him and saved me a job.' The link between Didier and me had gone straight over my dad's head, of course, but my mum knew better.

'Did you know he was going to be there?' she asked.

'I had no idea until the day before, and what's more, his plus one was his three year old daughter, Chlöe.' This time, my mum's eyebrows shot up and I laughed out loud.

'Well, he has been busy in your absence. Was his wife there too?' She looked a bit disgruntled now but I knew this was only out of loyalty to me.

'No, they're separated now. We did talk about what I'd said to him the day before and cleared the air a bit.'

My dad looked up and pushed his reading glasses on to his bald head. 'Are we talking about *that* Didier?'

My mum and I both rolled our eyes and didn't even bother to reply.

'Anyway, I think we've drawn a line under the past, Mum, which is great seeing as we're going to be working together.'

'So, tell us more about this job you'll be doing at the vineyard, sweetheart,' my mum asked, finally sitting down at the table for her own breakfast.

I told them all about Didier's plans to build a Visitors' Centre on the estate, and how he needed someone to manage the project and market it as well. Just telling my parents about the idea renewed my passion once again.

'It sounds like a great promotion for you. And you start tomorrow?' my dad asked.

'Yes, so I'll have to return this afternoon to get myself settled in my cottage before I start. I only had a brief tour of the estate and I want to make sure I know what I'm doing.'

'Oh, it's a shame you can't stay for longer. I wish Lottie had been able to stay long enough to see you too. Still, you can come home more often now you're nearer, and perhaps we could come and visit you, as well.'

'That would be lovely, Mum.' I didn't say anything more about Lottie. There was something odd going on with her, I was sure of it, but better to keep my concerns to myself until I'd had a chance to speak to her. 'Will you give my love to *Papi* too,' I went on, 'and tell him I'll see him next time?'

I hadn't seen my grandfather since my last visit either and we had a very special bond.

'Of course,' Mum nodded. 'He'll definitely want to catch up with you.'

After breakfast, I went for a shower and to pack my things before coming downstairs again and going outside into the garden for some fresh air. I sat down at the wooden bench with another cup of coffee, relishing the peace and quiet. As I sat there, I remembered saying goodnight to Didier the night before. For a brief moment I'd wondered if he was going to kiss me but, since I'd effectively told him to back off twice now, that seemed very unlikely. I hoped I hadn't upset him again. I sighed and stood up, deciding to go and look for my dad.

I found him in his shed, potting some plants before winter set in. The peaty smell of the compost enveloped me as the door closed behind me. My dad looked up and smiled and as he did so, his glasses fell down in front of his eyes. He laughed and so did I.

'Forgive me for saying this, but you will take care working with Didier, won't you? Remember, it took you a long time to get over what happened with him before and I don't want you to get hurt again.'

I opened my mouth to argue but of course I knew he was right. 'I know what you're saying, *Papa*, but I think we both have to share the blame for what didn't happen between us. And a lot has happened while we've been apart, to both of us. I'm not looking to start things up with him again. I just want to do my job.'

He brushed his hands off on his gardening trousers and smiled.

'It's time for us to find something nice for lunch, I think.' His eyes lit up and I laughed. Food and wine were my dad's two favourite things and always uppermost in his mind. He put his arm round my shoulder and we went back inside.

I gave Mum and Dad a hand in preparing some food before we all settled at the kitchen table together to tuck in. Dad had opened a bottle of Pinot Gris, which was crisp and refreshing enough to offset the richness of the cured meats and creamy salads. For a few moments, we fell silent, just enjoying the taste and smell of the wonderful food on our plates.

All too soon, it was time for my dad to take me back to the station. As I kissed and hugged them both, my eyes began to fill with tears. I really had missed seeing them so much, and I felt as though it was my own stupid fault for letting Paul stop me from coming home.

'Don't cry, sweetheart,' my dad told me. 'We'll see you again soon - perhaps at your cottage next time. You can show us the estate.' He took my bag out to the car while I said my goodbyes to Mum.

'You just take care, *chérie,* and good luck in your new job.'

I waved until I could no longer see her and tried to focus on the journey back to the station. I shed a few more tears as Dad dropped me off, and then I was back on the train again, heading towards Strasbourg and my new life.

Didier

'Have Chlöe ready for me to collect her from the courtyard at 3 please,' Isabelle informed me by text later that morning. *'I don't have any time to waste. I must be back in Strasbourg for an important meeting.'*

Isabelle had a way about her of annoying me with even the simplest request, so I was already irritated before she arrived. She didn't get out of the car, and left the engine idling as she wound her window down reluctantly to speak to me. She had her sunglasses on, as always, and her hair was piled in some sort of tower on top of her head. With her permanent uniform of heavy make-up, hair styling and ultra-fashionable clothes, I hardly recognised the woman I thought I had fallen in love with just a few years before.

'Hurry, please. I'm on a tight schedule.'

I gritted my teeth. 'Where are you going? And is Chlöe going with you?' I lifted Chlöe into her car seat and fastened her in.

'I have a meeting with my agent. Chlöe will be well looked after.' She tutted and looked pointedly at her Cartier watch.

I kissed my daughter goodbye and she gave me a little hug in return, falling silent as she always seemed to do when Isabelle and I were together. I put her bag on the floor in front of her and returned to Isabelle's window.

'Who is looking after Chlöe?' I repeated.

'The girls at the agency adore her and will look after her while I'm in my meeting. Now I must go. Stop fussing.' She pressed a button and her window started to rise, giving me no choice but to back away. I stared at the back of her 4x4 as she turned and drove towards the main road, whisking Chlöe away from me once more.

I returned to the cottage, doing some paperwork outside at the little table on the patio to take my mind off Isabelle and Chlöe. I didn't notice Fran approaching until she was almost in front of me. When I looked up and saw her struggling with a large suitcase, I grinned and jumped up to greet her.

'You should have let me know you were on your way. I would have come to meet you,' I said, relieving her of her suitcase. She surrendered it to me gratefully, rubbing her forearm a little. I led the way into the cottage, setting the suitcase down on the stone floor of the living room.

'Thank you so much for moving your things out, Didier, but you didn't have to do all that today. You could have taken your time.' She looked distressed at the thought.

'It was not a problem for me,' I touched her lightly on the arm. 'Chlöe and I had a lot of fun moving our things, and Henri pitched in too. I wanted it to be clear for your arrival so you could make it your own.' I smiled at her and she returned it.

'Thank you. That was really thoughtful of you.' She paused before changing the subject. 'Well, I'll get myself settled this evening and then I'll be ready to start work tomorrow morning. What time would you like me to meet you?'

'I have an early meeting in Strasbourg tomorrow, so I won't be here first thing, but Henri will show you around. Shall I tell him you'll meet him in the office at nine?'

Her face fell a little and I had the feeling that she was disappointed I wouldn't be there at the start of her first day. Then she pulled herself up and put on her brightest smile.

'Yes, that would be fine.'

I turned to go and she followed me to the door.

'Goodbye, then. *A demain!*' I stopped at the table to gather up my papers and sauntered off towards the château. It was only after I'd gone that I remembered I'd meant to tell her about the food in the fridge. I brought my hand to my forehead in irritation. Still, she would find it all for herself and at least she wouldn't go hungry on her first night.

Fran

I closed the little wooden door behind Didier and leaned against it, hearing my stomach rumble as I did so. I groaned. Not only did I have no food in the house, I also had no transport to go and buy any. My heart sank. I crossed the lounge to the kitchen area, planning to check out the fridge. I bent down in front of the door and held my breath, hoping there would be something inside. When I pulled the door open, I couldn't believe my eyes. The fridge was full of all kinds of delicious foods - cheeses, meats, a beautiful home-made quiche Lorraine and a chilled bottle of rosé, along with some other essentials too. I closed the door and released my breath. On the counter was a basket with a cloth draped over it. I pulled it aside and discovered a loaf of fresh bread. I sighed as I inhaled its sweet smell. Didier had been so thoughtful. I wished I'd known beforehand so that I could have invited him to eat with me.

The next morning, I was woken by a scratching sound at one of the doors. I'd slept so peacefully in the old-fashioned bed in my room that I didn't really want to get up to go and investigate, but I needed to be ready for work in just over an hour. Reluctantly, I pulled myself up. I grabbed my dressing gown, slipped my feet into my comfy slippers and padded down the creaky wooden staircase. I stood between the kitchen and the lounge, listening for the sound. When it came again a few seconds later, I went to the back door and peered out through the glass panel at the top. The dog that had greeted me so eagerly the other day was sitting there looking up at me quite forlornly. My heart melted at once and I opened the door to say hello.

'Hey you.' I crouched down to stroke the little red-coated dog. He responded with a soft whine and leaned into my touch. I glanced around to see if anyone was about but there didn't seem to be anyone with him. I went back in to get a bowl of water and was surprised when he stayed outside the door, waiting for me. As I came back, he stood up, tail wagging furiously and I only just about managed to put the bowl on the ground without spilling it everywhere. After watching him drink for a moment, I had to shut the door so I could go and get ready. I wished I had some food to give him but on the other hand, I didn't want to confuse him into thinking this was home.

I showered quickly in the rickety old bathroom because the water was barely warm, and then spent an agonising few minutes in the bedroom trying to decide what to wear. My suits from my old job in the City seemed far too formal and not terribly practical for the setting, but I wanted to look professional. I settled on a pair of smart black trousers and a short-sleeved cream blouse with a soft blue cardigan over the top. I had some black ankle boots that seemed the most sensible idea for walking around the estate so I slipped those on too. When I came back to the kitchen, I poked my head round the door but there was now no sign of the dog. He'd obviously got distracted by something, but I missed the company. After the quickest of breakfasts, I grabbed my jacket and notebook before setting off for the courtyard where I had first met Didier. It was only a short walk back across the lawn but it was the first time I had seen the estate this early in the day. A faint mist hung over the vineyards and the rising sun bathed the landscape in a spectacular range of reds and oranges as far as the eye could see. I wanted to get a professional photographer to take some photos of these views so we could show them off in the new Visitors' Centre when the time came.

I found Henri working in the office where I'd had my original interview. He was on the phone when I knocked tentatively on the open door but he waved me in and motioned towards the desk opposite. While I waited, I made some notes about my thoughts so far in my notebook. I was just finishing up when Henri came off the phone. He put out his hand towards me and I took it, shaking it firmly.

'*Bonjour, Mademoiselle* Schell! *J'espère que vous avez bien dormi?*' His kind enquiry set me at ease and I smiled at his friendly, open face.

'Yes thank you, Henri, I slept very well. Please do call me Fran.' I paused for a moment. 'So, what have you planned for me to do this morning?'

'Didier has asked me to give you a tour of the wine cellars this morning and he would like you to taste the wine as well so you become more familiar with it.' He had switched from French to almost perfect English in a second and I was very impressed.

'I'd love to taste the wine but that will be a bit later, won't it? It still feels a bit early yet.'

He chuckled in reply and stood up to go back out to the courtyard. I followed him and a second later the dog streaked towards us. Henri called him to heel at once and the dog sat adoringly at his feet.

'Is he your dog, Henri? He appeared at the cottage early this morning looking for some affection.' I reached out to stroke the dog again and he nuzzled my hand.

'It's a she actually and she belongs to Didier, but as he's always off somewhere or other, we all look after her, really. She'll probably come with us as we walk round. Shall we go?' He led the way and sure enough, the dog followed in our footsteps.

'What's her name?' I asked, looking back to check she was still with us. When Henri didn't reply, I glanced over at him.

'Her name is Princesse.' He grimaced, looking embarrassed at the mere mention of such a terrible choice of name for an animal, and I burst out laughing.

'I hope that Didier was being ironic!' Henri joined in laughing then and we were still chuckling as we arrived at the first stop on the tour. I had the feeling Henri and I were going to be good friends.

Henri held open the door of the ancient-looking barn I'd seen previously and gestured for me to go in. Instead of the dank, old barn I was expecting, there were large, gleaming metal tanks in front of me reaching right up to the roof.

'So, this is where the wine is made.' I gazed around wide-eyed.

'This is the winery, yes. We have the tanks you can see here for our white and rosé wines, and in the next part of the cellar you'll see the barrels for our red wines. The cellar is all temperature-controlled,' he said as we passed about a dozen tanks.

I noticed it was very cool in the first room too, so guessed there must be some kind of air-conditioning.

'It looks so ancient from the outside. It must have cost the owner a fortune to turn it into this modern winery.'

'Ah, yes, uh, we have invested a lot of money over the years, *Mademois...*' he began and then remembered at the last minute, 'er, Fran, yes.' He looked distinctly uncomfortable calling me by the shortened version of my name and I had to smile. He was quite formal for someone who must be around the same age as me. Having been in the UK for a few years, I'd forgotten the formality of the French language.

After inspecting all the modern equipment, we carried on into the next room which this time was full of old oak barrels, all lined up in rows.

'This is where we age our pinot noir wines.'

This room was darker and smelt of the oak, a smoky smell of wood imparting its flavour little by little to the wine during the ageing process. We emerged from this room into an empty space with a soil floor. Another smaller room lay beyond.

'Ah, so this is where you want the shop to be, I suppose?'

'*Exactement.*' Henri smiled at me. 'We want the visitors to go on a tour through the winery and finish in the shop for a tasting. We'd also like them to be able to buy the wines before leaving.'

'Have you looked at shops at any of your competitors' *domaines*?'

'Oh, yes, we have been to see what they've done. Most are very modern with sleek, wooden flooring and somewhere informal to taste the wines. You should probably go and have a look yourself.'

'And what's the budget, Henri? There's an awful lot of work to be done here. I hope the owner realises it could be expensive.' I looked directly at him and was surprised to see his face redden a little.

'Er, for that you will need to speak to Didier, I think.' I was sure he was fudging, even though he knew the budget. Intriguing, I thought. I would have to ask Didier about it, and find out when I might meet the vineyard owner, as well. Just then, the door to the estate opened and Didier's head appeared round it.

'So, what do you think of the cellars?' he asked me as he approached.

'Very impressive indeed.' I smiled. 'The owner has done a lot of work here. Henri and I were just talking about the budget for building the shop and tasting area.' Didier glanced sharply at Henri but the other man shook his head gently.

'If you will excuse me, er, Fran, I have some work I must be getting on with.' He nodded towards me, gave me a brief smile and set off towards the door.

'Well?' I asked Didier.

'Well, what?' he replied vaguely.

'What's the budget for building the shop? You've both been avoiding answering my question and this is something I'll need to know if I'm to do my job properly.' I held Didier's eye as I waited for the answer.

'We don't have a specific budget,' he replied at last with a sigh, 'but we do have some money set aside.'

'And how much is that?' I pressed.

'About fifty thousand euros,' he said quietly.

My mouth fell open for a moment, until I realised what I must look like and I quickly shut it again.

'Come, let us go and taste some wine.' He guided me out of the barn, taking advantage of my silence until we were standing outside, blinking a little in the now bright sunshine. He began walking away from me towards another smaller barn across the gravel path and I followed, still unable to fathom why they had thought this paltry amount would be anywhere near enough to pay for a new Visitors' Centre, let alone my salary.

CHAPTER EIGHT

Didier

I led Fran purposefully alongside a row of vines round the back of the house and into the smaller barn, leaving her no time to ask me any further questions about the money or who the vineyard owner was. As our eyes adjusted to the half-light, I could see a barrel had been placed on its end with some glasses arranged on it for our tasting. Behind this were rows of wooden barrels stretching far into the distance and, as always, I felt a surge of pride at all we had accomplished at the vineyard. Thierry, my winemaker, appeared from between two of the rows with a bottle of wine in his hand. He smiled broadly at us both.

'*Bonjour*, Didier, *mademoiselle. Comment ça va ce matin?*'

I grasped Thierry's outstretched hand and laughed as he pulled me in for a brief hug. I took in his familiar, lived-in, tanned face and his constant smile, marvelling at my old friend's easy-going nature once again despite all he had been through in recent times.

'Thierry, *je te présente* Françoise.'

'*C'est* Fran, *monsieur*,' she said, frowning at me and shaking Thierry's extended hand at the same time. I remembered then how she hated to be called by her full name. We both chuckled at her insistence and she smiled, graciously letting it go.

'*Vous voulez déguster du vin, non?*' Thierry asked, drawing the cork expertly from the tall bottle of white wine. He proceeded to sniff both the cork and the opened bottle gently to check the wine had not been tainted by the cork. Once satisfied that the wine was in good health, he poured out three tasting measures for us into the glasses standing on the barrel. He set the bottle down and Fran leaned in to study the *Domaine* label. I knew that she was in for a surprise when she saw what was written on it. There, in elegant calligraphy, it stated quite clearly *Domaine des Montagnes* and underneath it said *Propriétaire - Didier Le Roy*. She straightened and looked first at me, then at Thierry, and then at me again.

'Do you...? Are you...? I'm confused.'

'I do and I am. Does that answer your questions?' I replied.

'You are the vineyard owner! So, this is your family's vineyard? But why didn't you tell me?'

'I just didn't want to overwhelm you with all that. I wanted to keep things simple while we got to know each other again. There's plenty of time for everything else later.' I smiled, trying to reassure her that nothing had changed but I could see in her eyes that she felt something had, she just wasn't sure what.

'I would like to taste the wine, please,' she said eventually. She picked up her glass but Thierry stopped her, showing her how to swirl the glass gently to release all the flavours in the wine before she tasted it.

'*C'est un pinot blanc de l'année dernière,*' he said.

She took a sip of this fairly young wine and swallowed. Thierry and I both spat out our wine, having swirled it around in our mouths for a moment. I could see the obvious dismay on her face and I laughed.

'We are used to spitting because we taste so many wines,' I explained. 'You can simply enjoy it. Did you like it?' I asked.

'It's delicious. It's full of fruit and it makes my mouth water a little, if that makes sense?'

'That's a perfect description. Would you like to taste the rosé next?'

We went on to taste the rosé and a red and, by the time we had finished, Fran looked like maybe she should have been spitting out the wine after all. We said goodbye to Thierry and began to walk back across the lawn towards the cottage. About halfway, she stopped.

'So, this beautiful château and estate, as well as the vineyards, all belong to you? Is that right?'

I nodded.

'Will you show me the château?'

'Of course. Although I must confess, I haven't spent a lot of time there since I moved into the cottage.'

Fran

My heart sank as I remembered once again that I had made Didier homeless. We turned to retrace our steps. Closer up I could see the château really did need a lot of work doing to it. I wondered how expensive it must be to maintain it, let alone the rest of the estate. As we wandered through the downstairs rooms, looking at all the covered furniture and the dusty bookshelves still full of books, I began to feel sad that this house was so unloved. It felt almost abandoned.

'Why don't you spend time here?' I asked as we arrived at the bottom of the stairs.

'After my dad died, my mum couldn't bear the thought of staying here with the constant reminders of him around her. So, after living here for the whole of her married life, she moved out to a house in the village. It was my family home too, of course, and once they'd both gone, it felt strange without them. That's when I moved to the cottage.'

He walked over to the fireplace to pick up a photograph frame. He studied the picture for a second before putting it back and turning round to face me.

'Since my dad died, I have had to focus all my energy on running the estate. The château has fallen into disrepair while we've kept everything going. Thankfully, most of the people who work here have done so for many years, so we have been able to simply carry on what he started.'

'Are you sure spending money on a new Visitors' Centre is the right thing to do with the small amount of money you have spare?'

'To be honest, I don't know. There is so much to do I just didn't know where to start. My dad was very good at reinvesting in the estate, so I was surprised when I found out that he had managed to put any money aside. My mum and I discussed what would be the most efficient use of the money he'd saved. Our priority was to use it to help us raise more.'

'And that's when you decided on building a Visitors' Centre.' It was all making more sense now but I was still worried that it wasn't going to be a big enough budget for all he wanted to do.

We went up the stairs and I marvelled at the grandeur of the property. I could see quite clearly that it had once been a beautiful building. I stopped at one of the windows at the front of the house, to look out and admire the view of the gardens and the vineyard.

'I'm sorry about your dad passing away. I had no idea. You've done a great job here. I think your dad would be proud of you.'

'Thank you. That means a lot to me.' He came up to stand next to me.

'You know, in the longer term it would be a good idea to renovate the château too, and to open it up to visitors along with the winery and vineyard. I bet this old building has a tale or two to tell! How many bedrooms does it have?' I turned to look at Didier to find him smiling broadly at me. 'What is it?' I asked.

'It is you. Your enthusiasm - it is so infectious, and I was hoping you would have some good ideas about how I can manage the estate better in the future. To answer your question, there are six bedrooms. Why do you ask?'

'Well, if you could renovate the château, you could invite paying guests to stay here. How would you feel about that?'

'It sounds interesting but like a lot more hard work. Still, it's something we could keep in mind, especially if we have a good harvest this year. That's going to be the deciding factor, as always.'

We descended the once grand staircase side by side, and as I surveyed the dusty, unloved hallway below, I knew that if it was up to me, I would want to restore the château to its former glory so that it never looked like this again. We wandered back through the downstairs rooms, taking in the massive farmhouse kitchen, then passed through the old conservatory and found ourselves back outside. Glancing at my watch, I could see it was definitely lunch time.

'Are you hungry?' I asked on an impulse.

His eyebrows shot up at my question and I felt myself blush. 'Er, yes I am, but I wasn't planning to stop for long.' He ran his tanned fingers through his unruly mop of hair.

'You left me such a delicious selection of foods in the fridge in the cottage. It would be lovely to share it with someone. Well, with you, I mean.'

'That would be wonderful, thank you.'

I stared at him for a moment to make sure I'd heard him right. When I didn't move, he laughed. 'Shall we go then?'

By the end of the first week, I had managed to establish a good work schedule. Princesse woke me every morning and accompanied me to the office where I would be thrown into the next phase of my learning curve until lunch time, when Didier and I would usually stop for something to eat at the cottage. We talked a lot about the estate and my projects, but we hadn't discussed anything very personal since returning from the wedding.

On Friday, we sat outside the cottage once again, enjoying the last of the August sunshine. Princesse was sat at my feet, as always.

'You know, I had been thinking about getting myself a dog once I'd got myself settled here, but now Princesse and I have become friends, and she's spending so much time with me...' I paused, not wanting to upset him with what I was going to say next.

He looked up from his plate of charcuterie and gave me a cheeky smile.

'So, you want to adopt my dog now, is that it?'

'Well, I would love to have her with me all the time but I wouldn't want to deprive you of her.' I tried to look sheepish but didn't quite manage it.

'I bought her to keep me company when Isabelle and Chlöe left. I named her for my daughter but I haven't spent as much time with her as I would have liked. I think she really likes you and it helps that you're here at the cottage, which she still sees as her home. So no, I don't mind if you want to share her with me.'

'Oh, that sounds like a good idea. One thing though...' I hesitated again.

He rolled his eyes affectionately at me.

'Does she have to be called Princesse?'

He burst out laughing. 'You are very persistent. Did anyone ever tell you that?'

'Not for a long time, no. I think you're bringing that out in me.' We both fell silent then as we considered my words. I knew I felt stronger after only a week in Didier's presence. He asked for my opinion and deferred to me when I made good suggestions. My confidence was already boosted and I felt full of hope for my future.

'Do you have another name in mind?' he asked after a few minutes.

'Ruby,' I said, looking at her sleek, golden red coat. She looked up at me and whined and I reached out to pat her.

'Now that is an excellent choice. Henri will be very pleased with that. Okay, agreed.' He coughed slightly before continuing. 'There's something I wanted to ask you, actually.' My eyes widened. 'I wondered if you would like to spend the day with me tomorrow, visiting some other wineries nearby so I could show you what they have done with their set-ups. We could go for a nice lunch somewhere too.'

'I'd like that very much.'

Didier

We set off early the next day to visit some of the local wineries. There were lots of people milling around as we arrived at the first vineyard, which surprised me for a Saturday morning in late August. We were never that busy by this time in the month. We joined the tour and Fran made a few notes as we went round. The first winery wasn't as big as ours but it was just as modern. Once again, I could see that caring for visitors was big business. This tour included a visit through the bottling area, which wasn't something we offered our visitors.

After the tour was over, we emerged into a wine tasting room, where we sampled some of the wines before going through to the shop. I was drawn immediately to the wines for sale. I left Fran to wander round the shop in her own time while I went to study the display of *vendanges tardives*. I loved these sweeter, late-harvest wines and it had been a long time since I'd indulged myself by buying one.

'Have you found something you like?' Fran asked as she came up alongside me.

I laughed. 'Of course, I would like to buy them all but I might just have to buy only the one bottle today. There is a lovely half-bottle of Gewurztraminer in this display that I would love to try. How about you? Have you finished taking notes for now?'

'I've taken so many notes, it will take me ages to tell you everything I've had in my mind.' She pulled a face.

'Well, we're not going to go through your notes today. We'll do that next week when we're properly at work. For now, I want to buy this wine, and then go and find somewhere nice for lunch.'

We left a few minutes later, driving away from the little village and deeper into the Alsatian countryside. Everywhere we looked there were idyllic villages, with churches and castles all set among the vines, rivers and forests for which the region is famous. I heard Fran sigh.

'You sound like you're deep in thought. Are you okay?' I asked.

'Yes, it was a good sigh. I just feel happy to be back home after so long away. I didn't know if it was the right decision to come back at first, you know. I used to find life in the countryside so dull but now that I'm here, I'm beginning to enjoy it.'

I glanced at her to find her blushing slightly at her own admission but I didn't question her. I remembered only too well how keen she had been to escape to London.

I turned into the entrance of a small estate shortly afterwards and drove slowly along the gravel driveway. I pulled up in front of a beautiful country house, which was on two floors and covered with window boxes full of flowers. It was enchanting as always, and I couldn't wait to take Fran inside. I got out of the car and went round to her door to hold it open for her. Then I extended my hand towards her to help her out. As she stood up, I felt the warmth of her body next to mine and her intoxicating perfume filled the air. Her eyes explored mine and for a moment, time seemed to stand still. I let go of her hand and turned away from her, afraid to let things go any further. As I approached the restaurant, I was overwhelmed by the strength of my feelings towards her.

CHAPTER NINE

Fran

The restaurant was located at the back of the house, overlooking an isolated piece of land that faced out onto lush green vineyards, stretching as far as the eye could see. We sat at a table on the wide terrace and Didier ordered two glasses of *Crémant d'Alsace*. While we waited for the drinks, I struggled to think of what to say to break the ice a little after our close encounter outside. Didier beat me to it though.

'As I said, I don't want us to talk about work while we eat lunch, if that's okay with you?' I nodded gently. 'I think it's time we talked to each other properly, like we did last weekend.'

The drinks arrived giving me a breathing space, and Didier raised his glass to mine.

'*Santé*!' he said, giving me a broad, confident smile.

'What do you want to talk about?' I asked, trying my best to look calm while my insides were churning.

'I want to know more about what happened to you in London. You're not the same person you were before you left. Some of your spirit has gone and I wondered why.'

'I told you, I split up with Paul and your job seemed perfect for me. There was nothing left for me there, except my friend Ellie.' I dropped my gaze and began fiddling with my wine glass.

He shook his head. 'Come on. You've been working with me a week now. I think we've rebuilt our friendship enough for you to trust me.'

I sighed and turned to study the view of the vineyards, biting my lip as I did so. When I turned back to Didier, the understanding look in his eyes was enough to reassure me I could confide in him.

'Paul was...very controlling and you're right, I changed a lot during my time with him. I stopped doing the things I wanted to do, and did what he wanted instead. He could get very jealous if I spent time away from him. So my visits home became less and less frequent after I met him. My parents have no idea really what he was like.' I paused and took a deep breath. Didier's kind face encouraged me to go on, helping me overcome my embarrassment. 'I felt humiliated when I discovered him cheating on me but it opened my eyes so I could see him for who he really was and break away.'

'I'm so sorry. I don't know what to say.' Didier's answer was restrained but when I looked into his eyes, I could see he was angry. 'You already seem different after just a week here, if you don't mind me saying,' he continued. 'You seemed quite fragile when I first saw you again but now you are regaining your confidence, I think.'

'I am, yes. That's partly thanks to you.' I smiled at him and he gave me a heart-stopping smile back. 'I feel free for the first time in years to do what I want to do and not what someone else wants me to do. I gave in to Paul, rather than standing up for myself. I know now that I need to find my own identity again. Do you understand what I mean?'

'I do understand and I think you are already well on the way to finding yourself.'

'Yes, in the short term, I think I've taken the first step towards a new life by coming home. I don't know if this is what will be best for me in the longer term though. It's still early days.'

His smile faltered. I wanted to reassure him but I had no idea whether I could settle back into rural French life again after living in the city for so long.

'I'm so pleased we can be friends again,' I continued. 'And what about you? What happened between you and your wife that led you to decide to separate?'

Didier leaned back in his chair and took a sip of his wine. I kept my eyes on his as I waited for him to speak.

Didier

'Not long after you left for London, I met Isabelle at a wine tasting in Strasbourg, where she lived. She was trying to break into modelling and her assignment that evening was at the vineyard where the tasting was being held. Things became serious quite quickly between us and it wasn't long before I was spending a lot of time at her apartment. She was very much a party animal and wanted to be out every night, having a good time. In the beginning, that was fine.' I paused, remembering those happier times when I'd first met her. 'Then she fell pregnant and it seemed like the natural next step for us to get married. We were really happy for the first few months after Chlöe was born but then Isabelle started to get bored with being at home on the estate all day with no-one but a baby to talk to. She became angry that she was so far away from the city and couldn't maintain the social life she'd had before Chlöe was born. She'd kept her apartment but we hardly ever had time to get back there once I had to take full charge of the vineyard, and so resentment began to set in.'

I stopped and took in a deep breath. I found myself thinking about the way both Isabelle and Fran had found country life stifling, and how they couldn't wait to get away from it. 'We worked things out between us so Isabelle could get back to work. Then her career started to take off. Once she got herself an agent, she was getting jobs that involved travel across Europe and, later, across the world. I understood she wanted to further her career but soon she was hardly ever at home, and both Chlöe and I were missing her. We argued a lot in those days. Isabelle just responded by spending more and more time away from home. I didn't know what to do to bring her back, to restore the balance.'

I took a sip of my wine, finding it hard to talk about such difficult times. 'Then, after one particular trip away, she told me she'd had enough of the boring life we were leading out in the country and, just like that, it was all over. She moved out, taking Chlöe with her back to the apartment in Strasbourg. I was devastated. That was the last thing I wanted them to do. A few days later, she asked me to take Chlöe so she could go to an assignment, which I did without hesitation. And that's been the situation ever since. I never know when I'm going to see Chlöe because Isabelle won't agree to a regular arrangement. What I'd really like is for Chlöe to be with me all the time.'

'I'm so sorry. You've had a terrible time of it. Is there nothing you can do to gain custody of Chlöe?'

'Well, we're not even divorced yet, although it's been on my mind more and more to ask her about it. It's just that divorce is so final and I'm worried about doing what's best for Chlöe.'

She lay her hand on top of mine on the table, trying to give me some comfort.

'Love always seems to be complicated,' she said with a weak smile. 'When are you next seeing Chlöe?'

'Technically next weekend, but who knows?'

Shortly after this conversation, we made our way back to the car and drove to the next vineyard on our itinerary. We didn't get another chance to talk during the afternoon. The journey home seemed much shorter. I'd really enjoyed being in Fran's company and I knew that would end as soon as we arrived back at the vineyard. I pulled into the courtyard and we walked together towards the arch.

'Thank you for a lovely lunch. I'll write up my notes from the visits and we can talk about things again on Monday, perhaps?' Fran seemed awkward now it was time to say goodbye and I felt the same.

'Thanks, Fran. Enjoy the rest of the weekend and I'll see you on Monday.' I kissed her softly on the cheek and walked away.

Fran

I spent a bit of time on Sunday making the cottage feel more like home. I rearranged the furniture a little so it suited me more. Downstairs, I moved the two armchairs so that they faced the window, which allowed me to move the sofa next to the fireplace. I filled up some of the bookshelves with the few books I'd been able to bring with me and I moved the small breakfast table from the kitchen to the back of the living room, freeing up a lot more space in the kitchen. I didn't have time to start on the upstairs, but I would have to get round to it during the coming week because Ellie was coming at the weekend. We had enjoyed a long catch-up call together the previous evening and I was so excited about her visit.

'At long last!' she'd cried, when she answered the phone. 'I thought I was never going to hear from you again.'

'Oh, don't be mad at me please,' I replied, smiling at her high drama, 'I've had a lot going on and I have so much to tell you.'

'Well, come on then, don't keep me waiting!' And so I filled her in on everything that had happened since the last time we'd spoken. I confirmed that I had accepted the job as soon as I'd seen the cottage and then I moved on to the wedding, telling her what I'd learned about Didier's life during my absence. 'I can't believe he married someone else, Fran. I thought he was madly in love with you!'

'If he was, he didn't ever say so,' I said with sadness. 'I knew I was in love with *him,* though. Perhaps if we'd told each other how we really felt, it would have made all the difference to our decision to part. But it's too late for regrets, now. It's all over and done with.'

'It sounds like things are going quite well between you now.'

'Well, we're friends again, at least. Anyway, after all we've both been through, love should be the last thing on our minds.' I sighed, thinking about the gentle kiss Didier had given me yesterday.

'What you need is a good chat with an old friend, and I happen to know just the person. I'll pack a bag on Thursday so I can set off straight from work on Friday. Is that okay?'

'Of course it is. I can't wait to see you and to find out all your news.'

'Oh, you know me - same old, same old. I want to know all about your adventure!'

We chatted a bit longer before saying goodbye. I slept really well knowing Ellie would be coming to see me again so very soon.

Didier

As I approached the office after my morning inspection on Monday, Ruby came dashing towards me. We enjoyed a good catch-up cuddle for several minutes, and she lapped up my attention. I'd had to put on a thick jumper that morning, a sure sign of the season changing, and I'd even tugged my boots on in case the ground was boggy. My face felt fresh from the morning air and I could see my breath in front of me as I sweet-talked Ruby, watching her roll around on the gravel.

'Good morning. You look like you've been busy.'

I looked up as Fran approached and smiled, rising to stand next to her.

'I like the early mornings. It's my chance to walk among the vines before the day gets going, to see how they're faring. It looks like we're going to have a wonderful harvest this year if this weather continues.' I glanced up at the sky where all the answers lay for a *viticulteur* dependent on the sun and the rain. I stamped off my boots before going into the office and Fran followed me inside. On my way to the coffee machine, I glanced over at Henri who was already busy reading some papers.

'These are excellent notes,' Henri told Fran looking up from the papers.

I turned round. 'Ah, your notes from the visits we made on Saturday.' I took the papers from Henri as he finished with them and sat down at Fran's desk.

'I hope I haven't been too critical of the other visitors' centres or too bold with my suggestions for *Domaine des Montagnes*,' Fran murmured.

'We've finally received the letter from the *Mairie* confirming that we now have planning permission to develop our buildings into a Visitors' Centre,' Henri said, causing me to look up briefly again before looking back down at Fran's notes.

'Oh, that's great news,' Fran replied. 'So, when can we start the building works?'

'As soon as you can work your magic on the builders!' Henri answered. I noticed the cheeky grin he gave her.

'Have you spoken to any builders yourself yet?' she asked.

'No, we haven't had time. That's what we need you for.' He folded his arms and leaned back in his chair.

I glanced up and noticed Fran swallow apprehensively.

'Don't look so worried,' I said. 'I have a list of builders I would like us to approach.' I stood up and went to a drawer in the filing cabinet, returning a moment later with a shortlist in my hand. Fran looked at it, relieved.

I took a few more minutes to finish reading her notes as she chatted with Henri.

'This is an excellent summary of our visits from Saturday,' I said finally, smiling at Fran. 'I like your thinking. I do want us to be different and to have our own unique approach. I agree that people might not be so interested in seeing the mechanical operation of the bottling area, and that we must make sure to offer tours in different languages if we can, certainly in English and German. We also need to do some research on the best items to sell in the shop, rather than offering a whole list of things that people don't want.'

'Okay, well this list of builders will keep me busy for a while. Thank you,' she said.

I jumped up from her desk to let her sit down and get started. As I left, I gave Henri a smile knowing I could trust Fran to get on with the job in hand.

CHAPTER TEN

Fran

Despite the busy day I'd had in the office, I tossed and turned throughout the night. I finally dragged myself out of bed at eight the next morning feeling dog-tired. A long shower revived me a little but by the time I was ready to go downstairs for some breakfast, I still didn't feel ready for the day to come. Shortly before nine, my mobile rang and I snatched it up. I hadn't even noticed who the caller was.

'*Allo?*' There was a brief silence at the other end.

'Hello, Fran, it's me.'

'Paul? Is that you? What are you calling me for?' I suppressed a groan. He was absolutely the last person I wanted to talk to, especially in my current mood.

'I thought we should meet and talk. Where are you? Are you still in France?'

Damn, how had he managed to get through after I'd blocked his number? And I couldn't ask him either without giving away that I'd tried to block him. I ignored his question about where I was.

'I have nothing left to say to you after what you did to me. And trying to change the locks on me too - that was really low.' I banged around in the kitchen, making my anger very obvious.

'I am sorry about everything,' he said. 'I'd like to try and clear the air if we can and move on together. Tell me where you are so we can meet. Please. I'm trying to do the right thing.'

'For who? Not for me. I don't want to meet you and "clear the air". I just want you to leave me alone. I have to go now, bye.'

I rang off before he could reply. I checked my calls log and realised the call had come from the bank where Paul and I used to work. He had probably got in early so he could ring me before anyone else arrived. God, he was infuriating. I blocked the bank's number and set about making myself a very strong cup of coffee, taking out my frustration on the cups and kitchen utensils as they were the nearest things to hand. While I waited for the water to boil, I stood at the kitchen window looking out at the garden trying to calm down. Ruby nuzzled her nose against my clenched fist. I relaxed my hand and bent down to pet her. Maybe I would feel better once I got out for some fresh air and some thinking time. I decided against the coffee, threw on my coat and newly purchased wellies, and set off for a walk round the estate with Ruby.

I headed down towards the vineyard. Ruby had gone a long way ahead as if she knew where to go, so I just followed her lead. As I took in the vibrant red, green and gold of the estate around me, I tried really hard to forget about Paul's call. He was interrupting my new life, and just talking to him made me feel under his thumb again. I felt uneasy. Why was he so determined to keep in touch? I needed to stay in control and not let him browbeat me. I'd managed quite well in the conversation we'd had that morning. Now all I had to do was to keep that attitude up and not let him get under my skin again. I turned and made my way back to the cottage, feeling a bit more confident.

A few hours later, I was on my way back home after a long morning in the office, wondering whether I would see Didier for lunch today or not. As I passed through the archway, I made out a solitary figure peering in the windows of the cottage. As I got nearer I recognised Isabelle. She straightened up and turned as I approached, her elegant appearance and manner making me feel shabby in my waterproof jacket, jeans and wellies.

She looked me up and down with obvious disdain.

'Can I help you?' I managed to stutter out. I didn't think she remembered me from the church last weekend.

'Where is Didier?' she demanded.

'I haven't seen him all morning but I imagine he's busy in the vineyard.' Feeling uncomfortable in her presence, I turned to go into the cottage.

'Do you live here with him?' Before I could reply, she threw her head back and laughed as though the very idea was too ridiculous to entertain. My hackles rose and I found the strength to answer her back.

'I have just started working at the vineyard and this is now my cottage. Didier lives in the château. Perhaps you'd like to try there.'

She turned away, looking in the direction of the château as if she'd lost interest in me. I followed her gaze and blew out a sigh of relief when I saw Didier striding purposefully towards us. The relief was only momentary, however. I sensed the underlying tension emanating from her and I wondered if she was limbering up for a fight with him. I felt anxious and longed to get away before I had to witness anything unpleasant, but I thought I should show some kind of solidarity with Didier.

As he drew closer, I could see he was scowling in anticipation of a showdown. I saw the irritation on his face as he took in her beautiful but impractical outfit: sleek, tailored trousers, matching jacket and ridiculously high heels. Isabelle tapped her foot impatiently as she waited for him to arrive, and I wished I could be anywhere but here. I shifted awkwardly from one foot to the other, wondering whether they were about to have a massive row in front of me.

'Isabelle.' Didier nodded curtly in her direction before looking over at me and giving me a fleeting smile.

'I want to talk to you in private,' Isabelle said, 'but this woman tells me you no longer live in the cottage?' She said it as if she didn't believe it to be true and with as much scorn as she could manage. Didier gave me another quick glance, his gaze softening as though he were desperate to apologise for Isabelle's rudeness.

'That's correct. I don't live in the cottage. Come with me and we'll talk on our way to the château.' And with that, he turned on his heel and stalked off.

Didier

I turned round briefly to see Isabelle stumbling over the lawn until she finally decided to take off her high heels and walk in her bare feet. She caught up with me fairly quickly then but was still trailing along behind me. She was always immaculately presented but so out of place whenever she came here.

'What's this about?' I asked once I'd checked Fran had gone inside and we were far enough away from the cottage for no-one to hear.

'I need a special favour from you but I need you to listen to me. I can't do it while we're walking.'

I stopped and turned so abruptly she nearly bumped into me. I folded my arms and stared at her, knowing full well she was going to ask me to look after Chlöe again. All I wanted was a regular arrangement, with agreed visitation rights to see my daughter. These constant changes of plan were fraying my nerves.

'Well?' I said after a couple of minutes had passed and she still hadn't told me what she was talking about.

'The thing is I have been offered a modelling contract,' she began.

I noticed she was twisting her fingers together. That was odd in itself, because she was never nervous. She must want this job quite badly.

'So? You've had contracts before. What's so important about this one?'

'It's abroad.'

'You're not taking Chlöe abroad, Isabelle. That I will not allow.' I felt a stab of fear and braced myself for the onslaught of what she would say next.

She rolled her eyes at me. 'I don't want to take her with me, that's the point. I want her to stay with you so that I can go and do my work without having to worry about her.' She tutted at me and my mouth fell open at her cold-hearted approach to our child.

'Of course Chlöe can stay with me. I want her to be with someone who loves her as she should be loved and who can provide the stability that she needs. When are you going? And how long for?'

'I'm leaving on Saturday. And that's the other thing.' She paused dramatically. 'I'm going for a year.'

I was stunned by the thought of Chlöe staying with me for a year, delighted but anxious at the same time. I didn't want Isabelle coming back after a year demanding that everything return to normal. 'Then I think the time has come for us to start divorce proceedings and to agree on a formal custody arrangement.'

'What are you talking about? This is only a temporary situation. We don't need to get into all the formalities now.'

Her sudden anger caught me by surprise. 'A year is a long time, Isabelle, and we have already been separated for a while.'

It was as if she hadn't even heard me. 'Don't you want to know where I'm going?' she continued, full of her own self-importance. 'I will be in Toronto, in Canada, for your information.' She turned to leave, signalling the end of our conversation. It was just as well she wasn't looking at my face because I was sure a look of loathing must have passed across it as I struggled to contain my feelings. 'I'll bring Chlöe over on Saturday then, with her things,' she said over her shoulder. Then she sashayed off, leaving me reeling from her announcement.

Fran

After lunch, I kept myself busy all afternoon in the office, continuing with my phone calls to builders and slotting in appointments with them where possible. I had my first appointment lined up for the next morning. I needed to confirm that Didier could be there too, but there had been no further sign of him since he'd left with Isabelle. As I said goodbye to Henri at the end of the day, I worried about how their meeting must have gone. It was as if he was hiding himself away from us.

I was glad to get back to the refuge of my cottage at the end of such a rotten day, and I was just checking the contents of the fridge to see what I might be able to throw together for dinner when I heard a light knock at the door.

Didier was standing outside, looking very sorry for himself.

'Hey, you look miserable. Are you okay?' I gestured to him to come in, and he proceeded to collapse onto the sofa in front of the wood-burning stove. He stretched out his hands to warm them up. Despite his long face, he still looked gorgeous in his plain black t-shirt and jeans.

'Isabelle told me she's been offered a one year modelling contract in Toronto. She wants me to take care of Chlöe so she can go without having to worry about looking after her.' He stopped, a pained expression on his face.

'And how do you feel about that?'

'I don't mind if she goes to Toronto. I only care about my daughter's welfare and her future. I want to look after her, of course, but I don't want Isabelle coming back in a year's time and taking her away from me again.' He bowed his head and ran his hands through his curly hair in frustration. 'So, I told her that it's time for us to get a divorce and to sort out a formal custody arrangement for Chlöe but, judging from Isabelle's reaction, I don't think she will accept that easily. God knows why, she hardly spends any time with Chlöe as it is.'

'Have you spoken to a lawyer about this before?' I asked, sitting down opposite him.

'I spoke to someone when we first split up to check that I would be able to secure visiting rights to see Chlöe. He knew his stuff. I guess I could go back and talk to him about it in more detail now.'

I nodded. 'How did you leave things with Isabelle?'

'I told her I would be more than happy to look after Chlöe, but I didn't push her about the divorce or the custody.'

'Well, that sounds like you've done the right thing for now. When's she going?'

'Next weekend! I don't know what she would have done if I'd said no.'

'Does she have family nearby?'

'No, her mum lives in Paris and her dad's in America. They're divorced too, and haven't really shown much interest in their granddaughter so far.'

'Well, you can get on to the lawyer tomorrow and see what he has to say.'

'You're right.' He looked up at last and smiled at me. 'Thanks for listening, I'm sorry to dump all this on you.'

'Don't be silly, I'm glad if I can help. Changing the subject slightly, I was just going to make some dinner. Would you like to stay?'

He grinned and I was pleased I'd been able to help take his mind off his worries for a change.

I set about making a frittata using the leftover prosciutto and the asparagus spears I'd found hiding in the bottom of the fridge. As I was whisking the eggs, Didier stood up and came into the kitchen.

'It smells really good already,' he said, sniffing the air, 'Is there anything I can do to help?'

'Could you lay the table and pour out the wine while I get started cooking?' We sat down together at the table a short while later.

'*Santé*, and thank you for going to all this trouble for me. It looks and smells divine.' He tucked into his food, looking like he was savouring each mouthful. It was a pleasure to see how much he was enjoying it.

'You haven't told me about your day at all. I'm sorry I've monopolised the conversation.' He looked at me expectantly as he chewed his mouthful.

'I had a bit of a surprise call from my ex this morning.'

He raised his eyebrows. 'What did he want?'

'To meet and talk to clear the air apparently. I don't know what that was all about. I'd already told him it's over between us. I've moved on now, and I don't want to see him again.'

'You need to block his number from your phone,' Didier replied.

I nodded. 'That was the weird thing. I'd blocked him once already when he sent me a text but this time he called from the bank. I've blocked the bank's number now but he seems determined to stay in touch. It's important for me to maintain the new sense of purpose I've got since coming home. I don't want to fall under his control again.'

'Does he know where you are?'

'I did tell him I was coming home to France, but I haven't told him where I live precisely and he's never been here. But he could probably work it out if he wanted to from things that I've said in the past.' I chewed my lip as I considered how I would feel if he did come and find me.

'Was he...was he ever violent towards you?' Didier looked embarrassed even to ask me the question and I felt awkward about answering it. We were both silent for a few minutes.

'No, he wasn't physically violent towards me thank God, but he was threatening at times and I sensed he might hurt me if he didn't like something I said or did. To be honest, now I've had the chance to get away from him, I couldn't ever go back.'

After we'd finished our meal, we cleared everything away and Didier shrugged on his coat.

'Thanks for listening to my troubles,' I said to him as we walked towards the door.

'I should say the same,' he replied, turning to look at me. 'Thanks for a wonderful dinner too.' He leaned in towards me but this time he took my face gently in his hands and kissed me softly on the lips. The impact was electric but it was over far too soon. His warm breath caressed my face as he pulled back to look at me, his eyes searching mine for a reaction. I licked my lips, savouring the taste of him and trying to control my racing heart. When I didn't say anything, he dropped his hands and moved back.

'I'm sorry if that was too forward of me.'

'It wasn't. It was just unexpected, that's all, but in a good way.' I rushed to reassure him. In fact, it had been wonderful to feel his lips against mine again after all this time. I reached out to take his hands in mine. 'I just think we need to take things slowly. We need to be sure of what we want from each other.'

'I know, you're right. Maybe this is the wrong time for both of us to get into anything new. I'm sorry.' He turned to open the door again and a second later, he'd disappeared into the night.

I leant against the back of the door and groaned. Didier now thought I wasn't interested in him and that wasn't what I'd meant at all. I pulled myself upright and made my way to the sofa. I sat down and took a long sip of wine from my half-full glass. The truth was I didn't know what I wanted. I knew I still had feelings for Didier, that much was clear after just a few days spent with him again. But there was no escaping the fact that he was still married, and after what had happened with Paul, I just didn't know if I was ready to get involved with someone again so soon, regardless of who that someone might be. Not only that but I still hadn't made up my mind whether to stay in Alsace for good yet.

I took the wine bottle and glasses to the kitchen before making my way upstairs. I needed to talk to Ellie about the state of my love life - and everything else in my life as well. The weekend really couldn't come soon enough.

Didier

I rushed back across the grass towards the château. What had I been thinking? I knew she wasn't interested in another relationship, but her lips were so inviting and she'd been so lovely all evening that I'd let my heart rule my head. And she'd rejected me. It served me right for rushing in. I groaned out loud, causing some birds to flutter up into the sky in fright.

I reached the kitchen door at the back of the château and let myself in. I was so strung out after the day I'd had and then the embarrassing moment with Fran that I poured myself a glass of cognac and sank down into one of the kitchen chairs to drink it. I would need to back off a bit with Fran and revert to just being friends, nothing more. Perhaps it was for the best. I would have enough to deal with when Chlöe came to stay, not to mention dealing with my lawyer.

After a restless night, I took my morning walk round the vineyard before making my way to the office. Fran was already there and eager to talk to me about the appointments she had made with builders. She showed no sign of being annoyed with me so I tried to forget what had happened and bury myself in work as usual. In between the appointments with the builders, I tried to get Chlöe's room ready for when she arrived on Saturday. I made a quick trip into Strasbourg to order her a new bed and some bedding more suitable for a princess aged three. At least my little girl would have the basics she needed for her room. There was already a wardrobe and a chest of drawers. I worked each evening to clear them out and clean up her room for her arrival.

On Friday morning, I stayed at home to call my lawyer.

'*Bonjour,* Alain, *c'est* Didier Le Roy.' After the usual few minutes spent catching up, I explained all about the latest developments between myself and Isabelle.

'Are you sure about seeking a divorce from your wife now?' he asked after I'd finished.

'I don't think I have any choice. I want a formal custody arrangement for Chlöe and me. As soon as Isabelle hears I've gone ahead and put steps in place, she's going to be angry. I might as well get it all over and done with at the same time.'

'Just to clarify then: you are seeking a divorce from Isabelle and you want to agree a formal custody arrangement for visiting rights to Chlöe. Is that right?'

I blew out a long breath. 'To be honest, Alain, I would like to try for full custody if possible, on the grounds that Isabelle's job is her main priority and I don't think all the travelling she does is compatible with raising a child on her own. My life is more stable and I can provide Chlöe with a good home.'

'And you would be willing for Isabelle to have visiting rights instead?'

'Of course, but I would like it to be an agreed frequency. Perhaps every other weekend, unless Isabelle is away, in which case we can renegotiate. Does that sound reasonable?' I asked.

'It does to me but whether the courts will see it that way, we'll have to wait and see. I will draft the application and send it over for you to look at.'

After saying goodbye to Alain, I walked down into the village to the *école maternelle.* Chlöe was old enough to go to the village nursery school now, and I wanted to see if I could enrol her the following week. I had no idea how she would get on, so I was planning to bring her for a trial visit first. I knew Madame Albert, who ran the school, and she had a good reputation. I trusted her to look after my daughter. She told me she had space for Chlöe and asked me to bring her in first thing on Monday.

CHAPTER ELEVEN

Fran

With all my appointments with the various builders, the rest of the week flew by. By Friday afternoon, I'd become a lot more experienced about what questions to ask them, and I also had a much better idea of what Didier was looking for. Within a few more days, I'd have a shortlist of three for him to choose from.

Didier had been polite but distant since our dinner, and now his mind would be on Chlöe's arrival, and mine would be on Ellie's. I didn't know when we might get the chance to talk again. I was so looking forward to seeing my friend, I hardly had time to think about anything else. I was definitely going to get Ellie's advice on a few things during her stay. She sent me a text to say she would be arriving in Strasbourg at eight, so I decided to take a taxi to meet her from the train.

I arrived at the modern-looking station in plenty of time, and when the train pulled in I could hardly wait for her to reach me. When she saw me she let out a squeal that caused a few frightened looks among her fellow passengers. She was oblivious to them all, though, and that's what I loved about her. We hugged for a good few minutes and then she held me at arms' length.

'I think this country air must be good for you. You look really well.'

'I must admit I'm loving it so far. I wish I'd done it sooner.'

I pulled her small suitcase along the platform and it wasn't a long wait before we were in another cab and on our way back to the vineyard.

'Who knew you'd settle into this country life so quickly?' She rolled her eyes theatrically. 'I suppose you'll be buying some wellies now too?'

I smiled, blushing furiously. She smacked me playfully on the arm and we didn't stop laughing for the rest of the journey home. When the taxi dropped us off in the courtyard, I picked up her suitcase and guided her towards the arch. I was pleased to see she was wearing flat shoes so that she wouldn't have to struggle across the cobbles as I had done. We made our way towards the cottage in silence. As the house came into view, I heard her gasp. I glanced over at her, knowing her face would show her delight, and it did. I was glad I'd left the outside light on because the cottage looked heavenly in the half-light.

'Oh, I can see how easily you made your decision to take the job now. It's adorable!'

I opened the door and led her inside, turning on the lights as I went. The little house came alive and I felt proud of the slight changes I'd made to it to make it mine. I took Ellie's bag straight upstairs and she followed me, "oohing" and "aahing" along the way. By the time she saw her room, she had no words left.

'Well, what do you think?' I asked, smiling at her.

'Oh, it's so beautiful.' She moved her bag along the wooden floor so she could sink onto the bed. The furnishings were simple but it was all clean and homely.

'Come on then, let's go and get something to eat. I don't know about you but I'm starving.' I turned and went back towards the stairs. 'Go careful on these stairs, won't you? They're a bit rickety.'

Didier

It was busy in the bistro by the time we arrived, which was always a good sign. Henri and I pulled out seats and sat down at the bar to wait for Michel. Michel was Laurent's older brother and we had known each other a long time. He had run the bar in the village for a good few years but had only recently extended it to include the bistro. He was working really hard to make a success of the bistro, and now I thought of it, I couldn't remember having seen him at the evening reception for Laurent's wedding. Henri and I usually dropped in for a drink at least once a week to show our support. As we waited, I glanced around the bistro and noticed Elena, Michel's wife, darting around the front of house, making sure every table was being properly looked after. I watched as she took down an order at a small table in the corner. When she turned to leave, I realised Fran was at the table with another woman who I presumed must be Ellie, her friend from London. She looked animated as they chatted, and I was glad she had some company for the weekend.

'*Salut, les gars*. What would you like to drink this evening?' Michel gave us a broad smile but I noticed how tired he looked.

We ordered a glass of white wine each, and I sent two more over for Fran and her friend.

'Who is Fran with?' asked Henri, as I told him they were for her.

'She has a friend staying with her from London this weekend.'

Henri glanced round just as they both looked over and waved their thank you for the wine.

'What's Fran's friend called, do you know?' he asked after seeing Ellie's cheeky smile. I glanced at him to see a small grin appearing on his face too.

'Ellie, she said. I'm sure you'll get the chance to meet her this weekend if you'd like to.'

'I would definitely like that.'

I smiled knowingly. It had been a while since Henri had met anyone he liked. This could be an interesting weekend all round.

'Well, I'm sure I can help you with that. As a matter of fact, there's something you could help me with too.' He raised his eyebrows and I proceeded to tell him about the latest developments between Fran and me.

A short while later Fran and her friend stood up and came over to where we were sitting.

'Thanks so much for the extra glasses of wine. That was a lovely treat,' Fran said. 'This is my friend Ellie, by the way, as you've probably guessed.' I smiled and said hello but Henri jumped up at once to take her hand and kiss it ostentatiously. Ellie giggled. She and Henri hit it off at once, leaning in close to each other and whispering in each other's ears. Fran's eyes widened at Ellie's sudden change of mood. She rolled her eyes and then turned back to face me. Her beautiful face beguiled me.

'When's Chlöe arriving?' she asked, bringing me right back to the present.

'Some time in the morning. It's going to take a while for them to pack up all her things, I suppose. I don't know if she's going to be upset about her mother leaving or not. I'm quite worried about it all, to be honest.'

Fran glanced over at Ellie and Henri, who were chatting away like they'd known each other for years. Then she surprised me by reaching out and laying her hand on my arm and giving it a little squeeze. That small gesture conveyed that she understood how difficult things were for me but it also sent a jolt of electricity through my body, making me want more. She had no idea of the effect her touch had on me. It continued to surprise me too. I swallowed and tried to focus on what she was saying.

'Listen,' she said, 'would you like to get together tomorrow for dinner? All of us, I mean. We can help Chlöe feel a bit more at home.'

'That sounds like a lovely idea. I'll cook this time. I think Chlöe would be delighted to see you again, and to meet Ellie too. This will be the first time she's not stayed at the cottage so I don't know how she'll feel.' I bit my lip. She stared at my lips for a moment before looking away.

'Have you got a room ready for her at the château, with all her things in it?' She asked after a brief pause. I nodded. 'Then I'm sure she'll be okay.'

'Would you like a lift back with us to save you having to walk?'

'That would be great, thanks.'

We made our way outside and everyone clambered into the van. Ellie and Henri sat in the back together, continuing their conversation all the way. I wanted to bring up the subject of my kiss the other night but now wasn't the time. I had to hope Fran hadn't felt I was rushing her. I just wanted the chance to reassure her that I was prepared to take things one step at a time while we got to know each other once again.

Fran

The next morning, I was woken by sounds of breakfast being prepared in the kitchen. I was confused for a moment, until I remembered Ellie was staying with me. I jumped out of bed to go and join her.

'Morning, did you sleep well?' I asked.

'Like a log. The meal at the bistro was wonderful last night and I think this country air might be quite good for me, as well. I can't wait to explore today.'

'Yes, that was the first time I'd ventured into the village actually, and to think I have such a fabulous place to eat on my doorstep.

Maybe country living isn't so bad after all.' I smiled over the cup of coffee she'd poured for me and accepted the plate of toast she'd prepared. 'You seemed to be getting on very well with Henri last night,' I continued just before sinking my teeth into a slice of buttery toast.

'I know. I can't believe you hadn't told me about him already. I'd expected Didier to be gorgeous, of course - and he was, with his dark, curly hair and rugged looks - but Henri was definitely more my type, I'd say, and I can't believe how well we got on together. I hope I'll see him around today?'

'Well, he lives in the village, not on the estate, so you probably won't see him here.' Her face fell. 'But I did suggest to Didier that we all get together for dinner tonight to welcome his daughter, Chlöe.'

'Excellent! I knew this was going to be a great weekend. How about a walk into the village after breakfast, then?' She winked at me and I had to laugh at her thinly disguised plans to bump into Henri.

We were both dressed and ready in no time. We set off towards the château first of all, so I could show Ellie the vineyards across the estate, and so she could get a feel for the size of the place. As we walked, I told her about Ruby and about how I'd asked Didier if I could look after her.

'He's looking after her this weekend though, because his daughter's coming to stay.'

Ellie was completely entranced with the château, especially when I told her my idea about restoring it so we could let it out to visitors.

'That's a fantastic idea and you could throw in free wine tastings and tours as well, while they're here.'

I stared at her in surprise.

'That's a great idea. I'll have to remember to pass that on to Didier. It's going to be a long time before we get round to the château though, what with everything there is to do at the Visitors' Centre, but I think the idea's a good one.'

'There's a good chance that once you decide on a builder, you might be able to negotiate an even better deal for doing all the building work at the same time. They can devote all their energy to it, rather than having to come back another time to do the château as a separate project.'

'Hmm, I'll have to watch out, otherwise you'll be taking over my job! You're full of great ideas today.'

'It's the place, I think. It's very inspirational. You definitely made the right decision to move back here. You already seem so much more cheerful.' She threw her arm round me to draw me in for a hug and gave me a great big kiss on the cheek.

'You've no idea how much that means to me, Ellie. I do feel much calmer since I came here, and more like my old self, really, and that may have a lot to do with getting away from Paul.'

'I could see how much Paul was dragging you down when you were with him but I knew that strong spirit was still in there. I'm so pleased you've had the chance to reassert yourself, to break free of what he was doing to you.'

'The sad thing is that I don't really miss Paul. I wonder if that's because I didn't see that much of him before anyway so it's not a big change. He was always working late or out drinking with his work-mates and lately, we'd stopped doing much together, just the two of us. Now I'm relishing my freedom and taking the time to get used to life here again.'

'Have you heard from him at all?'

I told her about his recent phone call and how I'd had to block his number twice.

'I don't know if I should change my number now because otherwise, he'll just keep calling me using different numbers and I don't want to speak to him any more.' She nodded and fell silent.

We'd circled the château by now and we were back on the gravel, about to walk towards the courtyard and out into the village, when we saw Didier coming through the arch with Chlöe. The minute she saw us, her face lit up and she started running towards us both, arms outstretched, her little curls bobbing as she ran. I burst out laughing at the lovely sight, and so did Ellie. We both crouched down to welcome her and she crashed into us for lots of hugs.

'*Salut*, Fran!' she puffed and giggled, burying her face in my jumper as soon as she realised she didn't know Ellie.

'Chlöe, *je te présente ma copine*, Ellie,' I said once she'd got her breath back. Ellie held out her hand and waited to see if Chlöe would be brave enough. After a long minute, she stuck out her own hand and tickled Ellie, before giggling and running back to her dad.

'*Bonjour, mesdames!*' Didier cried.

'Oh, I feel about a hundred years old when you say that,' I chided him, smiling at the same time. He laughed.

'Are you taking Ellie on a tour of the estate?' he asked and I nodded. 'What do you think so far, then?'

'I love it! I can really imagine so many ways you could transform this place for visitors, and Fran is the woman to help you, for sure.' She beamed at him.

'Actually, Ellie has given me some great suggestions, Didier. Are we still getting together for dinner?'

'Absolutely. I've already told Chlöe, so no changing your mind now.'

'I wouldn't dream of it. We're off into the village. Is there anything you need?'

Didier asked me to pick up some ingredients for dinner and then we were on our way again, having said our goodbyes to them both.

Despite a long wander around the village exploring all the shops, as well as the market, we didn't manage to bump into Henri, much to Ellie's disappointment. Still, she was never one to stay down for long. On the way back, I stopped off at the château to give Didier his ingredients while Ellie returned to the cottage.

I got back to find her preparing omelettes and salad for our lunch, the lovely aroma filling the little cottage.

'I'm back,' I called out. 'What can I do to help?'

'You can pour out some wine and then sit down. I've got this and I want to do something nice for you. And you can tell me exactly what's going on between you and Didier. Have you even kissed him yet?'

I groaned. I knew that voice. It was the one she used to boss me about when she thought I was burying my head in the sand.

'He kissed me the other day,' I blurted out, more to shut her up than anything else.

'*What*? Why have you kept this from me for so long?' She stared at me for a second before continuing. 'Come on then, spill the beans. Where are things between you guys?'

'Nowhere, really,' I said with a sigh. 'I don't want to rush into anything, which is why I told him I just wanted us to be work colleagues. But now we've become friends again, and more than that, I know I still have feelings for him.' I frowned before telling her my real dilemma. 'Even so, I'm not sure if I'm ready to give things another try with him. The thing is, I don't know yet if I'll want this life in the long term, much as I'm enjoying it right now.'

'And have you told him any of this?'

'Well, yes and no. We haven't discussed whether we still have feelings for each other. We've really been keeping each other at arms' length. Then the other day, after he kissed me, I said I wanted to take things slowly but I think he thought I meant I didn't want to get involved at all. I haven't had a chance since that conversation to tell him exactly what I did mean.'

'Okay then, you need to do that as soon as possible and tonight, when we go for dinner, is a great opportunity. I'll keep Henri talking - ooh, that will be such a pleasure - and you can go and talk with Didier.' She rubbed her hands together with glee.

'I think you've forgotten about Chlöe. I can't say anything in front of her, can I?'

'Of course not, no. You'll find the right moment, don't worry, and you'll know just what to say when the time comes.' She patted me on the arm before collecting our plates.

Not long after clearing the table, I received a text from Didier.

'Henri is coming over at 4 to give me a hand with getting things ready. Would you both like to join us then?'

I read the text to Ellie, who promptly jumped up off the sofa where she'd been lounging.

'Tell him yes, of course, but we're going to have to hurry to get ourselves ready by then.' She ran off upstairs towards the bathroom. I had to chuckle at her excitement. I sent back a reply saying we'd be over as soon as we could and went to my bedroom to see what I could wear. I was still sitting on the bed, staring at my woeful selection of clothes, when I heard Ellie come out of the bathroom. When she called out my name, I let her know I was in my room and she poked her head round the door.

'You look miserable. What's up?'

'I just don't have anything that's right to wear. I only have city outfits or casual clothes. I really need to go shopping.'

'Come on, let me have a look.' Within minutes, she'd pulled out a pretty, cream, linen skirt embroidered with colourful pastel flowers that I hadn't worn for ages and matched it with a simple, violet jumper.

'I'd completely forgotten I'd even bought those clothes. It's been so long since I wore either of them. I'd better try them on again.' She rolled her eyes and left me to it. I slipped the skirt on and was relieved to find it still fit me with a bit of room to breathe as well, and the jumper went really well with it. I showed Ellie before jumping in the shower myself. I was just putting the finishing touches to my hair and make-up when she knocked lightly and came in.

'Ooh, you look lovely, Ellie,' I told her, admiring her dark linen trousers and her colourful tunic. 'Your hair looks great like that too.' She had such luscious red hair and her curls were to die for. I envied her. She was one of the only women I knew who loved her hair just as it was.

'That's it, then. I'm done too. Shall we go?'

CHAPTER TWELVE

Didier

By half past four, Henri and I were settled at the table in the enormous farmhouse kitchen, with our sleeves rolled up, preparing a feast for dinner. Chlöe was playing happily outside the French windows with Ruby - although she was still calling her Princesse - and I was hoping that Fran and Ellie would be arriving soon.

'Ladies, come on in,' I cried, when they appeared outside a few minutes later. I wiped my hands on my apron before kissing each of them on both cheeks and pouring out two more glasses of Kir. Chlöe followed them in, reaching out to Fran to be picked up. Fran happily obliged and they studied the food together. Ruby sat patiently at her feet, wagging her tail and waiting for her little companion to rejoin her.

'Can we help with anything?' Fran asked. I exchanged a glance with Henri, which I hoped Fran wouldn't quite be able to interpret.

'I know that you like cooking, whereas Henri, not so much.' Henri shook his head as if to confirm this and Ellie grinned, having probably guessed I wanted some time alone with Fran. A fleeting look of concern crossed Fran's face and I worried she might feel she was being manipulated. Henri had whipped his apron off by this time and he encouraged Chlöe to fall into his arms so he could take her back out to the garden. Ruby went first and Ellie followed them all, giving Fran a little wave and a wink before closing the door. Fran picked up the apron and put it over her head. I turned her round gently and tied the apron behind her. When she turned round again to face me she was smiling, and I felt my heartbeat quicken a little.

'Shall we get to work?' I said softly. She nodded and surveyed the work surface. There were ripe, red tomatoes, a whole romaine lettuce and some red onions.

'The *entrée* is *salade aux tomates*, I'm guessing,' she said.

'*Exactement*. Would you mind preparing it while I check on the main course?' I walked over to the large range oven and opened the door, releasing a wonderful smell of roast chicken into the kitchen. I took out the chicken and smothered it with a herb butter I'd prepared earlier. Then I put it back in the oven and returned to the work surface to begin preparing vegetables next to Fran. We worked in comfortable silence for a few minutes while I plucked up the courage to say something about the previous day. I heard Fran take in a deep breath too, but I didn't say anything.

'I...I think I may have given you the wrong impression the other day,' she began.

'How do you mean?' I asked, frowning a little.

'When I said I thought we should take things slowly. I didn't mean I didn't want us to get involved again, just that we both need to be sure of what we want before we take that step.'

I put down my knife and turned to face her.

'And do you want to take that step?' She wiped her hands and raised her head to look at me then.

'I think so but I don't want to rush things. I've only just come out of one relationship, and you're still married. Do you understand what I mean?' She looked up at me for reassurance. I bent towards her, slipping my arms round her waist, and kissed her gently on the lips.

'I do understand but I also know I would like us to try again. I think we both know we made mistakes before. Now, we can take all the time we need.'

With that, I let her go and returned to my food preparations with a smile. We had both said what we needed to.

Dinner was ready not long after that, and when I called out '*à table*' everyone came running, including Ruby. We all enjoyed the fresh tomato salad, with warm bread to mop up the juices, before going on to the roast chicken flavoured with an abundance of herbs and accompanied by a wonderful selection of vegetables. Chlöe enjoyed her meal as much as the adults and she chatted away happily throughout. Looking at her little face, I wondered if I had made the right decision not to tell her yet about her mother being away for a while. For dessert, there was fresh fruit and cheese, and then we all went to sit outside to enjoy the last of the daylight before it was time for Chlöe to go to bed.

'*C'est l'heure de te coucher, maintenant, ma chérie,*' I told her. Her little face fell and her lower lip pushed out when I mentioned bedtime.

'*Tu viens avec nous?*' she asked Fran, her dark eyes wide. Fran stood up at once, with a look of delight on her face, and I smiled at her gratefully.

Fran

We left Ellie and Henri to have a bit of time on their own while we whisked Chlöe through a very splashy bedtime and into her pyjamas. She was yawning widely by the time I kissed her goodnight. I left Didier reading her a story and went back downstairs to start clearing up the kitchen. I bashed some pans a little to make my presence known to the lovebirds outside, just in case they were getting on a bit too famously. I didn't want to walk in on anything. I put some coffee on for everyone, using a rather old-fashioned filter machine I found tucked away on a shelf, and coughed pointedly before emerging through the French doors. Ellie smiled up at me innocently and raised her eyebrows just a fraction. I couldn't say anything to that so I just took a seat.

'Thanks for tidying up the kitchen. You didn't need to do that,' Didier told me when he came back down a few minutes later. 'Fran has also put the coffee machine on so would you all like one?' I joined him in the kitchen to lend a hand and we brought everything out again shortly afterwards.

'Henri, will you be all right to stay here with Chlöe for a while if I take Fran home?'

'Of course, if that's okay with Ellie,' he looked over at her and she leaned in to him, patting his leg.

I stood up, kissed Henri goodbye and took Didier's hand as we walked off into the night, Ruby close at our heels. It wasn't long before the cottage came into sight and I knew Didier wouldn't be able to stay long.

When we arrived at my door, I took a small step towards him, hoping he would kiss me properly this time. I tilted my head up and the next thing I knew, his lips were crushing mine and he was kissing me again with a passion I hadn't realised I'd been missing. His hands were in my hair and my arms had naturally gone round his waist, pulling him closer to me as he pushed me gently against the wall of the cottage. When he paused for a moment, my lips were left tingling from the sensation of his mouth on mine. He stared deep into my eyes and I worried that he could read all my thoughts, which I wasn't sure he was quite ready for. I touched his lips with my fingers and then gently rubbed the stubble on his cheek.

'God, I've really missed you,' he said, leaning in to my touch and taking my hands in his.

'I've missed you too.' He stepped back and I felt the loss of the warmth of his body immediately.

'I want you to know I'm going to go ahead with the divorce, just so you know that I'm not doing anything behind Isabelle's back...or yours for that matter.'

'I'm sorry for all of you but it seems best for everyone.'

'It won't be easy but I want to be honest with you.'

I nodded and kissed him then, reassuring him I knew what I was getting into. He pulled away reluctantly a little while later.

'Will I see you tomorrow?' he asked.

'I hope so. It's Ellie's last day so I want to spend what time I can with her. Still, I have a feeling she might want to see Henri as well.'

He laughed then. '*Bonne nuit*, see you tomorrow.'

I watched as he walked away, and thanked goodness for fate.

I woke early the next morning and as I lay there in bed, enjoying the peace and quiet, I remembered waiting up for Ellie for a while but eventually going to bed without seeing her. I was thrilled that she and Henri had hit it off so well and couldn't wait to hear all about it. I had a quick shower and got dressed before going downstairs to see what there was for breakfast. Ruby jumped up as soon as she heard me coming, tail wagging furiously and I bent down to give her a long cuddle to make up for being so busy over the last few days.

As I was making breakfast, I heard Ellie getting up and creaking round upstairs. Shortly afterwards, she emerged into the kitchen with a great big smile on her face.

'Ooh, someone's cheerful this morning. I hate to sound like your mum but what time did you get in last night?'

'It was after midnight, I think.' She gave me a sheepish grin before continuing. 'By the way, you could never sound like my mother.' She then pulled a quite different face, leaving me in no doubt about how she felt towards her mum.

'Were you at Didier's all that time?'

'No, we walked into town to have a drink and ended up staying quite a while before walking back.'

'So, everything's good between you, then?' Her smile slowly fell away. 'What is it, Ellie?'

'It's just that I've had such a great time this weekend, being here with you and now meeting Henri as well. I don't want to go home, that's all. I hate my job and now I haven't got you there to cheer me up any more.' She sat down at the table with a sigh.

'Hmm. It has been a great weekend, you're right, and just as lovely for me having you here too. Have you thought any more about getting a new job? You've been so unhappy for such a long time. I know you could get something much better.'

'I'm always thinking about it, to be honest, but I can never get myself motivated enough to do anything. Being here this weekend has made me wonder whether the city is the right place for me, after all.'

I raised my eyebrows at that and she laughed as she took in my expression. Neither one of us had ever expected to hear her say that.

'Well, look, we need to come up with a plan of action to change your life but why don't we concentrate on doing something really fun today to bring the weekend to a nice close? I'm sure you have plans to see Henri at some point, don't you?'

'Oh, you're such a sweetheart. I do want to see him, of course, but I want to see you as well. I told Henri I'd text him once we were up and ready, so we can see what ideas he has.'

I sent a text to Didier too, and in the end we all went out together to the nearby *Jardins des Papillons*, which was something we would all enjoy. We took a picnic with us, hastily cobbled together from three different fridges before we bundled ourselves into the van. The weather was already starting to cool as summer gave way to autumn but the day was still warm enough to enjoy being outside. It was only a short drive to the gardens, which was just as well because Chlöe was almost giddy with excitement before she'd even got into the van. I glanced round to see her chatting away animatedly to Ellie who was nodding often despite not knowing many words of French at all. I laughed and turned back to finding Didier smiling at me too.

We went straight into the butterfly house when we arrived, having tried to explain to Chlöe that it would be very hot inside because that's how butterflies like it. She was still completely taken aback by the humidity when we walked in, puffing out her little cheeks in surprise.

'*Oh, qu'il fait chaud, Papa!*' she exclaimed, as we closed the screen doors carefully behind us. She began fanning herself at once but as soon as Didier pointed out the first butterfly, she forgot about the heat in no time. There was a stunning display of exotic butterflies inside the house and they kept us all entertained right through till lunchtime. We managed to find a lovely picnic spot in the village but it wasn't long before Chlöe was running around again, leaving only the adults to lounge about on the assorted blankets.

Didier

'What do you do in London, Ellie?' I asked as we all tried to recover from the heat of the butterfly house, coupled with our generous lunch.

'A very boring job at a bank in the City, I'm afraid,' she replied, rolling her eyes.

'What would you prefer to do?' We all looked at her, wondering what she would say.

'Well, I've always liked working with the public. Customer services, that kind of thing.'

'Ah yes, I can see you in that kind of job, certainly.'

'The thing is I've always loved being in the city but this weekend has made me wonder whether it's time for a change.'

We strolled around the gardens for an hour or so after lunch until it was time for Ellie to get ready to catch her train. No sooner had we strapped Chlöe into the car than she fell asleep. The journey home passed quietly as we all retreated into our own thoughts. When we got back to the *Domaine*, Henri offered to drive Ellie to Strasbourg.

'Would you mind, Fran? I don't want you to be upset but it would save you the hassle.' Ellie looked torn.

'Of course not, silly,' Fran replied, looking like she was trying her very best to hold it all together.

I lifted Chlöe from the car and started walking back to the château, giving Fran a quick smile as we left. I was disappointed we couldn't stay for longer but there was nothing I could do. I saw Henri give Ellie a quick kiss before disappearing back to the courtyard to pick up his own car, with a promise to return to collect her later.

I thought about my kiss with Fran as I made my way back to the château, and I was glad that we had taken that first step. I had no doubts that the immediate future was going to be difficult, though. Besides the custody and divorce proceedings, I also worried about whether Fran would commit to staying with me this time. Was she really ready to settle down?

I tucked Chlöe into her new bed and made my way back downstairs, trying not to let myself get too carried away. For now, I needed to take care of my daughter in her mother's absence. The practicalities were going to be challenging to say the least. I would have to ask my mum for help, if I was going to continue running the vineyard as well. I knew she wouldn't mind but I felt guilty for having to rely on her. I knew that Isabelle must also have experienced these practical concerns, but then, she had left me, not the other way round. If I was going to make the case for full custody of my daughter, I needed to be able to show I could manage to take care of her alongside the running of the vineyard, and I had to be able to offer her a more stable life than the one Isabelle would be proposing.

CHAPTER THIRTEEN

The next morning, as I drove back to the vineyard, I was overwhelmed by how difficult it had been to leave Chlöe at the nursery. She had been perfectly content and the staff had assured me everything was fine but I missed her. The strength of my love for her surprised me.

Fran was coming out of the office just as I pulled up in the courtyard. I climbed out of the van and strode towards her, pulling her in for a hug without a word. She put her arms round me at once and I relished the feel of her soft body against mine and the sweet smell of her hair as it brushed my cheek.

'Hey, what's the matter?' she asked after a minute.

'I've left Chlöe at the *école maternelle* in the village for the first time.' She pulled back to study my face. Her expression softened with understanding.

'I didn't realise that was your plan for this morning. I'm sorry,' she said.

'Actually, we were just going for a visit but she loved it so much, they asked if she wanted to stay until lunchtime. Now I just feel lost without her.'

She hugged me again, rather than trying to make me feel better with platitudes.

'Come on,' she said, 'I have things I need to talk to you about in the office. It will take your mind off thinking about Chlöe.'

I followed her inside, stopping in front of Henri's desk on my way to the coffee machine. This was a very different Henri to the man I was used to seeing every day. One look was enough to tell me he had it bad. He had bags under his eyes, his face was unshaven and his clothes were mismatched.

'Bad night, huh?' I asked him. All I got in return was a feeble nod. He slumped down further at his desk.

'*Je n'ai pas dormi. C'est terrible.*' He clutched at his heart as if to emphasise his point. I wasn't sure if he had ever felt like this about a woman before. I struggled not to chuckle, knowing that to him it was very serious.

I poured him a cup of coffee, patting him on the shoulder as I placed the cup in front of him. Then I sat down between his desk and Fran's and watched as he shuffled his papers around for a few minutes. Finally, he released a big sigh and settled on dealing with just the one piece of paper. I turned towards Fran, knowing there was nothing I could do to help him.

'So, what's on the agenda?' I asked.

'I want to reduce my list of builders down to a shortlist of three. And I also want to ask you what you think of an idea Ellie had when she was here.'

We agreed on the shortlist in no time. Ellie's suggestion that we have the château restored at the same time as the building work took a while longer to discuss.

'I have no idea how much both jobs would cost, that's all,' I said.

'There's no harm in asking the question, is there? What about if I ask them to quote for the separate jobs and then for both jobs together, so we can compare?'

'Okay but let's not rush into anything. Our funds are limited, as you know.' I stood up. 'I need to go and check the vines. It's touch and go about the best time to start the harvest. By the time I've done that, it will be time to go and get Chlöe. Why don't we all have lunch together today?' I included Henri in my suggestion.

'Great. We'll see you at the cottage later.' Fran gave me a smile but poor old Henri didn't even seem to hear.

Fran

At lunchtime, little Chlöe was full of excitement, with stories of new friends and new activities from nursery. Didier had booked for her to attend every morning from now on, and I could see what a weight off his mind that was going to be, especially with the harvest coming up. He was already working all hours in preparation for the start of picking.

We had just finished clearing up when I received a call from my mum. I left the others to go on ahead.

'*Salut, Maman, ça va?*'

'*Oui, et toi, chérie?*'

'I've just had Ellie here for the weekend, and it was so good to see her.' In fact, the cottage still seemed empty without her and I was missing her terribly. Having Ellie to stay had made me realise what a good friend she was. We had hugged each other fiercely when the time had come to say goodbye.

'I hope we'll get to meet her soon,' my mum replied. 'I'm calling because I've asked *Papi* to come over this weekend and I'd like us all to have a big family get-together. I've heard from Lottie again as well, so I've asked her to come too.'

'You've heard from Lottie twice in the last couple of weeks. I take it she's back for good?' I realised with a pang of guilt that I still hadn't texted Lottie since I'd been home.

'I'm not sure if she's staying but she is coming to visit this weekend. Please say you'll come. It would mean a lot to me and your dad for us all to be together again.'

'That sounds like a lovely idea, *Maman,* but I can't decide on the phone right now. I'll need to check and call you back, okay?'

'Okay, but please don't leave it too long.'

I rang off quickly and decided to send a text to Lottie straight away.

'Salut! Sorry I missed you last time. Good to hear you're back. Will you be going home this weekend for sure? Would be great to see you after all this time xx' I pressed send and then looked up as I heard the front door squeak open.

'Is everything okay? I was worried when you didn't follow us.' Didier stood there looking at me with concern. I told him about the call from my mum.

'Well, of course it's not a problem from this end if you want to go.'

'I haven't seen *Papi* or my sister for a long time so it would be good to go. I've just sent Lottie a text. I'm quite worried about her actually.'

'Why's that?'

'Just before I went home last time, my mum told me Lottie was back. She's been away travelling for the best part of a year, but we hadn't heard anything much from her while she was away. We've always been close so I was really excited to see her again. But before I'd even arrived, she'd left. It was almost as if she didn't want to see me.'

Didier put his arms round me. I rested my head on his shoulder and didn't say any more.

'I'm sure that isn't true but if you do go this weekend, you'll be able to find out how she really is, won't you?'

'As long as she turns up.'

Despite being busy all afternoon trying to plan a brief for the builders, I struggled to stay focused on anything. My mind kept coming back to my mum's call and what was going on with Lottie. By the time I was ready to go back to the cottage, I still hadn't received any reply from my sister. I berated myself for not having contacted her sooner.

Henri's mood had not improved all day, and Didier had had to leave early to look after Chlöe, so my walk to the cottage was a troubled one. I decided to call Ellie to see how her day had gone and to get her take on my situation.

'Hey, how are you?' I asked brightly as soon as she answered.

'Miserable without you and Henri.'

'Well, if it's any consolation, he was desolate without you today as well. And I still miss you too.'

'That does make me feel a bit better.' I could hear the smile in her voice at the other end of the phone.

'Promise me you'll come back soon.'

'You know I will. That was the first time in ages I'd met someone I really fancied and could actually get on with.'

'Oh, I see. You don't care about seeing me, just Henri.' We both laughed.

'How about you? You sound a bit fed up too,' she said.

'Oh, it's just that my mum rang earlier to invite me for a family get-together at the weekend but I'm worried about whether Lottie will actually come.' I filled her in on more of the background and the fact that I hadn't seen Lottie for such a long time.

'Look, I'm sure everything's fine but I'll call you tomorrow. Maybe by then you'll have heard from her.'

Didier

The appointments with the builders kept me so busy that the rest of the week passed in a blur. Fran had scheduled them for the mornings so I could attend without having to worry about Chlöe. I was also occupied with more frequent vineyard inspections. The harvest was drawing closer and we became obsessed with checking sugar levels in the fruit.

By Friday, I could see Fran was distracted by her family troubles.

'Are you okay?' I asked for what must have been the third time that morning.

'I'm sorry. It's just I decided I would go home this weekend. Now I'm on edge.'

'How about I take you out for a drink later on this evening to take your mind off things?' I raised my eyebrows.

'What about Chlöe?' she asked, after a long delay. I wasn't sure what to make of that pause but tried hard not to read too much into it. Perhaps she was just preoccupied.

'I've already asked Henri to look after her for me this evening. He's desperate for something to take his mind off Ellie.'

'Okay. Shall we say about seven?'

At seven precisely I knocked on the door of the cottage. I was greeted by a wonderful sight. Fran wouldn't have had a lot of time to get ready after leaving the office but she had definitely used the time well. She looked gorgeous in a colourful dress and heels. She had left her dark hair to hang loose around her shoulders, rather than tying it back as she usually did. I took a step closer to her and kissed her softly on both cheeks.

'You look amazing,' I said, unable to take my eyes off her. She didn't say anything but I heard her soft gasp as she took in my appearance too. I'd wanted to tidy myself up for a date with her but I'd tried not to overdo it. I'd gone for dark jeans and a black, v-necked sweater, teamed with a leather jacket.

'Hey, are you in there?' I said finally, with a chuckle.

She blushed. 'You're so beautiful,' I told her. 'You'll need a coat, though. It's got chilly since earlier.'

She grabbed her coat, slipped it on and pulled the door shut behind her, and we moved swiftly to get in the car. I closed her door for her and soon we were off.

'I decided on a little village about fifteen minutes away, if that's okay. It has a cosy bar, with a nice log fire. I think you'll like it.'

We sat in silence for the first few minutes, adjusting to each other's company. For my part, I was trying to decide how to get the conversation going.

'Have you heard from Ellie this week? I haven't had a chance to ask you, it's been so busy.'

'Yes, she's okay, although she's already missing Henri in a big way.'

'Well, they've obviously fallen for each other. He has been miserable all week, hasn't he?' We both laughed.

'I'm pleased for them both, though,' Fran said. 'They're a good match and Ellie has had some awful boyfriends.'

'Has she? I'm surprised by that. Ellie seems a good judge of character.'

'Well, it happens to us all, doesn't it?'

'Yes, unfortunately it does.'

We continued chatting for the rest of the short journey. When we arrived, I jumped out to open her door for her again, offering my hand to help her out.

A few minutes later we were sitting at a quiet table near the fire. I watched Fran take a sip of her wine. She was biting her lip, as if trying to calm her nerves. Her action drew my attention to her full lips and I was oblivious to everything else for a second. When I reluctantly tore my eyes away to look at her face, I found her staring at me, her hazel eyes glittering in the firelight.

'What is it?' she asked me in the end.

'I suppose it feels a bit funny to be going out on a date with you when we were together for such a long time.'

'Yes, I know what you mean. We've both changed in the meantime, though.'

'I know, but fundamentally we are still the same people, you and I.'

'Being in a relationship does change you, though. You were married - and I was about to be - so we were both committed to other partners. Now, we're both forever changed by what those relationships did to us.'

I took her hand and brought it to my lips. She shivered, and I wondered if she was even aware of doing so. My feelings for her were still every bit as strong as they'd been all those years ago. I just hoped she was feeling the same way.

'Would you like to eat here?' I asked. I was eager to spend more time with her and hoped she felt the same.

'I didn't know if we would eat dinner or just have time for a drink before you have to get back for Chlöe. But I'd love to, if you're sure.'

'Henri is in charge,' I replied with a smile. 'I think it will do him good to have someone else to think about apart from Ellie for a bit.'

I signalled to the waiter and asked for the menus. Once we'd ordered, we both relaxed back into our chairs.

'So, have you heard from Lottie since you texted her the other day?' I asked.

She shook her head. 'No, and I haven't had a chance to call my mum to ask if she's heard from her, either.'

'How old is Lottie?' I asked.

'She's twenty-five. She's been travelling around Europe for the past couple of years. I haven't seen her since I went to London and we've only been in touch occasionally. It must be coming up for a year now since we last spoke to each other.' She rubbed her temple. 'I know she would have got in touch with me if she'd been in trouble but we've never gone this long without talking.'

The waiter returned with our meals and for a while we focused on enjoying our food rather than talking.

'So, apart from your worries about Lottie, are you looking forward to going home this weekend?' I asked.

'I am. It will be wonderful to see my grand-dad. We're very close too. If Lottie is there, it really will be great to see everyone again.'

I gave her a warm smile and I was glad that she'd felt able to tell me about it.

Fran

I was deep in thought on the journey back to the *Domaine*, wondering about my family and how the weekend would go. I didn't feel half as confident about it as I'd said I was to Didier. My worry about Lottie continued to nag at me.

Soon, we were standing outside the cottage. He took me in his arms and kissed me, gently at first but when I responded, he kissed me more firmly and I felt my knees weaken. I ran my fingers through his hair as we kissed, enjoying the feel of his thick curls. His hands moved to the small of my back and he pressed gently. I couldn't help but arch my body towards his. He pulled me in closer but I had to break the kiss for fear of running out of breath. We were both breathing heavily.

'God, you're doing something completely unexpected to me,' he panted, stepping back.

'What do you mean, unexpected?'

'It's just that I've had my guard up for so long and now, you're beating it down with no trouble at all. You're making me nervous and excited all at once.' He chuckled and it was a lovely sound.

'Would you like to come in?' I asked hesitantly.

'I thought you'd never ask.'

I didn't know what to make of his reply but I was hoping that we were thinking along the same lines. I opened the door and went to check on Ruby. She needed a walk but as I'd taken her for a long one earlier that day, I was happy to just let her out in the garden. I stood at the back door, folding my arms against the cold. Didier came up behind me and put his arms round my waist. His body was so warm and inviting, I relaxed back against him without a moment's thought . When he gently moved my hair to kiss my neck, I let out a moan of pleasure.

He paused, and I took the chance to call Ruby back in and lock the door. I turned to face him and he took my hand to lead me out of the kitchen along the hall. We stopped at the foot of the staircase to kiss again. I lifted my hands to his shoulders, pulling him closer. He kissed the sensitive spot behind my ear and continued his way down my neck. My breath caught in my throat and my pulse quickened. Once we reached my bedroom, Didier pulled gently on the tie at my hip. My dress came undone, and he pushed it off my shoulder and kissed my skin, sending shivers down my spine. My nipples puckered in response and I sighed as he stroked the side of my breast. He slipped my dress off my other shoulder and caressed my arms, then began to leave a trail of kisses across my breasts. I was desperate to feel his skin against mine. I started to unbutton his shirt and at the sight of his well-defined chest with the smattering of dark hair, I sucked in my breath with pleasure. He led me gently to the bed and before long, our bodies were entwined. From that point on, we abandoned ourselves to each other, holding nothing back until we both reached the edge of our release. The intensity of the moment enveloped me.

As we lay there in the dark afterwards, I knew we belonged together. I sighed with contentment, feeling all my barriers disappear.

'What are you thinking about? I can hear your brain whirring.'

'I was thinking how lucky I am and how wonderful that was.'

He turned towards me and propped himself up on his elbow. 'Making love with you was just as good as I remembered.' His eyes twinkled and he pulled me towards him for another kiss. 'In fact, it was so good that I'd like to do it again,' he said in between kisses.

CHAPTER FOURTEEN

I woke the next morning to find Didier was no longer beside me. I wondered if it was late. Had he had to leave already? But as I came to, I heard sounds around the cottage. My heart warmed to know he was still there, after all. I sat up, pulled on my camisole and shorts, and padded down the stairs to find him. He was in the kitchen making breakfast, looking gorgeous in just a pair of boxer shorts and his t-shirt. I stole up behind him and put my arms round his waist. He turned and pulled me into his arms for a good-morning hug and kiss that almost knocked me off my feet.

'You look far too tempting for this time of the morning,' he told me, holding my body firmly against his.

'I could say the same to you,' I teased him. 'What time is it?'

'It's really early. I have to get back to Chlöe but I didn't want to just disappear on you. I wanted us to spend a little bit of time together after last night and before you go off for the weekend.'

I smiled at him gratefully.

'Thank you for making breakfast. I would have understood if you'd had to leave, you know.'

His eyes locked onto mine. 'I wouldn't have left without saying goodbye,' he promised.

We sat down to eat scrambled eggs on toast, with juice and coffee.

'Mmm, this is so good. You really are a great chef, you know. Where did you learn to cook like this?'

He grinned. 'My mum taught me. It's something I love to do but nothing is so good as hearing how much you like it. Well, maybe there are some other things.' He winked at me and I had to laugh.

'You're being very flirtatious this morning.'

'I know. You bring out the worst in me. I wish we could just stay in bed all day...but we really can't.' He reached across the table and took my hand. 'I hope I can see you again tomorrow when you get back, if you're not busy?'

'Ooh, I'll have to check my social calendar to see if I have time to fit you in.' I suddenly realised what I'd said and we both burst out laughing. I cleared up the kitchen while he went to get dressed and I remembered how nice it felt to have more than one person in the house. I saw him off from the door a bit later with a final lingering kiss.

It took me a while to get going after he'd gone. I kept daydreaming about our wonderful night together and wondering if we might be able to do more of the same again soon. It was nearly ten by the time I was on my way back to Strasbourg to catch the train home for the great family get-together. The journey passed quickly and soon I was stepping out into the car park of Colmar station once again, looking round for my dad. I spotted his car and began walking towards it.

A moment later, the car door opened to reveal my grandfather, with a broad smile on his tanned face. He raised his hands in greeting and as I ran up to him he pulled me in for one of his bear hugs. He kissed me on both cheeks. I felt I was truly home in the comfort of his embrace.

'Françoise! *Ça fait trop longtemps, ma mignonne.*'

'Oh, *Papi,* it's so good to see you. You're right, it's been far too long.'

I let him go reluctantly and climbed into the back seat.

My dad turned round and smiled at me too, and all at once, the prospect of a weekend with the family seemed to be just what I needed.

Didier

After leaving Fran, I walked back to the château with a real spring in my step. At last we had shared our innermost feelings and it felt wonderful. Even though she was going to be away for the weekend, I could look forward to her coming back with renewed passion.

'Hey, Henri, thanks so much for agreeing to stay over last night. I really appreciate it,' I told my friend as I entered the kitchen.

'It was no problem, *mon ami.* Chlöe was no trouble at all and it was my pleasure to help you out in your hour of need.' He raised his eyebrows subtly and I beamed in return, leaving him in no doubt that Fran and I were back together.

'Fran did tell me Ellie's missing you just as much as you're missing her, so that's a good sign, isn't it?'

'It is, I suppose, but it will still be a long time before we see each other again.'

'Well, why don't you go and see her? You could easily do that in a weekend, and if you want longer, you know you only have to say the word.'

His face lit up. 'Now that is a brilliant idea. I'm going to get on to that straight away.' He ran to Chlöe, gave her a kiss and a hug, and was soon running across the grass towards his car.

I picked Chlöe up for a hug and she tucked her head underneath my chin, rubbing gently at the stubble on my jaw.

'*Alors, j'ai une idée pour aujourd'hui, ma petite.* We're going to surprise your grandma!'

Chlöe's eyes grew round in her face. It was a while since she'd seen her grandma. After a quick shower and change of clothes, we set off for the village on foot, with a bottle of wine in hand. We stopped at the market in the village for a bunch of flowers and arrived at my mum's house a few minutes later. Instead of going round the back of the house to go in as I usually did, I asked Chlöe to knock on the front door. I left her on the doorstep and stood to one side so my mum would see her first. I kept peeping round the corner, and when I saw my mum's face as her grand-daughter greeted her with a bunch of flowers, it was worth it.

'*Oh, ma chérie, que tu es grande maintenant,*' she cried, as though she hadn't seen her for years. I stepped out from the bushes, laughing, and I was surprised to see tears in my mum's eyes.

'Oh, Didier, *je te remercie! C'est merveilleux de la revoir*. Come in, both of you!' She set Chlöe down and waved us in, and we went straight out to the garden. My mum brought out drinks a few minutes later and we sat outside in the sun to enjoy them. Chlöe sat on her grandma's lap to drink, studying my mum's rings while she did so.

'You didn't tell me Chlöe was coming this weekend,' my mum said. 'Was it another last-minute thing?'

My mum knew all too well how Isabelle called on me at short notice. I swapped into English to explain what Isabelle was doing.

'*C'est pas croyable!*' my mum cried, when I'd finished. 'I can't believe that she's just abandoning you both like that.'

'Well, look, Mum, I'm delighted to have my daughter with me but I want to make it official now, if you know what I mean,' I said, glancing at Chlöe to make it clear she didn't know what was happening.

'That is the best idea you've had in ages. If you need any support, just let me know.'

'I will, I promise. And I hope you won't mind continuing to help me look after Chlöe. She's going to nursery every morning but there will be times when I'm sure I'll need your help.'

'Of course. You know I am always willing to help where Chlöe is concerned.'

'There's something else I want to talk to you about.'

'There is?' she raised her eyebrows.

'It's about me and Fran.'

She stared at me for a moment. 'I see.' She folded her arms. This wasn't going to be as easy as I'd thought.

'Let me explain before you jump to any conclusions. We're giving things another go and I think it's about time you met her and got to know her.'

'You're right,' she said to my amazement. 'Life is too short for regrets. If you're both ready to try again then I wish you the best of luck and happiness. I would love to meet her.'

Fran

Before long, we were sitting outside admiring the beautiful back garden at home, sipping at a cup of coffee my mum had brought out for us. Thankfully, my mum had heard from Lottie and she'd confirmed she was still coming but not till later. I took the opportunity to catch up with my grand-dad.

'So, what's new, *chérie*?'

'Well, where shall I start? I've split up with Paul...'

'*Oh, non*! What happened?'

Tears sprang to my eyes - I was so emotional lately. 'He cheated on me.'

'That bastard! I never liked him.'

I smiled through my tears. My grand-dad's fierce loyalty was one of the many reasons why I loved him.

'There's more to it than that, *Papi*,' I went on.

'What? There's worse to come?'

'I don't know if you know but we'd only just got engaged.' I fell silent and looked over at him to see his reaction.

'*Oh, c'est terrible*. I am so sorry.' His wrinkled face was unusually solemn for a moment.

'I know. I could hardly believe it either.'

'But where are you living? Are you still in London? Surely you have kicked out that despicable Paul?'

'I moved out, *Papi* to take up a job here. I've got a job on a vineyard up near Strasbourg and I'm living in a little cottage on the estate.'

'And you're sure that this is what you want long term?'

'It's early days yet but I do feel so much better since coming home. It turns out the vineyard is owned by Didier, the man I was dating at university. I don't know if you remember?'

'Is that the man you left behind to go to London?' he asked pointedly.

'The one who wouldn't come with me,' I retorted. 'Look, *Papi*, Didier and I have talked about it. He had his reasons for staying, and I wanted to go off and explore the world - well, London, at least. What's done is done and we've both grown up since then. The good news is, we're giving things another go.'

'Well, that all sounds wonderful. So now, all we have to do is to wait for Lottie.'

'I haven't seen her since she went travelling, *Papi*. To be honest, I'm quite worried about her. We've hardly spoken either, while she's been away. She came home briefly the other week but was gone by the time I arrived. I haven't said anything to Mum and Dad but they must have noticed her odd behaviour too.'

'Well, we'll know more when she gets here, won't we? I'm sure everything's fine and you're worrying for nothing.'

Didier

The next morning, I noticed that Chlöe was very quiet on our walk to the *boulangerie*. Even though we had Ruby with us to keep her company while Fran was away, it didn't seem to lift her spirits at all. On the way back, I decided to stop at the park to see if it might cheer up, but she just stayed on the bench next to me.

'*Qu'est-ce qu'il y a, ma petite?*' I asked finally, worrying what she would say, if anything at all. 'Are you missing *Maman?*'

'*Où est Maman?*' Her eyes were huge in her face. I owed her the truth but how to explain to a young child?

'*Elle est au Canada.* It's another country, a long way from here.'

'Will she come back one day?'

I scooped her onto my lap then. 'Of course she will come back but it is too far away for her to visit you very often. You're going to stay with me for a while. *Ça va?*'

She seemed to consider that for a while before nodding. '*Oui, ça va, Papa.*' She fell silent for a moment, then continued. 'And do you love Fran now, not *Maman*?'

I felt like I'd been hit by a train. All my breath disappeared with her question. I considered what to say for the best. I hadn't even talked to Fran about my feelings yet. In the end, I decided it was best to tell the truth.

'*Oui, j'aime Fran.*'

'*Moi, j'aime Fran aussi.*' She stood up then and ran off to play on the swings. My heart ached from all that had happened to her in her little life. I determined right then to call Alain the next day and chase him about the divorce papers. We needed to get past this limbo and Chlöe needed stability.

While Chlöe played, I sent Isabelle a text. I hated having to contact her but Chlöe needed to hear her voice.

'Please can you call Chlöe? She asked where you were today and she's worried you're not coming back.'

There was no reply, which I expected because it was still quite early in Canada, but I hoped we might hear from her later. By the time we'd walked home, Chlöe seemed her happy self again and went off to play with Ruby. I sat outside to do some paperwork but my mind kept returning to Chlöe. When I wasn't thinking about her, I was thinking about Fran and the night we had spent together. I also wondered how she was getting on at home and if I should have offered to go with her. I could at least offer to pick her up from Strasbourg to save her having to get a cab. I sent off a quick text asking her to let me know when she would be arriving.

Before long it was time for lunch and, after a quick wash and brush up, Chlöe and I made our way into the village to meet Henri. I'd promised to keep him company, knowing how much he was missing Ellie. I also wanted to find out if he'd managed to make any plans to visit her, as I'd suggested.

CHAPTER FIFTEEN

Fran

The silence of the garden was broken by the crunch of a car's wheels on the gravel driveway. I exchanged a look with *Papi*. Lottie must have arrived. We stood up and made our way to the gate to say hello, joining Mum and Dad who were already there. Lottie got out of the taxi and paid the driver. Rather than come round to greet us all, she waited for the car to drive away, then bent to pick up her bag. As she straightened and came into full view, I realised why she had stayed away. A gasp escaped my lips at the sight of her small but perfectly formed baby bump.

'*Salut,* Fran,' she said, coming towards me and kissing me on both cheeks. I still hadn't managed to work out what to say but I was glad to see that she had a healthy bloom about her. I watched as she kissed *Papi* before moving on to my parents. We stood in stunned silence.

'What? No questions?' she asked. She appeared confident, as she beamed at everyone with her head held high, but I could tell from the way she glanced quickly between us that she was worried about our reaction.

'Oh, Lottie, congratulations!' I gave her a warm smile and pulled her in for a proper hug, feeling her relax in my arms. 'It's a bit of a surprise but I'm really pleased for you.' Soon everyone else came forward for a hug and to give their good wishes, as well. My dad took her bag and I led the way inside.

We settled around the kitchen table while my parents bustled about organising drinks.

'I'm sorry I didn't reply to your text, Fran,' Lottie began, 'I just didn't know how to tell you.'

'It's okay. I was just worried about you, that's all.' I paused for a moment. 'When you'd gone before I even came home the other weekend, I was so disappointed not to have seen you. It made me realise that I hadn't spoken to you for ages, let alone seen you. I'm so sorry.'

'Mum told me about you and Paul. What a slimy bastard.'

Everyone round the table laughed but with me, not at me, and I was overcome with love for my family and the safe haven they provided.

We had all sat down around the table by now and it seemed to be the right time for Lottie to tell us what had been happening in her life as well.

'So, I have two bits of news,' Lottie said brightly. 'One - as you may have guessed - is that your first grand-child, great-grand-child and first niece or nephew is on the way.' She looked at each of us in turn as she spoke. 'Two, you won't be walking me down the aisle just yet.' She glanced briefly at my dad. Then, seeing the look of sorrow on his face, she promptly burst into tears. My mum jumped up at the same time as I did, and we stood either side of her to envelope her in a hug. My dad passed her a tissue across the table, and when she'd dried her tears, we all sat down again.

'Are you up to telling us what happened?' my mum asked.

'I met someone when I was in Greece and I really liked him. Well, obviously.' She rolled her eyes, whether at herself or at him, I wasn't sure. 'We got on so well and we started dating, and I suppose I relaxed into it a bit and stopped being as careful as I would usually be. The next thing I knew, I was pregnant, and he didn't want to know any more.'

'Why didn't you just come home, love?' My dad spoke this time.

'I was embarrassed, and afraid.' Her eyes filled with tears again and I reached out and took her hand. Was there more to this than she was telling us?

'Afraid of what, Lottie?'

'I was afraid you'd all be ashamed of me. You know, pregnant and unmarried.' She blushed and covered her face briefly with her hands.

'Oh, Lottie, no-one would ever be ashamed of you. It happens.'

Lottie's mouth dropped open at these words from her grand-dad and I couldn't have been prouder of him at that moment.

'Come on, it's time for some food. We can talk more while we eat.' Dad took over and after another hug with Lottie, Mum joined him to prepare lunch.

The next morning was so quiet, it was spooky. I still wasn't quite used to that level of silence, having lived in the city for the last few years. I felt rested, though, which was an improvement. As I lay in bed, slowly beginning to wake up, I realised that there were birds tweeting quite noisily outside. I hadn't registered them at first. Perhaps I just wasn't used to the sound of birdsong. My mind turned to Didier, and I reached across to my bedside table for my phone to check whether I'd had any messages from him. My face lit up.

'Missing you and your lovely body this weekend. Would you like me to pick you up from the station? Hope everything is going well at home xx'

I sent a quick reply taking him up on his offer and then went downstairs to the kitchen in my pyjamas. *Papi* was busy making himself some breakfast. Mum and Dad were already outside working in the garden. I imagined Lottie was still in bed. She probably needed the rest more than anyone else.

'*Bonjour, chérie*. Did you sleep well?'

'I did *Papi*, thanks. How about you?'

'Not too badly for an old man. What time will you need to get away today?'

'I probably ought to go straight after lunch. What shall we do this morning?'

'How about a walk across the vineyards? It looks like it's going to be a reasonable day.'

'That sounds wonderful.'

After breakfast, I had a quick shower and got dressed before saying hello and goodbye to my parents. Then we set off through the trees towards the footpath that led through the vineyards.

'So, what do you think about Lottie's news?' he asked, after we'd been walking for a while.

I glanced at him and smiled. He was still so in tune to my feelings, even though we hadn't seen each other for ages.

'Well, I'm relieved everything's out in the open now and that we can help her get through the pregnancy. It would have been awful for her to go through all that alone. I hope she decides to stay at home, where she will be well looked after and cared for.'

'One thing we all know about Lottie is that she's headstrong and she likes to make up her own mind. We won't be able to pressure her into doing what we think is best.' I stopped to admire a bright pink wild flower before catching up with *Papi* a few feet further on.

'Hmm. I hadn't thought of that. I don't want to pressure her. I just want her to be safe but I can see she might view that differently. She loves adventure. It's why she went travelling in the first place, after all.' We started walking again and I found myself thinking about how similar Lottie and I were.

'She needs a sense of purpose. She's not the sort to sit around waiting to have the baby.'

I'd missed Papi's wisdom in the years that I'd been away.

'Yes, you're right. The last thing she'll want to feel is trapped into staying here. I know that feeling only too well.'

He paused for a moment before continuing. 'Anyway, that's enough talk about Lottie. Tell me more about you and Didier.'

'Things are going pretty well,' I said with a smile, 'now that we've accepted we both made mistakes before. So, we're not blaming each other any more and we've both agreed to try again. I do feel a bit wary about whether to get completely involved again, though, especially so soon after splitting up with Paul.'

'Well, that's the trouble with our hearts, isn't it? They rarely do what they're told.' His eyes twinkled, despite his serious tone. 'You have to take a leap of faith in deciding whether this is the right man for you. There's always a risk that things might not work out between you. You know this already. Only you can decide whether it's worth the risk to your fragile heart. I think if you loved each other before, you can love one another again. Perhaps you should see this as a second chance to put right the wrong decisions you both made before.'

'Oh, *Papi*, you've summed it all up very well, as always, thank you.' He took my little hand in his big, crinkly one and I felt protected from the outside world at once. 'Maybe I'm just naturally wary, although I know Didier is a good man and I can still see all the goodness in him. I know he would care for me. We've both learned a lot in the time we've been apart.' I fell silent and turned to admire the panoramic view of the thriving, green vineyards. As we'd been walking for about half an hour or so, we turned to circle back home for some lunch.

'You and Lottie have both experienced that need to go out and explore the world. Now, for different reasons, you both have to decide whether you're content to settle back into life here.'

Didier

On Sunday morning, I took Chlöe to the supermarket to shop for the things we'd been unable to get at the market the previous day. She loved helping me to find things and to put them in the trolley. When she got tired, I lifted her into the seat where she delighted in giving me instructions.

We were going to my mum's for lunch, and Henri was invited too. I was hopeful that grandma might even look after her little granddaughter while I went to pick up Fran. It would be good to spend a bit of time with Fran on my own. Chlöe and I had spent a lovely afternoon with Henri the previous day, during which he'd told me all about his plans to go and see Ellie the following weekend.

'I couldn't believe it when I heard her voice at the other end of the line,' he'd said. 'She sounded exactly the same, and I knew I had to see her again as soon as possible.' He went all dreamy-eyed, and Chlöe and I had laughed at him.

'So, she liked your suggestion of going to stay for the weekend?'

'She screamed down the phone!'

Chlöe giggled again and he blushed.

'When are you planning to go?' I asked, passing round a bowl of plums.

'Would it be okay for me to leave on Friday so I can meet her when she finishes work? I'd like to stay till Sunday afternoon as well, if that would be all right. That means I'll be in late next Monday too.' He'd never had a day off in all the time I'd been working with him. With no close family of his own, the vineyard had become his way of life.

'That's absolutely fine Henri, don't look so worried, really. We'll manage without you.'

Henri was still smiling when we arrived at my mum's just before lunch. I teased him about it as soon as Chlöe disappeared off to the kitchen.

'You are like a puppy, you are so lovesick.'

'I am in love for perhaps the first time in my life. What do you expect?' He patted his heart.

I realised it would do him good to get away and that by Friday, Fran and I might well be glad to see him go. For now, I patted his arm and stood up to go to the kitchen and find out what my mum was cooking for lunch.

'So *Maman*, can I do anything to help?'

Chlöe had a little apron tied round her waist that I recognised from when I was a child myself. She was busy shelling peas for the main course. Meanwhile, my mum was preparing a salad for the starter.

'Please can you prepare the apples for the *tarte aux pommes* while I make the pastry?' She passed me a bowl of apples and the apple corer and I rolled up my sleeves.

'I wanted to ask you a small favour,' I said, once we'd both got started on our jobs. She looked up briefly from rolling out the pastry. 'Fran is coming back from her parents' today and I offered to pick her up from the station. I wondered if I could leave Chlöe here while I go and get her?'

'Of course. You'll pick Chlöe up on your way back, will you?'

'Yes.'

'Would you like to bring Fran in with you?'

'Not this time, Mum. I think she'd need a bit more notice but I do want you to meet her soon.'

She nodded and we left it at that.

Fran

Papi and I arrived home just in time for lunch. Lottie was up and looking a lot brighter than the day before. I gave her a hug.

'You look so much better. Did you sleep well?'

'Like a log. It was my best night's sleep in ages. I've been sleeping on my friend's couch for the past couple of weeks and it was incredibly uncomfortable.'

'Are you going to stay here now, then?' I kept my voice light so she wouldn't think I was pressuring her.

'I don't know yet, Fran. I have a lot to think about. I'll be here for now, though.' She gave me a lovely smile and I felt like she'd turned a corner.

It was soon time for me to leave. I stood on the doorstep, hugging first *Papi* and then Lottie tight, not really wanting to let either of them go. When I finally released them, we all had tears in our eyes.

'*Je t'aime Papi*,' I mumbled.

'*Moi aussi, ma mignonne*.' He coughed to mask his emotions and put his arm round my mum.

I turned to Lottie. 'If ever you need a break and want to come and stay, just let me know. I have a spare room and there's always plenty going on at the vineyard.'

'The harvest can't be far off now, can it? I'd definitely be up for that.'

Everyone stood on the doorstep, waving at my dad and me as we drove away, until we turned the corner and could see each other no more.

Later, on the train, I wondered about Lottie's plans for the future. My parents were worried about how she was going to bring up a child on her own, and so was I. I just hoped she would accept their offer of support.

As the train approached Strasbourg, my mind turned to Didier. I was so looking forward to seeing him again and feeling his warm embrace. I thought about what *Papi* had said about taking that leap of faith and I realised he was right. Didier and I had wasted too much time on the wrong people. It was time for us to find out if we were really meant to be together.

I stepped out on to the platform at Strasbourg station a short while later, looking for signs of Didier and little Chlöe. I spotted him at once. He was on his own. I had a sudden moment of panic - was Chlöe okay? - but Didier was smiling and looking very relaxed. He also looked gorgeous in his dark, figure-hugging jeans and long-sleeved t-shirt. I couldn't wait to feel his body and his lips against mine. He reached out his arms for me and kissed me as though he hadn't seen me for days. I slipped my arms round his neck, tangling my fingers in his curly hair and pulling him as close as I could. The sounds and smells of the station faded away as I lost myself in his kiss and the taste of him I loved so much. When we finally broke apart, we were both out of breath. He picked up my case and took my hand, guiding me out of the crowds and into the car park.

Once we were safely inside the car, I felt able to speak again after our breathtaking kiss.

'I missed you, you know.'

He reached out and took my hand. 'I missed you too. I wish we'd come with you.'

'I know. I'm annoyed I didn't even think of asking you. You must come next time with Chlöe. Where is she, by the way? Is she okay?'

'She's with my mum and she's fine.'

'Good. I must tell you all about Lottie and her news.' And for the rest of the journey, that's what I did.

CHAPTER SIXTEEN

Didier

The day after Fran returned from Colmar, I received the divorce papers from Alain. They were waiting for me when I got back from dropping Chlöe at nursery. Even though I knew this was what I wanted to do, seeing it all in black and white was hard to handle. There would be no coming back from it. I put the papers to one side and decided to read everything through properly later when I was a bit less raw about it all.

There had been no word from Isabelle and I was angry with her. Chlöe seemed happier since we had spoken but a phone call from her mother, however brief, would make her feel better. I had the feeling, though, that once Isabelle received the divorce papers via her lawyers, she would be straight on the phone but for none of the right reasons. I sighed as I threw on my jacket and left the château for the walk to the office. I wished that Isabelle had listened to me when I'd tried to talk to her about it previously.

After my inspection the day before, I was fairly sure we would start the harvest sometime in the following week. The next few days would be critical. For some of our grape varieties, it was now almost forty-five days since the *véraison* - or the point when the grapes begin to ripen - and the regulations stated that the harvest should begin when that time was up, or thereabouts. We would begin harvesting those grapes that were fully ripe then and carry on with the process as each variety ripened.

I reached the office, took off my boots and walked inside, grateful for the warmth from the office heater. Fran was on the phone. She waved hello.

'*Salut,* Henri, *ça va?*'

'*Oui, et toi?* How are the grapes looking?'

I filled him in on the situation.

'I'd better make sure I'm back for that next week, then. You'll need all the hands you can get.'

We always had to call on lots of friends and family members to get the harvesting process done. Although it was an exciting time, it was also back-breaking work picking the grapes by hand. We could have moved to mechanical harvesting to make things quicker but not if we wanted our wines to be graded as top quality.

'Are you going to start with the pinot blanc grapes?'

'Yes, I'll be watching them very carefully this week.' Thierry and I would need to make sure we reached the optimum amount of sugar, balanced with a decrease in the amount of acidity, before we started to pick the grapes that go into our *crémant* or sparkling wine.

'I'll pray that it doesn't rain for you.'

I grimaced as I made a cup of coffee. Rain was the most disastrous thing that could happen to us at this point, and it could make the difference between a successful harvest and a disaster. The impact it could have on our finances didn't even bear thinking about.

'Would you like a cup?'

Henri shook his head, as did Fran when I gestured to her. She was on the phone to one of the builders discussing minute details about their quote. The first quote must have come in today following the appointments last week. I was looking forward to studying it, although dreading the cost as well.

I looked at Fran again as I drank my coffee. She was just as stunning, even with her hair now tied up again and her business-like air in place once more. I remembered the way she'd looked on Friday night with her hair resting on her shoulders. She was gorgeous with or without her clothes on. She glanced up at me, sensing me studying her, and a faint blush crept up her face as if she could read my thoughts. I cleared my throat, not wanting to embarrass her, and turned away to look at some paperwork. Anything to try and help me focus on what I should be doing.

Fran

I sensed Didier's eyes on me from the moment he walked into the office that morning. Although I welcomed his attentions, I began to wish we were back in my bedroom at the cottage and not in a public place. I felt myself blush while on the phone. Thankfully, he must have seen because he turned away. It was all I could do to listen to the builder after that. Finally, I managed to finish the call. I took a moment to pull myself together.

'Good morning, Didier,' I said with a grin.

He turned round to face me and the wicked look he gave me rendered me momentarily speechless.

'Morning. So, you've had a quote in from one of the builders already?'

I swallowed and took a deep breath, wanting more than anything to remain professional in front of Henri, who had also looked up.

'Yes, I was querying something on the quote with them.'

'Can I see it, please?'

I passed it to him and our hands brushed, making my heart skip a beat.

He turned over the pages, looking for the final figure. I held my breath, waiting for his reaction.

'*Mon dieu! C'est pas croyable!* €100,000 for just the Visitors' Centre and €300,000 for the château.' His face fell.

'I know. It's ridiculous, and that's what I was trying to tell him. He has priced up without doing enough research into the materials, I think. I told him to have another go at it, but this time I only want to see a realistic quote.'

'Good. It will be interesting to see what the other quotes are like in comparison. As you say, it is a bit soon for them to have sent in a quote. That suggests they are not very thorough.'

'I agree. Anyway, if they're not up to it, I can still go back to one of the other builders on your original list.'

'That's true.'

My phone buzzed, catching me by surprise.

'I'm sorry, I should have turned that off,' I told Didier. I glanced down to see an unfamiliar number. A little butterfly lodged itself in my stomach. It had to be another message from Paul.

'It's not a problem if you want to read it.'

I bit my lip anxiously. 'That's the thing. I'm not sure if I do want to.' My finger hovered over the button for a second and then I pressed it.

'*Still waiting for you to get in touch with me. I want to see you and I'm not going to give up. Paul.*'

Tears of defeat sprang to my eyes.

'Are you okay?' Didier asked, coming up next to me. 'Who's it from?'

I passed him the phone and he quickly scanned the text. He put the phone down on the desk and, crouching down next to me, took hold of my hands. 'I think you should change your number now. That's the only way to stop this.'

A tear rolled down my cheek and he wiped it gently away before standing up and taking me into his arms. I heard Henri mutter something about needing to go to the village, and then we were alone.

I rested against Didier's shoulder for a few minutes, feeling protected from the outside world by his warm embrace. Then, reluctantly, I stepped back. I reached for a tissue from the box on my desk and wiped my eyes before sinking into my chair.

'I know you're right but it will make him even more angry if I do that. Do you think I should reply?'

'No, definitely not. It's his problem, not yours. Get on to your phone company at once. You'll feel much better if you do.'

I stared at my hands, feeling guilty as always, but hating the way that this was what Paul reduced me to. I took in a deep breath and straightened my shoulders. Then Didier tilted my chin up so I was looking at him. He smiled at me and I gave him a grimace before sitting down at my desk to get on with the torturous process of changing my number and letting everyone know.

Didier

It was a long, difficult day in many ways. To cap it all, Chlöe was grumpy at bedtime, which completely threw me, so it was nearly eight by the time I managed to sit down with the divorce papers. Once I adapted to the legal speak, it didn't take me long to go through them. Alain had kept things simple, as I'd asked, with no blame attached on either side. He had asked for full custody of my daughter on my behalf, with visiting rights for her mother at a minimum of every other weekend or by negotiation. He also stipulated that as we shared no assets, there was no estate to be divided up between us. As soon as I had read it through, I sent him a quick message asking him to send the papers off to Isabelle tomorrow, by email if possible so that we could sort things out quickly. I was sure she would have something to say about the custody issue but I thought I had a good case to argue.

I'd just poured myself a small glass of the sweet *vendange tardive* wine I had treated myself to on my day out with Fran, when I heard a light knock at the back door. I popped my head round the corner to see Fran standing there with Ruby.

'Hey, this is a lovely surprise. Come on in.' I reached for her hand and pulled her to me for a hug, closing the door behind her. She took off her coat and we moved to sit on the sofa in front of the wood-burning stove where Ruby had already bagged a space on the floor.

'I hope you don't mind me dropping in like this. I was just out for a walk and I thought that Chlöe was probably already in bed.' She raised her eyebrows and I nodded. I leaned forward and kissed her gently on the lips, pulling her body closer to mine and savouring the very taste of her. She smelt of the outdoors, smoky yet fresh at the same time.

'Mmm, I have been waiting to do that all day,' I said as we pulled apart after a long moment.

'Yes, I could see what was on your mind this morning when I was on the phone,' she replied with a chuckle.

'It was more than kissing.' I glanced over at her. 'I'm sorry if I embarrassed you.'

She leaned towards me, her whole body pressing against me. 'Don't ever be sorry. You make me feel wonderful and I love feeling like that - like you want me. It's been a long time since anyone made me feel that way.' Her hazel eyes were warm and so inviting but she moved back again to settle against the sofa. Neither one of us was ready to take that step yet with Chlöe just upstairs, even though we both wanted to.

'Would you like a drink?' I asked, standing up to try and ease the sexual tension in the air.

'Yes please, I would.'

I poured her a glass of the sweet wine and settled back next to her on the sofa.

'I just approved the divorce papers my lawyer sent me. He should be sending them on to Isabelle tomorrow.'

'Was everything as you expected?'

'Yes, I think so. I just hope Isabelle will see sense and let me have full custody.'

'I hope you don't mind me saying but Isabelle doesn't strike me as a woman who really has much common sense. Having said that, she is Chlöe's mum so I'd expect her to fight for her daughter.'

I thought about that for a moment and in my heart, I knew Fran was right. 'You think I should be prepared for a struggle?'

'I hope not but it would be better to be on your guard, I think. The trouble is you're reasonable and you expect other people to be the same, but they're often not. It's the same thing for me with Paul.'

I turned to face her on the sofa, folding one leg under the other so I could look at her properly. 'It's one of the things that makes you special though.' I reached out to caress her cheek and she leaned into my hand with a sigh, closing her eyes. In that moment, I knew for sure that I had fallen in love with her all over again.

Fran

I walked back from Didier's feeling ten times better than when I'd left the cottage. I'd given him my new phone number, telling him it would be live in twenty-four hours. I'd already called my mum and dad to tell them the news. The only other person who would need it now was Ellie.

I was so deep in thought that when my phone rang, it startled me. I was very pleased to see Ellie's name and accepted the call at once.

'How are you? It's been ages!' she cried as soon as I answered. I cheered up immediately just from hearing her voice.

'The quick version? Everything is wonderful between me and Didier, Lottie is pregnant but there's no sign of the father and I've had to change my mobile number because Paul just won't stop ringing me.'

'Oh, my God, I go away and all hell breaks loose. Still, I'm so pleased about the Didier part. I presume that means you've had sex?'

'Ellie!' She really had no shame.

She burst out laughing at the other end of the phone. 'Fran, it's okay, everyone does it, you know.'

I could feel myself reddening even though we couldn't see each other. Then I felt a fool.

'Yes, well, we don't all feel the need to discuss it in minute detail, like you do.'

'That's the best bit! Anyway, how is Lottie? Is she okay about having the baby on her own?'

I quickly filled her in about the weekend and about the text I'd received from Paul earlier. She whistled softly.

'Do you think I've done the right thing?' I asked.

'Of course. Paul's a devious rat. Better to cut him off now before he gets his hooks into you again. Once you've got your new number, you can forget all about him and just enjoy yourself with Didier.'

'Talking of which, I hear you're going to have a romantic visitor of your own this weekend. Henri is so looking forward to seeing you again.'

'I know, me too. I couldn't believe it when he rang and suggested it. It's going to be brilliant.'

'Well, look, have a wonderful weekend and try to show Henri some of the sights at least.'

'I'll call you early next week to tell you all about it...in minute detail!'

I gave her my new number and then we said goodbye.

CHAPTER SEVENTEEN

Didier

On the Friday morning, I took Chlöe to nursery and then half-walked, half-ran back to the cottage. Fran had invited me round for breakfast before work. Henri would be on his way to London, and so we had the chance to spend a little time together. I couldn't wait to see her but it wasn't breakfast I had on my mind, despite the bag of pastries I was carrying in my hand.

She opened the door and I dropped the bag on to the table, swept her into my arms and kissed her until both of us were gasping for air.

'Didier,' she breathed. Her eyes were bright with passion. I took her hand to lead her upstairs to her bedroom. Her hair was still damp from the shower and she smelt of peaches and vanilla. I moved her hair gently to one side and kissed my way down her neck to the dip in the middle. Her hands were in my hair and she sighed with pleasure. I lifted my head to kiss her lips, as I gently undid the
...t. I pushed it off her shoulders. Her skin was so
...s and I wanted to feel hers against mine. In one
...ed my t-shirt over my head and we moved to the
... trembled as I reached behind her to undo her bra,

and the sensation of skin on skin was almost too much for either of us to bear.

'You are truly beautiful,' I whispered as she arched her body against me. We helped each other to remove our remaining clothes and we joined together. After so long waiting, we were hungry to show each other how we felt.

Once we had finished making love, neither one of us wanted to let the other go. We lay in each other's arms, until her stomach rumbled and I laughed.

Later, when we were both sat at the table downstairs munching on croissants, Fran seemed lost in her own thoughts.

'Hey, are you okay?'

She looked at me and smiled a heart-stopping smile. 'I am more than okay. You make me very happy.'

And I believed her.

'You deserve to be happy.' I reached out to take her hand and bring it to my lips. 'I suppose we ought to go and do some work really.'

'It will be strange without Henri there, won't it?'

'Yes. He's become a permanent fixture. I can't remember him ever having taken any time off.'

'I'll send Ellie a text later to check he's got there safely.'

Fran

When Didier went out to do his inspection of the vines later that morning, I took advantage of the time on my own to reflect on what had happened between us. It had done my confidence a power of good to know he wanted me so passionately. He had been so attentive to me, never pushing me to do anything until I was ready. The only cloud on our horizon was his divorce but he'd been honest with me about that, and I had told him everything about Paul. Now that I'd changed my number, I hoped my ex would also be out of the picture, so we had a clean slate and could move forward. For the first time in a very long while, I felt full of hope. I couldn't remember when I had last felt this good. Even my doubts about staying in Alsace were starting to fade as I looked towards the future.

I decided to send off a quick text to Ellie about Henri, knowing they were about to spend a great weekend together too.

'Hey, just wanted to wish you a fabulous weekend together. Will you let us know when Henri gets there? He hasn't had a day off in ages :)'

'Will do. Can't wait to see him and then spend all weekend ravishing his body ;)'

Her reply almost made me spill my coffee.

I carried on working through the newest quote I had had in from one of the three builders. Their estimate for both jobs was much more realistic. They were a small, local company. Didier knew the family, and they had also agreed to stagger the work and the associated payment. This would allow us to see how the harvest went before we committed to spending the full amount; however, I still had one more quote to come in, as well as the amended one from the first builder, so I was keeping an open mind.

Lunchtime rolled around and I realised Didier must have gone to pick up Chlöe. I started the walk back to the cottage with Ruby on my own. I had only just crossed the courtyard when a car pulled in. I stopped in case the visitor needed help and was surprised when a young woman climbed out, followed by little Chlöe. Chlöe ran straight up to me and took my hand.

The young woman gave me a hesitant smile. 'I'm Laura from the *école maternelle.* Monsieur Le Roy didn't come to collect Chlöe at the end of the session this morning so I've brought her back as it was starting to get late. Is Monsieur Le Roy here?'

'He is here but he must have got tied up with something and not realised the time. Thank you so much for bringing Chlöe home.' She smiled but she looked reluctant to leave as she didn't know me.

'*Où est ton Papa, alors?*' I smiled at Chlöe, noticing the slight wobble of her lower lip. I wandered over to the archway with her, trying to distract her from her tears. Thankfully, I spotted Didier in the distance running towards us. The young woman had followed behind us and when she spotted him, she said goodbye, climbed back into her car and drove off again.

Didier

I was in the château, changing out of my wet clothes after the vineyard inspection, when the phone rang. Isabelle. I pressed the button with trepidation.

'Didier?' her voice was sharp. I glanced quickly at my watch, conscious it was nearly time to pick up Chlöe.

'Yes, Isabelle, it's me.'

'What the hell do you think you're doing sending me divorce papers? And you want full custody as well? Do you have any idea what you're taking on?'

'I did try to talk to you about it when you came to tell me you were going to Toronto but you wouldn't listen.'

'I had no idea you were being serious when you said that.' She paused to take in a breath. 'I don't understand why you had to make it all so...so formal.' Her voice caught and I was surprised.

'We've been living apart for two years now. It's time for us to move on.' I spoke gently, trying to make her understand my intentions. 'As for Chlöe, she's already going to be living with me for the next year and my lifestyle is a bit more stable than yours. I only want to do what's best for her.'

'Well, I'm not happy about any of this at all,' she said, recovering her usual confident tone. 'I will be talking to my lawyer and you will be hearing from them very soon about what I want.'

'What do you want, Isabelle? Why don't you tell me?' I was trying to keep my voice low and not get annoyed with her.

She made a scoffing noise at the other end of the phone. 'What about my share of the estate? If we're married, I think I am entitled to half your assets if we get a divorce.'

My throat went dry, even though I was pretty sure that the law was on my side on that point.

'If that's the way your mind is working, I think we need to communicate only through our lawyers now, like you said.'

With that final word, I hung up.

'*Merde*!' She really knew how to wind me up. I looked at my watch again. It was past time for picking Chlöe up. I threw on my coat, grabbed my keys and dashed out of the door hoping she was safe at the *école maternelle*. As I strode across the grass, I spotted Fran and Chlöe in the distance at the archway to the courtyard and blew out a big sigh of relief. I ran the rest of the way, anxious to reassure my little girl that everything was okay. I was glad to see that Chlöe was laughing with Fran and seemed perfectly fine. I crouched down and she fell into my arms for a hug.

'*Ça va, ma petite?* I'm sorry I was late, I was on the phone.' I looked up at Fran and she reached out to squeeze my shoulder.

'*Ça va, Papa, pas de problème*.' Chlöe ran off with Ruby, seemingly none the worse for what had happened.

As we walked towards the cottage to go and get lunch, I told Fran about my conversation with Isabelle. She was frowning and looked as stressed as I felt when I'd finished telling her everything.

'It's odd that she was so upset about the divorce, isn't it? She must have been expecting it surely?'

'I know, I didn't understand that either.' I wiped my hand over my face, trying to erase the memory of the phone call.

'And she didn't say anything more about the custody issue. It sounds to me like it was all a bit of bluff and bluster.'

I stared at her, confused for a minute by the phrase she had just used. 'What is this "bluff and bluster"? I don't understand, sorry.' She laughed and the lovely sound brought a smile to my face. She took my hand and swung it as she tried to explain.

'The closest I can get to that English phrase is "*des paroles en l'air*" I think.'

'Okay, yes, maybe you're right but if she goes after half the estate's value, I don't know what I'll do. I feel pretty sure she's just clutching at straws but it has still made me very nervous.'

'Are you going to call your lawyer?'

'Yes, I will, straight after lunch. I think he needs to know what we're going to be up against as soon as possible.'

Fran

After lunch, Chlöe stayed with me while Didier went back to the château to call his lawyer. We walked back to the office and I collected my paperwork so Chlöe could play at the cottage while I tried to do a bit of work. I decided the next time I was at the château, I would ask her to pick out some of her toys and books to keep at the cottage in case she was with me again.

Around half an hour later, we heard voices outside. We both looked up. Chlöe stood up and went to the door to find out who it was and I hurried after her in case it was someone she didn't know. We emerged outside to find Didier talking animatedly in very fast French to a smart older woman. It took me only a second to notice the resemblance between them and then to work out that this must be his mother.

'*Maman, je te présente ma copine,* Fran.' He made an apologetic face at me, which I took to mean that I was much more than his friend but I understood that he didn't want to say more in front of Chlöe.

I put my hand out towards his mother and she took it. '*Bonjour, madame.*'

'I'm so delighted to meet you at last, Fran. I have heard a lot about you over the years.'

'It is lovely to meet you too, Madame Le Roy.'

'You must call me Sylvie, I insist.' She looked so regal, with her elegant clothes and hair styling that it was all I could do to stop myself from curtseying in her presence. She had a warm smile, though, and she seemed genuinely glad to meet me. While we were talking, Chlöe had made her way over and was now hugging her grandmother's leg. Sylvie bent down to embrace her and took her hand.

'I am going shopping, Didier. Would it be all right with you if Chlöe came with me this afternoon? And perhaps I could cook dinner for us all this evening.'

'That would be wonderful, *Maman.* Shall we come round about seven?'

'Perfect. Now, *ma petite*, shall we go?' Little Chlöe nodded and with one last wave, the pair of them walked back towards the courtyard.

'What did your lawyer have to say?' I asked Didier as we made our way to the office.

'He remembered my mother's concern about the estate when he drew up our marriage contract. He said he would double-check what the contract entailed but as far as he remembered, after my dad died, we decided to split ownership of the estate between us, with me managing all the day-to-day running. My mother's input is invaluable and I wouldn't have wanted it any other way. Anyway, for that reason, it was important to draw up our marriage contract so that the estate was regarded as an asset before marriage and therefore mine alone.'

'Well, that sounds as though Isabelle can't get her hands on it.'

'I hope so. I really can't face fighting her over that too.'

CHAPTER EIGHTEEN

Later that afternoon, I received a text from Ellie telling me Henri had made it safely to London. Didier and I both breathed a sigh of relief to know they were together at last.

We worked steadily through the afternoon, trying to catch up with everything. Didier even managed to fit in another vineyard inspection towards the end of the day. He was pretty sure the harvest would begin early next week and he wanted to do more frequent checks as a result.

At half past six, Didier picked me up from the cottage to take me to his mother's house for dinner.

'Hey, what's up? You really don't need to be nervous.'

'Are you sure about that?' I replied. 'She's your mum and I'm sure she feels very protective towards you.' I thought of how my mum had reacted when Didier and I had split up. I couldn't help worrying that Didier's mum might feel equally resentful towards me for hurting her son.

'She worries about me but not overly so. She has given us her blessing and she wants me to make the most of this second chance with you. That's what I'm doing.' He smiled, kissed me firmly on the lips and took my hand to lead the way.

Didier's mum lived in a typical Alsatian house, right in the heart of the village. It was painted a pale pink on the outside and had timber beams running down the front of it. There was a small garden in front, full of colourful pots overflowing with petunias, geraniums and daisies, but Didier led me round the back of the house, through an ironwork gate and underneath an arbour covered with yellow roses. The smell was heavenly. I stopped for a moment while it assaulted my senses in the best possible way. Didier went on ahead, oblivious to the beautiful open space around him, but I trailed behind, taking in all the plants in the borders, a little pond with a tinkling water feature and a summer house in one corner. It was stunning and I loved it. Even in the fading September sunshine, it was beautiful. By the time I reached the patio, I had a great big smile on my face. Sylvie reached out to embrace me fondly, and I relaxed at once.

'Oh, your garden is so wonderful! I could explore for hours.'

'Thank you! Well, you are welcome to come and explore any time. My husband and I used to love gardening but sadly, he never had much time because of his work in the vineyard.'

'I was very sorry to hear about your husband's passing, Sylvie. You must miss him so much.'

'I do miss him still, but he is always here in my heart.' She patted her chest to emphasise her words and I felt tears spring to my eyes. 'Come on Fran, let's go inside and you can see what Chlöe and I have been getting up to.' Her eyes twinkled and I was relieved to feel completely at ease in her company.

Inside, Didier was crouching down next to Chlöe, helping her roll out pastry circles. Her face was covered in flour.

'*Regardes Fran, j'ai fait des petites tartes aux pêches!*' She pointed proudly to some finished peach tarts.

'*Bravo*, Chlöe. *Ça va être délicieux!*'

She carried on rolling while we went to sit at the large kitchen table, where Sylvie poured us all a glass of her own *crémant* rosé.

'So, Fran, how are you enjoying working and living at the *Domaine*?' she asked, sitting down opposite me and Didier at the table. Didier's hand closed over mine beneath the tablecloth.

'I'm really enjoying it. The job came at just the right time for me. I'd been wanting to come home for a while, and now I'm glad I did.' I glanced sideways to find Didier studying me while I talked. He gave me a reassuring smile.

'And your family is from Colmar, is that right?'

'Yes, my mum and dad still live there.' I could see Sylvie had planned a full-on inquisition for me. I tried to remain calm.

'Are you staying in Alsace for good now?'

'Well, yes.' I paused before adding, 'For the time being anyway.'

Didier pressed his lips together. I sensed his disappointment in my reply but he said nothing, merely giving my hand a brief squeeze before standing up.

'*Maman*, is there anything we can do to help with dinner?' It was a signal that it was time to end the Q&A, and I was grateful to him. I still wasn't sure if I had passed the test though.

'*Non, non, c'est déjà fait*,' she tsked. She stood and made her way to the oven to check how the quiche was getting on before going over to check on Chlöe's progress.

With a smile, Didier pretended to wipe his hand across his forehead, suggesting I'd survived the first round of grilling, at any rate. We sat down to dinner shortly after that, starting with a delicious salad of pears and walnuts, a classic combination that I hadn't enjoyed for a long time. This was followed by a home-made quiche Lorraine and vegetables, which Didier paired with a spicy Gewurztraminer.

'This quiche is delicious and goes so well with the wine,' I commented in between mouthfuls. 'It is so good to have Alsace food again.'

Sylvie smiled and seemed more at ease.

'Have you decided when you're going to start the harvest?' Sylvie asked, turning her attention to Didier.

'I'm pretty sure it will be Tuesday now. Have you already mentioned it to our regular helpers?'

Sylvie nodded as she stood up after the main course to help Chlöe put her little tarts in the oven.

'All the usual crowd have said they'll be there.'

Chlöe's peach tarts cooked in no time and soon we were tasting them along with a spoonful of vanilla ice cream. Sylvie took a photo of Chlöe eating her creation and she looked every inch the proud young chef.

'Can I bring Chlöe over on Monday afternoon, *Maman*? I was hoping that you could take her to and from school every day during the harvest, if that's okay?'

'Of course, that will be fine. Will you give me a hand with the coffee now, please?'

When they returned a few minutes later, Didier was beaming and I couldn't think what they might have discussed to make him look so pleased.

I stood up and started clearing plates but Didier stopped me with a kiss and gestured for me to sit down again. He disappeared into the kitchen and I went to see what Chlöe was up to. I'd thought she was playing with Ruby but realised she had fallen asleep, resting on Ruby's side. I gently lifted her up and carried her to the sofa. She smelt of pastry and peaches, and her little face was warm against my cheek. I laid her down carefully and pulled a throw over her. I stared at her for a moment, and I realised just how much I'd grown to love this little girl. When I looked up, I found Didier watching me from across the room. I blushed slightly at the tender look he gave me.

'We ought to get this little one home to bed,' I said softly, sweeping Chlöe's hair gently away from her forehead.

'Mum has asked if she could stay here tonight. I'll take her upstairs and lay her down in bed.' He came over and kissed me gently before lifting Chlöe into his arms and padding upstairs.

I stood up, smoothing down my skirt, and went over to look at some photos on the dresser in the corner of the room. They were all of Didier's father. Almost every photo showed him working in the vineyard and from his constant smile, I understood that was where he had been at his happiest. He had the same dark, curly hair and captivating smile as his son. All the photos of him and Didier showed them laughing together. I sighed.

'Are you okay, Fran?'

I turned, surprised by the sound of Sylvie's voice in the quiet room. 'I was just admiring these photos of your husband with Didier. He and Didier seemed very close. I'm so sorry your husband has gone. He can't have been very old.'

'No, he wasn't. He had cancer and he was definitely far too young to die. I miss him and I know Didier does too, every day. He would love to be able to talk about the vineyard with his dad and to seek his advice. He had to grow up very quickly when his dad was diagnosed.'

'How long did he have before he died?'

'He was given six months to live but in the end he had just three months left. The doctors were sadly misinformed about how aggressive the cancer was. It rocked us all. We just weren't ready to be without him.'

'When did he pass away?' I asked.

'It was just after you left for London,' she said softly.

I gasped. 'So, Didier already knew his dad was dying when I told him I was going to London?'

She nodded. 'Why didn't he tell me? I would have stayed.'

'I think you have your answer right there. He knew you wanted to pursue your dream. He would never have wanted to hold you back. That's how much he loved you, Fran.'

I looked at her with dawning horror. When Didier had needed

me most, I'd left to "pursue my dream." And look where it had got me. I didn't know what to say.

'What are you two whispering about?' Didier suddenly appeared beside us. I paled when I thought about how much I must have hurt him. He put his arm round me and I tried to force a smile.

'We were looking at some photos of you and your dad. Fran hadn't seen them before.'

'Come on then, Fran, shall we go? Chlöe's fast asleep now. Thanks for dinner, Mum.' He kissed and hugged his mum goodbye and I was struck by how attached they were.

'Thank you for a wonderful dinner, Sylvie.'

'It was my pleasure both of you. Now off you go and enjoy the rest of your evening together. I'll bring Chlöe back after lunch tomorrow.' She gave me a smile and a warm hug before releasing me. Didier held my coat out and soon we were back outside in the cool night air.

Didier

Fran didn't say anything much on the way back. I didn't know how to broach the subject of what might have passed between her and my mum while I was upstairs with Chlöe. Every time I looked at her, she was biting her lip anxiously. By the time we reached the cottage, I was starting to worry. She pushed her hands deep into her coat pocket, searching for her keys, but she didn't bring them out. She just stood there, with her head hung low.

I lifted her chin so I could see her face. Her eyes were full of tears. I folded her into my arms then.

'Let's go inside and you can tell me what this is all about,' I said after a few moments.

She passed me the keys and I opened the door, holding her hand the entire time. Once inside, I led her to the sofa, neither of us bothering to remove our coats. I waited for her to speak but the minutes became long and still she didn't say anything.

'Please will you talk to me? Whatever this is about, we can sort it out.'

'I feel ashamed of myself,' she said, so quietly I almost didn't catch it.'

'What do you mean? You have nothing to be ashamed of yourself for.'

She took in a deep breath, physically pulling herself together for what she was about to say. 'Your mum told me about your dad's cancer diagnosis and the fact that you knew about it already when I told you I was going to London. And now I hate myself for pursuing my own selfish desires at a time when you really needed me.'

The tears rolled down her cheeks. I had a sudden image of her on the day we'd said our goodbyes. She'd been sobbing and I had so desperately wanted to comfort her but I couldn't find a way without telling her the truth.

'I wish you'd told me, Didier. I would have stayed. I thought you didn't really love me because you *didn't* ask me to stay. Things might have been so much different for us both if we'd told each other our real feelings.'

I stood up and began pacing in front of the fire.

'I didn't tell you because you had your own life to lead. I knew you would have given everything up to stay with me. If I'd told you, you might blame me now for stopping you. You weren't selfish; you were young and carefree and full of dreams waiting to be fulfilled, and I didn't want to be the one to stand in your way.'

'I just wish I'd talked it all over more with you, rather than digging my heels in and thinking only of myself. I wish I'd given more thought to just how much you meant to me and made more of an effort to compromise. We've wasted all these years.' She covered her eyes with her hands.

'I told you once that I can't see the point in regrets. Life's so short as it is. Perhaps this is fate, us meeting again and getting a second chance. And that's all I want from you. I want the chance to see if we were meant to be. I want to love you now, and to know you love me in return. I want to look forward into the future and not waste time with regret about the past. And I want to know if you want that second chance too.'

I stopped pacing. She lifted her head to study my face, and then she stood up and came to me. She reached out and I pulled her closer without hesitation. Then she kissed me tenderly.

'I *do* want that second chance. I want to make up for lost time between us and I want to be able to show you every day just how much I love you.'

I crushed her lips with mine, eager to show her the depth of my passion and commitment. As her lips parted and our tongues tangled together, my desire for her was renewed.

'I love you too. And I want you to come to my bed in the château this time.' I was locking the door again when I heard her call my name. When I turned round, she was running across the grass towards the château. I laughed out loud and set off to catch her.

Fran

When I woke the next morning, I didn't remember where I was at first and then it came back to me. I remembered our wonderful night of lovemaking the night before and turned to watch Didier sleeping for a moment. He looked so peaceful and so gorgeous.

I glanced round the room, taking in the rustic furniture: an old wardrobe, bedside tables and a pretty chest of drawers. There were few personal items in the room. The plaster walls were painted a creamy colour and there were pale blue curtains at the window. I noticed how clean the room was. In fact, the whole house seemed very clean and tidy. I was impressed by the way he had spruced up this part of the château before Chlöe's arrival, and by the way he looked after himself and his daughter.

I thought back to Paul and remembered just how messy he had been. I wondered for a moment what it would be like to live with

Didier and found myself excited by the idea. I had surprised myself by revealing that I loved him. But I really did. I had come to love every little thing about him over these past few weeks. I looked over at him again, and I knew that if he asked me to stay, I wouldn't have to think twice, especially after what he'd said to me the night before.

He stirred and I reached out to touch his hair. I snuggled my body up against his and his arms came round me at once.

'*Bonjour, chérie*. How are you this morning?' His dark brown eyes stared into mine intensely.

'I'm okay, I suppose,' I teased.

He gave me a wicked grin. 'That's not nearly good enough as an answer. I think we will have to do something about that.'

'Have you got any ideas?'

'*Certainement*,' he growled and kissed me fiercely before proceeding to show me exactly what those ideas were.

Some time later, we decided to get up and face the day. I had no idea what the time was and although I had nowhere else to be, Didier had to think about Chlöe, who would be coming back after lunch. I showered while he went downstairs to prepare breakfast. When I emerged, I felt fresher and a bit more with it.

A wonderful sight met my eyes when I went downstairs. Didier had laid out a delicious looking breakfast of fresh coffee, juice and a selection of pastries.

'How did you manage to do all this in twenty minutes?'

'I could pretend to be Superman, of course, but I have a housekeeper who comes in and helps me keep on top of things. She brought breakfast in for us this morning so that we could have a lie-in.' He grinned at me.

'When did she come?'

'While you were in the shower. I gave her a call.'

'Oh, okay.' I was reassured to know his housekeeper hadn't been in the house while we were upstairs in bed. 'I'd been thinking you were incredibly clean and tidy and I was impressed. Now you tell me that none of it is down to you at all,' I joked.

'So, I am not your hero after all?'

'No, you've disappointed me. You'll have to make it up to me some other way.' I raised an eyebrow. He pulled me to him and kissed me firmly on the lips, patting my behind at the same time.

'I'll have to give some thought today to how I can meet that challenge but for now, come, sit and have some breakfast.'

I was ravenous and so was Didier. There wasn't much food left after we'd finished. I was glad to see that it was only now ten o'clock so we still had some time together before little Chlöe would be back.

Didier went off to have a shower and I cleared up before wandering over to my bag to check if there were any updates from Ellie. There was nothing from her so I knew they must be having a really good time. That thought brought a smile to my face.

I stood at the French windows looking out at the back garden, admiring the view and wondering just how many people were needed to keep the abundant flower beds and borders looking so beautiful. I sensed Didier come up behind me and then felt his hands on my shoulders, followed by his lips on my neck.

'What shall we do with these couple of hours?' he asked.

'Will you take me on your vineyard inspection? I know it's very close to the harvest now and I want to see what that looks like.' I turned to face him and he gave me a warm kiss on the lips before we grabbed our coats to set off on a brisk walk to the vineyard.

CHAPTER NINETEEN

Didier

I couldn't have been more delighted when Fran asked me to show her the vineyard. She'd seen it from afar many times of course, but now I was proud to show her the results of all our hard work since my father's death.

It only took us a few minutes to reach the first rows of the vineyard. As always, there were a number of people still hard at work, removing leaves from the vines to increase the exposure of the grapes to the sun. Many of the workers waved as we approached and called out greetings to me. I was lucky to have such good staff. They had really pulled together around me when I suddenly found myself in charge. I would never have got through that first harvest without their help.

Fran was silent as we strolled along between the rows of flourishing vines.

'What are you thinking about?' I asked.

For a moment she said nothing. I had the feeling she was shy about baring her soul to me but I hoped that she understood by now that I only wanted to know her better.

'I was just thinking how much everyone likes you. It makes me feel proud to be with you.' She didn't look at me as she spoke. I stopped her and lifted her chin.

'I am proud to walk alongside you too. You are beautiful and I'm so glad I can share all this with you. The vineyard means so much to me.' I waved my arm to indicate I meant the estate. Then I coughed, feeling a bit embarrassed. 'I'm sorry. I'm just so passionate about it all.'

Fran took my face in her hands and kissed me firmly on the lips.

'I love your passion, Didier.'

I smiled at her and we started walking again. In no time, we were deep in the heart of the vineyard, with row upon row of vines sloping down as far as the eye could see. It was an amazing sight. Even though the land was mine, I felt a great sense of awe at the size of our vineyard and our operation.

'How big is the vineyard?' Fran asked. 'And how does it compare to others locally?'

'We have about 20 hectares here, which makes us a small-sized vineyard in Alsace. Most of the local ones are similar in size. A *Grand Cru* vineyard would be double the size of ours though. Last year's *vendange* was a good one because the weather was pretty good. We were able to produce a small amount of red and rosé, together with large quantities of our white wines, making just over 150,000 litres.'

Her eyebrows shot up and her eyes widened. I chuckled at her response. We continued our tour, stopping every now and then so I could check the grapes with my refractometer.

'What are you measuring with that instrument?' Fran asked after one such stop.

I straightened up and showed her the reading. 'This measures the balance between sugar and acid in the grapes, as well as the pH levels. I compare the reading to an index and it gives me an idea of the weight of the unfermented grape juice. This, in turn, tells me the potential alcohol of the grape juice during fermentation. It's not as complicated as it sounds.'

'What are you thinking about the harvest? Is it time?'

'It's definitely time for the pinot blanc grapes, which is what we usually harvest first for the *crémant*. I'd like to make a start on Tuesday or Wednesday, as long as I can get enough people to come and help.'

'How long will the harvest last from beginning to end?'

'If we have enough people for the hand-picking, it will take around a month and a half. And we will be working eight hours a day every day for that time, both picking and pressing.'

We started walking back up the hill towards the château, now shimmering in the distance in the haze of the midday sun. I wrapped my arm around Fran's shoulders.

'Where do you get all the people from?' she asked.

'People come to France just for the harvest every year. They either contact us directly or they come via an agency. Some of them have been coming back for several years. The rest are family, friends and other locals who step in to help us. It's truly a community job. Everyone helps out somewhere.'

'I'm very excited to pick grapes for the first time.'

'I'll remind you of those words in a couple of weeks' time, Fran. It's back-breaking work, you know.'

She lifted her chin in that determined way of hers and I had to smile.

'Are you trying to tell me I'm not up to the job, *monsieur*?'

'I wouldn't dare. Have I ever told you how sexy you look when you get that gleam in your eye?'

I kissed her and pulled her closer to me.

'Are you hungry?' I asked her.

'I'm starving,' she replied, 'but not necessarily for food.' Her eyes twinkled. She pulled away and began to run. I chased after her, enjoying the wind in my hair and against my face. I couldn't ever remember feeling more content.

Fran

As we lay in bed after making love, I was surprised to hear the kitchen door open downstairs. I froze as Didier jumped out of bed and pulled on his trousers to go and investigate. I was sure I would have heard Chlöe's little voice by now if it was her and her grandmother. I got up and started to get dressed again, hearing the door close while I was doing so, followed by Didier's footsteps on the stairs.

'Who was it?' I asked.

'Don't worry, it was only my housekeeper. I asked her to drop lunch off for us so we wouldn't have to worry today.'

'You think of everything, you really do.' I gazed at him with admiration and he reached out for me.

'I am wooing you with food and wine,' he murmured, bending his head to kiss me in the sensitive spot just below my ear.

'I warn you that if you kiss me there, we will never get to eat today.' He carried on kissing me until I dodged away and made for the stairs.

'You can be such a spoilsport, you know,' he told me, laughing at me.

'Well, I really am hungry for food now so you'll just have to wait and ravish me later.' Behind me, I heard him groan but then he followed me downstairs anyway. When I reached the bottom step, I glanced over at the kitchen table to see a beautiful wicker picnic hamper waiting for us, along with a chilled bottle of *Domaine* rosé. I couldn't wait to open the hamper and find out what was inside. Didier gave a rich laugh behind me, as I threw back the lid of the basket. I was overwhelmed with a whole host of heavenly smells. There were fresh baguettes, a delicious looking onion tart, a selection of charcuterie and various salads and - for the remote chance we might actually have some room left - there were also some homemade desserts. I smiled as Didier passed me my glass of wine.

'You look very content,' he said before taking a sip of his wine.

'I was already before we found this wonderful hamper but now I really am in heaven. It's a proper banquet!'

We began by tasting the onion tart, which was still warm and every bit as delicious as I'd expected.

'I hope Ellie and Henri are enjoying their weekend as much as I'm enjoying mine,' I said, closing my eyes as I savoured the smoky flavour of caramelised onions - a glorious match with the fruity wine.

I helped myself to some bread and charcuterie before passing the plate to Didier.

'I'll send Henri a text today,' he said. 'I ought to let him know we're planning on starting the picking on Tuesday, just so he's prepared when he returns.'

'That's a good idea. Will it be all right to leave the office unattended during the harvest?'

'It's what we usually do. Most people realise if we're not there at this time of year, it's because we're busy. I take your point though. Maybe we should put up a sign or something this year.'

'I can do that on Monday. I'll call the builders as well, and tell them what's happening.'

'Are you any closer to a decision yet?'

'I liked the look of the second quote and the company very much, so unless the third one is outstanding, I think we should probably go with them. If we do decide, could they make a start while we're doing the harvest do you think?'

'Mmm, yes, possibly.' Didier swallowed a mouthful of potato salad before patting his firm stomach in defeat. 'That was delicious but I really can't eat any more.'

'What about dessert?' I teased, moving over to lean against him.

'I think I've probably had more than my fair share of dessert already today.' He patted me on the bottom, giving me a cheeky grin. I kissed him with delight and rested against him.

'This has been lovely, thank you.'

'You deserve every minute, and it has been my pleasure.'

Didier

When I woke up on Sunday morning, I could feel a change in the weather. Before I'd even got out of bed, I could see there was no sun peeking through the blind, and it seemed a tiny bit darker than the day before. It was definitely time to start the harvest.

I walked along the corridor to Chlöe's room and peeked in. She was fast asleep, another tell-tale sign that the new season was coming. Chlöe was a good sleeper, luckily, but she was usually up with the birds. Today was noticeably different. I went downstairs to put on a pot of coffee. As the machine gurgled, I stared out of the French windows at the early morning dew, fretting about leaving the picking too late. At least it hadn't rained. If it had, leaf rot would be a major concern.

I poured myself a strong cup of coffee, no milk, no sugar. As I sat at the table, I remembered about sending a message to Henri regarding the start date for the harvest. I picked up my phone and was surprised to find a message already waiting for me, sent late the previous night.

'Salut, Didier. Sorry to have to tell you but Fran's ex was here at Ellie's tonight demanding to know where Fran is. We said nothing but he was very aggressive. Wanted to warn you.'

Damn. I sucked in a breath at the man's nerve.

'Only just read this, sorry. Are you both okay? How did you leave it with him?'

I waited anxiously for a reply but it was an hour earlier in London. Should I tell Fran or would it just worry her, perhaps unnecessarily? Or perhaps Ellie had already told her. I sent off another text to Henri.

'Did you tell Fran about this? If not, please don't. She doesn't need the worry. I was going to text you today to say that we start the harvest on Tuesday, just to let you know. So sorry you had to deal with all that trouble. See you tomorrow.'

I worried then for a while about whether Fran would be waking up to this news. She would be sure to panic but I had no idea what we could do. I decided to go over and see her as soon as Chlöe and I were dressed.

By the time I'd showered, Chlöe was downstairs playing in the living room.

'*Bonjour, Papa.*' She looked up at me with a smile and then promptly yawned.

'Hey, sleepyhead. You must have been very tired this morning after your sleepover with *mémé*.' She nodded. 'Why don't you go and get dressed, and we'll go out and get some breakfast?'

While she went upstairs, I checked my phone again.

'We're both okay but Ellie's still quite shaken up today. We threatened to call the police and he went. Ellie has already sent Fran a message, sorry. See you tomorrow.'

I ran my hands through my damp hair. Christ, what a mess. I had no idea her ex was like this. I was glad he had cheated on her. It had given her a damn fine reason for leaving him. I ran upstairs to help Chlöe finish getting dressed.

Fran

I was still in my pyjamas enjoying a lazy start to Sunday morning when I was surprised by a knock at the door of the cottage. Didier was on the doorstep, a worried frown on his face. He brought Chlöe inside, where she settled down with Ruby in front of the fire, and then guided me out to the kitchen out of her hearing.

'I take it you haven't looked at your phone since last night?'

I shook my head. 'I didn't look at it at all yesterday evening. I went to bed quite early, with my book. What is it? What's happened?'

'Ellie's sent you a message. It's not good news, I'm afraid.' That scared me to death as I imagined all kinds of terrible things happening to her and Henri. I let out a gasp and ran to find my phone. 'Sorry, Ellie and Henri are both okay,' he added quickly.

I found the message and groaned. 'How dare he do that to my friends? The bastard.' I spoke in a fierce whisper so Chlöe wouldn't hear. I read Ellie's message out to Didier.

'Paul came round tonight looking for you. He was drunk and shouting about you hiding from him. He kept asking us where you were and when we wouldn't tell him, he became aggressive. Henri stood up to him and when we said we'd call the police, he went. We must do something to stop him, Fran.'

'Oh my God, I just can't even begin to process this. What am I going to do?'

'Look, why don't you call Ellie? I'll go with Chlöe to get breakfast and we'll talk some more when we get back. Okay?'

Didier helped Chlöe put her coat on again, whistled to Ruby and then they were gone. I sank down onto the sofa while I worked out what on earth I was going to say to Ellie. How could I make this up to them both?

'Ellie, hi, it's me. I've just read your message. I'm so sorry.'

'Let's get one thing straight right away: this is not your fault, okay? I will not have you blaming yourself for Paul's behaviour.'

'Okay, but what the hell happened?'

I gnawed on my lip as I listened to her story.

'We'd been out for dinner and were just getting ready for bed when there was a terrible banging and shouting from the hallway outside the flat. I went to the door and Henri followed. I recognised Paul at once of course, and I could see he was really drunk. He kept shouting your name over and over. I realised he thought you were staying with me, so I told him you weren't, and that you were still in France. Then he accused me of lying and barged into the flat looking for you. That's when Henri stepped up.'

I gasped. I couldn't believe Paul had actually gone to these lengths to find me.

'I screamed that I would call the police and he started to back off.

He was making such a commotion that other people came out of their flats too. At least that means we have a lot of witnesses. Just before he went, he said he would find you, that you couldn't hide away from him forever. He kept demanding your new number but I didn't say anything.'

'Oh, Ellie, God, I'm so sorry. Are you both all right?'

'We're fine, honestly. I do feel a bit shaken up still but I'm most concerned about what he'll do if he finds you. I really think you should call the police about him, Fran.'

'The thing is he hasn't done anything to me, has he? I don't think they would be interested to hear from me unless he does something. I can't understand what's got into him. When I spoke to him before I left, he was upset but he seemed to have accepted it was over between us. Why has he changed his mind?'

'I really don't know but I'm worried for your safety.'

'Look, please try and enjoy your last few hours with Henri. I'll call you tomorrow. Thanks so much for sticking up for me.'

'Any time. Take care now.'

I rang off just as Didier and Chlöe came back with breakfast.

CHAPTER TWENTY

Didier settled Chlöe at the table, and while she was busy eating her *pain au chocolat,* I relayed my conversation with Ellie to Didier as quickly as I could.

'What do you think I should do? I'm wondering about calling Paul and threatening him with a court order.'

'Has he ever been to your family's home?'

'No, he was never interested in coming to France, thank God. I did tell him I was coming home for Amandine's wedding, and Ellie confirmed I stayed on afterwards.'

'He can't connect you with the vineyard, though, so that's good. I don't think you should make any further contact with him. He's not someone you can reason with, from the sounds of it.'

'I suppose you're right. It's just I hate the fact that Ellie and Henri have been dragged in to something that's nothing to do with them. It's my mess and I feel I should do something.'

'No, it's not your mess. This is all down to Paul and you're not responsible for him.' He pulled me towards him and I rested my head gratefully on his shoulder as he stroked my back, trying to soothe all my worries away.

'Are you going over to your mum's for dinner today?' I asked, changing the subject to take my mind off Paul.

'Yes, would you like to come too? She asked me to invite you.'

'I'd love that, thank you.' We shared a long kiss and then he jumped up.

'Come on, Chlöe, let's go and get you properly washed and dressed before we go to grandma's this afternoon. We'll pick you up around midday, Fran, okay?'

After Didier had gone, I thought carefully about what he had said. I knew he was right but I couldn't help worrying about it all. I had a quick shower and got dressed and then decided to give my parents a call and get their advice.

'*Papa, c'est moi.*'

'*Oh, ça va, ma chérie?*' He sounded weary which wasn't like him at all.

'Dad, what's the matter? You sound as though you have the weight of the world on your shoulders.'

He sighed. 'It's Lottie. She's taken herself off to Strasbourg to visit a friend for a few days. We tried to talk to her about her future plans and she pushed against us, thinking we were pressuring her. Now we haven't heard from her, and your mother's worried sick.'

'Come on, Dad. She's always been a free spirit and she does what she likes, you know that. She's just annoyed because she can't wriggle out of this. She has to face her responsibilities now. I'm sure she'll be fine in Strasbourg for a few days.'

'But she's pregnant, Fran, that's the difference this time. We are very worried about her.'

'And she's not answering her phone, I take it?'

'No. Have you been in touch with her?'

'Not since that weekend, no. I'll send her a text today and see if I can persuade her to get in touch with you. Listen, I called because I need to talk to you about something.'

'I think Didier has given you good advice,' my dad said after I'd explained what had happened. 'And thanks for warning us. I don't think Paul will come and bother us but if he does, at least we'll be prepared. Anyway, how's everything going for you? Tell me some good news, please.'

'Things are great, Dad.' I smiled as I thought of how wonderful things were between Didier and me. 'We're going to start the harvest this week, which I'm really excited about. How would you and Mum like to come up and help out? We start on Tuesday, and we need as many pairs of hands as we can get for the next month or so.'

'It's been years since we helped at a grape harvest but I think it might do us good to get away from home for a bit. It will take our minds off things. I'll have a chat with your mum and let you know. You won't forget to contact Lottie, will you?'

'No, Dad, I promise.'

Didier

Monday morning rolled around quickly. I was up early to get Chlöe to school before doing my morning inspection. Aside from a period of light drizzle on Saturday afternoon, the weather had remained mostly fine over the weekend but I would have to keep a close eye on it.

I made my way to the office straight after the inspection, looking forward to seeing Fran after not being able to spend the night together the evening before.

'Morning, sweetheart,' I said. I leaned over her desk for a kiss, not noticing the look in her eyes until it was too late.

'Ah, just as I expected. You two have been carrying on behind my back.' I swung round with a start at the sound of Isabelle's brittle voice behind me. 'I doubt you've even thought about the impact your sordid little affair will have had on Chlöe,' she continued as she came up next to me. She must have been behind the door as I came in and I'd given Fran no chance to warn me.

'We're not having a "sordid affair". We are very careful about how we behave in front of Chlöe. What are you doing here?'

'I wanted to see for myself just how stable your lifestyle is and whether it really is suitable for Chlöe. Now I know.' She reached out and tapped my forearm with one of her long, manicured fingernails, the blood red varnish looking out of place here, just as she did. I went to sit at Henri's desk in an effort to remain calm.

'I am very busy, Isabelle. Is there something specific you want?'

'Of course, I want to see my daughter. I have really missed her these past few weeks.' My head snapped up then.

'You have a very funny way of showing how much you miss her. You haven't spoken to her in all the time you've been gone. Chlöe is at school and my mother will be collecting her because I am trying to get ready for the harvest, so now is not the best time. If you want to see her, please give me notice of when is a good time for you. Better still, sign the paperwork and then we can sort out a more official arrangement.'

She walked over to Fran's desk, trailing her hand along the edge as she drew closer. I stood up then, worrying what she might say to Fran. I looked over at Fran, to see her staring right into Isabelle's eyes.

'I hope you don't think for one minute that you can replace me in my daughter's affections,' Isabelle sneered.

'I don't need to. Chlöe knows me for who I am - her friend. I have never tried to be anything else.' Isabelle whirled round and made for the door.

'I will be in touch with my lawyer today to sort all this out once and for all.'

She swept out in a cloying haze of perfume and we both breathed enormous sighs of relief. I went towards Fran immediately for a reassuring hug.

'I'm sorry I couldn't let you know she was here.'

'Well, it can't be helped. I just hope there won't be any more surprise visits from her.'

Fran

Didier left mid-morning to collect Henri from the station. I took a break from poring over builders' estimates and picked up my phone to compose a text to Lottie.

'I'm sorry I haven't been in touch since the other weekend but could you give Mum and Dad a ring? They're really worried about you. And so am I xx'

I stared at my message for several minutes to be sure I was satisfied with it and then pressed "send." I didn't expect to hear back from her for ages, if at all, but her reply came back at once.

'I'm in trouble, Fran.' Oh God.

'What do you mean? I thought you were with friends?'

'No, I just said that to get away from Mum and Dad. I'm in Strasbourg. Can you come and get me?'

I stopped texting and dialled her number. It rang for ages. I thought she wasn't going to pick up and was just about to hang up when she finally answered.

'Lottie? What's going on?'

She sighed loudly down the phone. 'Look, you ought to know by now that my life is a mess. Please could you just come and get me?'

'Okay, look, hang on a minute. I might be able to sort something out more quickly than you think. Stay there and I'll call you back.'

'Okay.'

I hung up and dialled Didier's number.

'Fran, is everything all right?'

'Not really, no. I'm on to the next crisis now. This time it's my family. Lottie is in Strasbourg and needs picking up and bringing back here. Where are you? Would you mind collecting her?'

'I'm just coming in to Strasbourg now. Where is she?'

'I have no idea. Please could you just wait until I call you back?'

I rang off and called Lottie back. Relief flooded through me when she answered.

'Fran? Are you coming?'

'Where are you Lottie? Didier is just arriving in Strasbourg. He's going to the station to pick up a friend. Are you anywhere near there at all?'

'I...I'm in the station café. I wanted to go back home but I was scared Mum and Dad would be mad at me after all I've done to disappoint them.'

I sucked in a large breath. 'Lottie, they love you no matter what, and so do I. Look, stay there and I'll get Didier to come and get you. Is there something you have with you that would help him identify you?'

'I have a bright blue rucksack with me. Your old one, do you remember it?'

Crikey, that was years old. 'Yes, I'll tell him. Lottie, please wait for him, won't you? Don't change your mind. He'll look after you and bring you to me, and then we can sort everything out, okay?'

'I'll stay right here. Thank you.' She started to cry and my heart nearly broke.

'Lottie, please don't cry. Everything will be okay, I promise.'

Reluctantly, I rang off and called Didier back with all the details. Then I waited while he went to get Henri and then to get Lottie. Five minutes passed and I nearly chewed off all my fingernails in that time, but then my phone rang again.

'Fran, it's me. I'm on my way home with Lottie and Henri safely in the car.'

I blew out a big sigh of relief, staring at my trembling hands.

Didier

Today was turning into the worst day imaginable. I concentrated on driving to the station, pulling into the first available parking space when I arrived before going to find Henri. I strode quickly inside, scanning the arrivals board for the TGV train from Paris. I had no trouble finding Henri as the crowds had already started thinning out by the time I reached the platform.

'I'm so sorry that your weekend with Ellie was spoilt by that madman.'

'It's over now and he won't be bothering Ellie again. She called the police about it and they'll be going round to his place to talk to him today, if they haven't done it already.'

'Listen, Fran's sister is in the station café. She's coming home with us.' He raised his eyebrows wanting to know more. 'Don't even ask.'

I passed him the car keys, then circled back past the taxi rank and round to the café, looking out for a young woman with a bright blue rucksack. Luckily, the café wasn't busy and I found her straight away.

'Lottie?'

Fran's sister looked up. There were big, grey circles under her eyes and her clothes were a mess. God only knew what had happened to her.

'Didier.' She stood up and I took her bag.

'Thanks for coming to get me,' she said softly, and gave me a weak smile.

Henri and I chatted quietly in the front of the car on the way back, as he told me about all the sights he'd seen in London. I kept sneaking quick looks in the rear-view mirror every now and then to check on Lottie.

'I thought Isabelle was in Toronto?' Henri asked after I told him about her surprise visit this morning.

'She said she was missing Chlöe but she was more keen on catching me with Fran. Anyway, let's not talk about her. It sounds like you and Ellie got on very well in London.'

'Yes. I can't believe how well we got on actually.'

Henri fell silent. I glanced over at him to find he had a faraway look in his eyes that I recognised as love. From what Henri had told me about his previous relationships, I knew this would be his first real love and I was glad for him.

The next time I looked in the mirror, I saw Lottie had fallen asleep, exhausted.

CHAPTER TWENTY-ONE

Fran

As soon as Didier called to tell me Lottie was in the car with him, I rang my parents to let them know.

'Thank God,' my mum cried. 'Is she all right?'

'I don't really know, Mum. She didn't sound good on the phone. She said her life was a mess and asked me to come and get her. I'll talk to her when she gets here and ask if she wants to help with the harvest. It will give her something to do to take her mind off all her troubles. Did Dad mention to you about helping out at the harvest?'

'Yes but we won't be able to get away till the end of this week. I'm sorry.'

'Not to worry. I'll keep in touch about Lottie. Just come when you can.'

'Thanks so much for reaching out and showing her some love when she needed it most. I'm proud of you.'

'Oh, Mum, she's my sister. I wouldn't ever want anything bad to happen to her.'

'I know, sweetheart. Bye for now. Speak to you again soon.'

It was lunchtime when I came off the phone. I was expecting

Didier back shortly. I walked out into the courtyard just as he pulled in. Didier came over to me at once and gave me a hug and a kiss. Then Henri climbed out giving me a little smile. I took one look at his face before bursting into tears.

'Henri, my God!' I hugged him tight. 'I'm so sorry you and Ellie got drawn in to my mess.'

'I'm fine and so's Ellie. She reported Paul to the police so that should be the end of it.'

'Thank you, Henri. I really am so grateful. I hope you still managed to have a wonderful time with Ellie.'

He shot me a massive grin. 'It was fabulous. I can't wait to see her again.'

I patted him gently on the chest before ducking to look for Lottie in the car. She was fast asleep.

'I'm going into the village with Henri,' Didier told me. 'I'll leave you to spend some time with Lottie, and I'll see you after lunch.' He pulled me in for another hug and kissed me deeply, before letting me go.

'That sounds like a good plan,' I said. 'Thanks for everything you've done this morning.'

As the two men walked away, I went to the car to wake Lottie. Although I shook her gently, she had a glazed look in her eyes when she sat up.

'Lottie, it's okay. You're with me at the vineyard. You fell asleep.' I smiled at her and she gave me a tentative smile back. 'Let's go and get you settled in the cottage.'

She took my hand, climbed out of the car, and then threw her arms round me. She hugged me so tightly, I almost lost my balance.

'Thank you for helping me, Fran. You have no idea how much it means.'

I picked up her bag and took her hand to lead the way to the cottage. Lottie was going to need a lot of love and understanding over the coming weeks.

Didier

It was hard to leave Fran on her own to deal with Lottie but I understood they needed some privacy. I resisted the urge to look back at her as I set off with Henri, trying instead to focus on what he was saying.

'So, we're starting the harvest tomorrow, you said in your message,' Henri said as we walked along the track from the vineyard to the village.

'Yes, that's definite now. I'll check with Mum at lunchtime exactly how many people she's managed to round up and remind her about buying all the food and drink.'

'It's going to be a busy time again, isn't it?'

'It's always frantic, I know, but it's fun too, when we're all working to the same end. I must make sure Thierry's inspections tally with mine this afternoon.'

'Any news on the builders?'

'Fran's had all the quotes in now. All she needs to do is to make a decision. They may even be able to start work during the harvest.'

'I'll see you after lunch, then.' He turned to go towards his apartment above the *boulangerie*.

'Take your time,' I told him. 'You probably need a rest after that long journey.'

He waved in reply and then disappeared round the corner.

When I arrived at my mum's house, she was just serving lunch up for the three of us. Chlöe ran towards me and I lifted her up into my arms relishing the sweet smell of her skin.

'*Hey, ma petite, comment ça va aujourd'hui?*'

'*Ça va, Papa, et toi?*'

'*Comme ci...*'

She finished for me, '*Comme ça!*'

We waved our hands at each other in the way we'd always done and she giggled.

'*A table, tout le monde,*' my mum said. I set Chlöe down and she went off to wash her hands in the bathroom.

'Isabelle turned up at the office this morning, Mum, and caught me kissing Fran,' I muttered quickly under my breath before Chlöe came back. My mum glanced sharply at me, as she put lunch on the table.

'What did she say?'

'She accused us of seeing each other behind her back.' My mum made a harrumphing sound. 'Then she said she wanted to see Chlöe, that she'd missed her, so I told her to give me more notice next time. Then she tried it on with Fran and lost.'

My mum smiled at that one. 'So how did you leave it with her?'

'She said she'd be in touch with her lawyer to sort it all out once and for all.'

The sound of the bathroom door opening and running footsteps in the hall signalled that Chlöe was on her way back. She rushed back in a minute later, picking up her favourite doll before sitting down at the table. My mum and I joined her.

'Have you heard anything more today?'

'No. It has been one heck of a morning what with one thing and another, but I'll check my emails this afternoon. The good news is Henri is back in one piece from his big adventure.'

'His big adventure? What do you mean?' I told her all about his trip to London and the incident with Paul, trying not to say too much in front of my little one. 'And we also have Fran's sister staying with us. She might be able to help out with the harvest, actually, when she feels a bit better.'

My mum raised her eyebrows but I nodded in Chlöe's direction, not wanting to say any more. We passed round bowls of salad and potatoes, while my mum dished up some pork fillet.

'I've managed to round up about twenty people to start on the harvest tomorrow,' Mum said, sitting back down again. 'With all of you as well, you'll be fine for the first couple of days.'

'Fran's parents said they might come and help too, but I'm not quite sure when. Are you going to be all right to get the food for lunch and dinner every day, Mum? I don't want to overload you.'

'It's all in hand, don't you worry, *mon chéri*.'

We fell silent for a few minutes while we ate.

'So, what did you get up to at school today, Chlöe?' I listened attentively while she told me all about her various activities.

Fran

We walked slowly back to the cottage, giving Lottie the chance to wake up and take in her surroundings.

'Your cottage is beautiful. What a lovely setting!' She paused for a moment, admiring the colourful flowers round the door and in the front garden.

I smiled as I opened the door and let her in. I put her bag down on the floor.

'I have to get to work this afternoon, Lottie. I thought you might want to catch up on your sleep a bit. Perhaps we can talk about things tonight, if you're up to it?'

'That sounds good. Thanks again, Fran. Did you speak to Mum and Dad?' She bit her lip nervously.

'I just rang to let them know you were going to stay with me. Mum was relieved to know you're all right. They're coming up here at the end of the week to help with the harvest.'

'When does the harvest start?'

'Tomorrow. I thought you could help too, if you feel up to it, but no pressure.'

'I think I will have a lie down.'

'I'll show to your room. There's plenty of food in the fridge if you want something.'

I led the way upstairs, carrying Lottie's bag for her, and left her to settle in. I made myself a quick sandwich and went straight back out towards the office, closing the door quietly behind me. I stood outside for a moment, breathing in the clean air and noting the hint of autumn on the cooler breeze. I pulled my jacket and scarf tighter around me - I would need to invest in a proper winter coat soon.

As I crossed the lawn back to the courtyard, I noticed a man coming through the gates. He was too far away for me to identify properly. Something about his confident stride seemed familiar but I couldn't put my finger on it straight away. Didier and Henri were still at lunch, and so I made my way to greet him. By the time I reached the courtyard, he'd turned away.

'*Bonjour, monsieur!*' I called out.

At the sound of my voice, the man turned and I froze. Paul was standing there with a wicked smile on his face.

'*Bonjour,* Fran. It's so good to see you again.'

'How did you... how did you...?'

'Find you? Oh, it was easy. Your friend's pathetic excuse for a boyfriend led me right here. All I had to do was to follow his path from London.'

I groaned at how easy it had been for him to find me after all. He took a step towards me and I was suddenly aware of how alone I was.

'Stop right there!' I held up my hand. 'I've made it clear I don't want to see you again.'

He crossed the remaining distance between us in seconds and made a grab for me. I yelped as he caught my arm and squeezed it tightly.

'I've come to take you home with me, to get you back under my control, where you belong.'

At that moment, I heard the squeak of the office door opening and thanked God someone must be there.

'What the hell are you doing here?' Henri's voice cried out behind me and the gravel crunched as he came closer. I wished Didier was there too.

'I'm taking back my fiancée.' Paul snarled at him, tightening his grip.

'Let me go, Paul, you're hurting me,' I whispered, fear constricting my voice.

'Good. Now you know what it feels like to suffer as I have.'

I closed my eyes briefly in despair. How on earth had things come to this?

'Paul, please. Don't do this.'

'Let her go, you bastard!'

Didier appeared out of nowhere and hauled Paul away from me. I ran to Henri and threw my arms round him, holding on until I was steady. A few seconds later, Didier landed a punch right in Paul's face and Paul staggered back onto the ground. His nose was bleeding and the look he gave Didier was full of fury. I ran to the shelter of Didier's arms.

'I'm so sorry, Didier, are you hurt?'

'Shhh, Fran, I'm fine. You have nothing to be sorry about. I just wish I'd known what an awful man he is.' He nodded towards Paul. Then he put his arm round my shoulders, pulling me in close to his side and kissing my hair. 'Are you all right? You're shaking.'

'My arm hurts a bit but I'll be okay.'

Paul finally stood up and Henri came alongside Didier and me to support us.

'I'm sorry, Fran. I shouldn't have come here. I just...I missed you so much.' I had never seen Paul look so guilty.

'You can't have expected Fran to go back with you after you treated her like that,' Didier said.

'You love him,' Paul said, keeping his eyes firmly on me. It wasn't a question but I nodded.

'You need to leave before we call the police.' Henri took a step towards Paul but Didier stopped him. They both stared at Paul and for a moment, I thought he would retaliate but after one last look at me, he turned and left, disappearing out the gate. Thankfully, he didn't say another word. A taxi drove by a minute later taking Paul out of my life for good this time.

We walked back to the office in stunned silence. I collapsed at my desk, relieved the ordeal was now over.

Didier

I followed the others back into the office, away from the nightmare we'd just experienced. I went straight to the coffee machine. I glanced over at Fran and was relieved to see the colour coming back into her cheeks, but it was going to take some time for her to get over what had happened.

'I could have killed that bastard for daring to lay his hands on you,' I murmured as I passed her a cup of coffee. She didn't reply but tears welled in her eyes. I touched her cheek briefly and was overwhelmed by the love for me in her expression.

'So, where are we all at?' I asked brightly, deciding to carry on as normal rather than thinking about what might have happened.

'Lottie is at the cottage and my parents know she's here with me,' Fran said after a moment's hesitation while she gathered her thoughts.

'After a fantastic weekend, I am raring to catch up before the harvest starts tomorrow,' reported Henri.

'My little girl is safe at home with her grandma. Thankfully, Mum has sorted out pickers for tomorrow and she's also got all the food organised.'

'I'm about ready to make a decision on the builders too,' Fran told me. 'Although I'll wait for you to sort your stuff out if you need a few minutes before we talk about it.'

'Why don't you bring Henri up to speed while you wait?'

'Good idea.' She gave me a brave smile and we settled down to our own tasks.

I scanned my email inbox for a message from either Isabelle or her lawyer and breathed a sigh of relief when there was nothing. There was no word from Alain either, so I sent him a message explaining what had happened when Isabelle had turned up that morning. I outlined it all succinctly, making sure I stressed the importance of my daughter's custody. I had no idea what Isabelle's reaction would be and that was what worried me the most. After sending the message, I stood up and stretched before pulling up a chair and sitting down next to Fran's desk. She still looked pale and a bit shaky.

'Are you sure you're okay, Fran? We don't have to talk about the builders now.'

'I'd rather keep busy,' she replied. She took a deep breath before continuing. 'I think we should go with the local building firm, Hahn et fils, who you already have links with. Theirs is a sensible quote with staggered payments as they complete each phase of the work. I talked through the pros and cons of all the builders' estimates with Henri and he agrees that the local firm's is the best. What do you think?'

'It sounds like you've given it a lot of thought. I'm very grateful. Would you mind if I asked my mother to look over their quote? She's had a lot of experience and in the end, it is her money too.'

'I think that's a really good idea. Why don't you take this paperwork with you when you go down for dinner tonight? I'll put it together in a file for you.'

'Thanks. Henri, can you stay with Fran for the rest of the afternoon and take her back to the cottage at the end of the day, please?' He nodded and I gave Fran a brief kiss before putting on my coat and setting off to meet with Thierry.

I trudged across the gravel once more, making my way to the winery to find out what Thierry's view on the pinot blanc grapes would be. We'd been checking in with each other for several days and our thinking had been completely aligned so far, so I was hopeful he would agree with me about starting the harvest now.

I found Thierry in the winery, doing his final checks on all the equipment in readiness for the harvest.

'Are you ready to start tomorrow, Thierry?'

'Yes, I agree now is the best time. I've checked samples of berries every day for the past week. The balance between the sugar and acidity in the pinot blanc grapes is just about perfect, so we should definitely start picking those first. We're within the decreed dates for the start of the harvest so everything's good.'

'We've got pickers ready to start tomorrow morning. Have you got enough staff to cope this end?'

'Yes, I've already warned everyone but they were expecting it anyway.'

'Great. I'll see you in the morning.' I hesitated for a moment, wanting to ask how he was but feeling a bit awkward after so long.

'I'm fine, don't worry. See you tomorrow.' He smiled at me but the look in his eyes was still so sad. I shook his hand and walked back outside. It had been over a year since Thierry's wife had died but the pain he suffered was still as strong. I wished there was something any of us could have done to spare him his agony. I shook my head, refusing to go down that painful path again. All I knew was I had another chance with Fran and I was going to take it with both hands.

CHAPTER TWENTY-TWO

Fran

When I stood up to go home, I was grateful Didier had asked Henri to come with me. Although work had taken my mind off things a little, just walking across the courtyard was enough to leave me feeling weak at the memory of what had taken place with Paul. By the time we approached the cottage, though, the trembling in my hands had stopped and I was beginning to feel stronger again. Thanking Henri for looking after me, I said goodbye and turned to go inside.

A very different Lottie was sitting on the sofa from the one I had left behind at lunchtime.

'Hey, you look better I'm glad to see.'

She gave me a warm smile. 'All I needed was a sleep, a shower and a good meal. I'm so grateful for all you and Didier have done for me today.' I gave her a hug, relief flooding through me to find she was more like her normal self. 'How was your afternoon?' she continued.

I crumpled on to the sofa and, taking a deep breath, I told her about Paul.

'God, Fran! You should have come back here. What were you

thinking staying at work? You're probably suffering from shock or something.'

'Thanks for worrying about me, but there's no need, honestly. It was better for me to work through it and not dwell on it. I'm okay now so let's not talk about it any more. I want to think about something else,' I said, more assertively than I felt. 'Are you ready to talk to me about what's been going on in your life?' She hesitated for only a brief moment, still worrying about me no doubt.

'I think that's the least I owe you after all that's happened.' She took a deep breath.

'After you left the other weekend, Mum and Dad wasted no time in asking me how I was planning to provide for the baby once it's born. I know they mean well but I can't stand it. They're always badgering me for answers to everything so I told them I was going to stay with a friend in Strasbourg, and I left.' She shrugged.

'Did you actually have a friend to stay with?'

'No. The friend I stayed with last time was away so I've been sleeping rough. I just wanted to escape and it seemed like a good idea at the time.' She had the grace to look shame-faced.

'You're going to have to face it all some time, Lottie, and to realise you're looking after someone else as well now. You can't keep running away from your problems.'

'I know that only too well but I wish you'd all stop reminding me.' She tutted, refusing to meet my eye.

'Have you had any thoughts yourself about what you'd like to do?' I asked gently.

'I'm going to have to get a job but I'll need someone to help care for the baby if I'm going to work every day. And that's as far as I get each time. If I don't work, I won't have any money to care for the baby with.' She threw up her hands in despair.

'Okay, so you're already well on the way to working something out based on your thoughts so far. Now you need to consider your options.'

She rolled her eyes at me. 'I don't have any options. That's the point.'

'What I meant was that one option is to stay at home and to ask Mum and Dad to help care for the baby some of the time so you can get a part-time job. You and the baby would have somewhere to live and on-site babysitting too.'

'That's my only option as far as I can see but the downside is I have to live at home again, in the back end of nowhere, with Mum and Dad breathing down my neck.'

'Another alternative might be to work now and save as much as you can before the baby's born to give you a head start afterwards. You could perhaps look for something you could go back to once the baby is old enough.' I paused for a moment to let it all sink in. 'You do have a choice, you know. You don't have to just lie down and take it all.'

'That's quite a good idea,' she conceded, 'and one I hadn't thought of. What could I do, though?'

'Is there anything you'd really like to do?'

'There are lots of things but I can't do them with a baby in tow.'

'But we're talking about before the baby is born. Have a think about that first. Listen, you're more than welcome to stay here with me for a while. The harvest starts next week and we need lots of helpers if you'd like to give a hand.'

'You have no idea how much I would appreciate that. I should have taken you up on that suggestion the first time you made it.' She sighed, looking like a great weight had been taken off her shoulders.

I moved to sit next to her on the sofa and put my arm round her. 'You've already taken the first step, Lottie, by talking to me and I'm really proud of you for that.'

She started to cry and I stroked her hair while she let it all out.

Didier

I woke at five o'clock on the first day of the harvest, ready to greet the pickers who would be arriving for breakfast at six. Thierry joined me from the winery as I made my way to the courtyard and we walked side by side across the still dewy grass. Fran and Lottie were leaving the cottage as we passed. Fran gave me a sleepy morning smile and I only wished I was seeing it under different circumstances. I took her hand in mine and smiled at Lottie, introducing Thierry.

'How are you today?' I asked Fran.

'Better, thanks, just tired.'

There were already plenty of people in the courtyard sitting at the tables set out for breakfast. They were tucking into cheeses and meats my mum had brought over in the car, as well as breads and pastries sent over by Liliane from the *boulangerie.* My mum had the shed open and had started the urn for hot drinks. Chlöe was standing by her side chatting with pickers as they came and went.

'*Bonjour, ma petite,*' I said to Chlöe, swinging her into my arms for a good morning kiss, before leaning over to greet my mum. 'Thanks so much for organising all this, Mum.'

'It is my pleasure. You know how much I love it.' She smiled up at me in between pouring out more cups of coffee. Fran and Lottie were helping out as well and I was glad we had got the harvest off to a good start.

After a few minutes, I whistled to get everyone's attention.

'Thank you all very much for coming again to help pick grapes at *Domaine des Montagnes.* It is wonderful to see so many familiar faces, and to meet some new ones too. I hope to get to know you better over the coming days and weeks. We'll serve a quick *casse-croûte* around ten and lunch will be at midday. If we could gather over by the archway in five minutes, please, I'll lead you down to the vineyard.'

I looked around for Thierry because I needed to find out whether all the baskets were already down in the vineyard or whether we should collect them on our way. My eyes widened when I found him deep in conversation with Lottie. His face lit up at something Lottie said and I wondered how long it had been since he'd last looked so vibrant.

'Hey, remember me?' Fran came up, giving me her special smile.

'Sorry, I was distracted by Lottie and Thierry for a moment. It's good to see them both looking happy.'

'Well, I know about Lottie of course, but I didn't know Thierry had problems.'

'It's a long story but I will tell you one day.' I bent my head to meet hers and kissed her soft lips. 'I hope you and I will have the chance to spend some time alone together soon, otherwise I'll go mad.'

'How about tonight?' She looked forlorn, in case I said no. I leaned towards her, letting our bodies touch and she put her arms round the back of my neck, gently rubbing with her fingers. A lovely tingling feeling reverberated through my whole body.

'I wish you could come now, given how you're making my body feel at this moment but I suppose tonight will just have to do.'

I left Fran to go and check with Thierry about the baskets. Soon everyone was gathered and ready to go. I was looking forward to getting started but I knew from years of experience these would also be the hardest few weeks of the year.

Fran

My body was aching all over after only a few days of the harvest but I hoped it would get easier as the weeks went by. As more pickers joined us, we moved on to harvesting the other grape varieties and settled into a good routine.

We were just finishing our morning snack on the Friday morning when my mum and dad's car pulled in to the courtyard. I went over to meet them, calling out to Lottie on the way. As soon as she saw who it was, a guarded look came over her face and she dragged her feet.

'It's great to see you.' We exchanged kisses and hugs before they turned round searching for Lottie. I waved her over, noticing Thierry taking in everything that was happening.

'Why isn't Lottie coming over?' asked my mum in an anguished voice.

'She's probably nervous you're angry with her, that's all.'

My mum started walking towards Lottie and they met in a flurry of hugs, kisses and tears. Thierry had followed behind so I introduced him to my dad. As soon as Lottie and Mum had finished, my dad swooped in for a hug as well and I breathed a sigh of relief.

Didier called everyone back together shortly afterwards and we started to follow before I realised I hadn't introduced my parents to Sylvie.

'Mum, Dad, hang on, I want you to meet Didier's mum.' Lottie followed Thierry back down to the vineyard, and I led my parents over to meet Sylvie.

'Ah Fran, I was hoping you would come over to talk to me.'

'Actually, Sylvie, I wanted to introduce you to my parents. They've come to help in the vineyard.'

She wiped her hands and shook theirs in turn, giving them her broadest smile.

'It is lovely to meet you at last,' she said. 'Thank you so much for coming to help. It is very hard work and we appreciate every pair of hands.'

'We wanted to do our bit to help and we also needed to see Lottie. And you too, Fran, of course,' my dad continued hurriedly, trying not to put his foot in it with anyone.

'I would love it if you would all come to dinner tomorrow evening. You can meet Chlöe, my grand-daughter, as well.'

'That would be lovely, Sylvie, thank you,' I replied.

'Fran, I know you need to get back but I just wanted to tell you I agree totally with you about the choice of builder. You have done an excellent job in researching this project for us. Well done!'

My cheeks heated at her unexpected praise. 'Thank you, Sylvie, that's great news. I'll give them a ring this afternoon to find out when they can get started.'

We said goodbye and made our way across the estate towards the vineyard to get picking.

'How is Lottie?' my mum asked as we passed through the archway.

'She's much better, Mum. The picking has definitely helped take her mind off things. I think she just needed a bit of time.'

'Is she going to come home with us?' Dad asked.

'I don't know what she's decided but she needs to tell you in her own time.' Both Didier and I had noticed the friendship developing between Lottie and Thierry, which was sure to impact her decision about what to do next.

'We just want to look after her, Fran.'

'I know that Dad but you must understand that if you keep pressing her to make decisions, she'll only feel like she's in a corner again. She needs some space to think everything through without any pressure. She's safe here with me while she does that.'

Dad shook his head and sighed, impatient to step in and sort everything out for Lottie as he had always done. He still didn't really understand how to handle her despite my efforts to explain, but he would have to learn quickly or risk pushing her away for good.

Didier

Although the first week of the harvest had gone well, I was exhausted trying to split my time between the harvest and the wine-making process, as well as keeping an eye on the business. On top of this, I was trying to see Chlöe too.

I'd been going back to the office after the *casse-croûte* every day to catch up on anything critical. As I pushed open the door, I noticed a large, formal-looking envelope on the floor in the middle of all the other post. I stared at it, after placing the rest of the letters on the desk. It was from Isabelle's lawyers. My heart was in my mouth as I opened the envelope and quickly scanned the contents. As I read through their demands, my heart sank lower and lower.

'Alain, *c'est* Didier Le Roy,' I said when I was put through to my lawyer a few minutes later.

'I expect you're calling because you've received the paperwork from Isabelle's lawyer.'

'Yes, and to be honest, I'm surprised you haven't called me sooner, Alain.'

'I'm sorry, Didier. I've actually been doing a lot of research to try and sort things out for you.'

'It's all right, I know you're doing everything you can.' I massaged my temple with my free hand, trying to keep calm. 'Have you managed to find anything out?'

'Well, Isabelle's demand for half your assets, including the vineyard, is a non-starter. I will just quote French law at them on that one. Don't forget, she's using a Canadian lawyer and I assume they just haven't done their research.'

'That's a relief, at least.' My shoulders relaxed a little at that news.

'The issue of custody is more complicated,' he went on. 'Isabelle is contesting your request for full custody of your daughter.'

'On what grounds?'

'She does not believe you can offer Chlöe any more stable a lifestyle than she could offer herself.'

'And yet she had no problem leaving Chlöe with me while she took this latest job for the next year.'

'In the paperwork, she cites the fact that you have the vineyard to run, which she says means you have to lean on your mother for childcare. She also refers to your relationship with Fran as an unsuitable environment in which to bring up your child.'

'I can't believe I'm hearing this. What does she want then?'

'They're suggesting you split custody. My personal feeling is that that would be tricky with Isabelle's job. I believe you have a good case for being able to offer her a stable lifestyle - your mother's support is an advantage in my view. The awkward factor is her citing your relationship with Fran as a negative reason why you shouldn't have custody of Chlöe.'

'What do you mean?'

'It's really a case of which one of you the judge feels could offer the more stable home life for your daughter. I'm speaking as your friend now but I wonder if it might be best for you and Fran to stop seeing each other until this is all sorted out.'

'How would sending Fran away make any difference to the situation? If I get custody of Chlöe, what's to stop Isabelle from saying the same thing all over again if Fran and I subsequently get back together?'

'I know it's difficult but you're going to have to consider your options very carefully. I'll leave you to think about it over the weekend but I'd advise you to get back to me on Monday, if you can.'

I put the phone down with a heavy heart. I'd missed Fran so much during this week and I had no idea when we might next get some time on our own. The occasional kisses and fleeting touches we had shared had been barely enough to sustain me.

Now I really would have to talk to her but not under the circumstances I had in mind.

CHAPTER TWENTY-THREE

Fran

Didier slipped away after the *casse-croûte* and I wished I could go with him. It had been a long few days apart and now my parents were here, I was even less likely to get away.

When he came back to the vineyard, it was nearly lunchtime. He was frowning and his shoulders were hunched. I caught his eye, trying to give him a visual hug in the absence of anything else, and he gave me a little shrug back. When we broke for lunch, Didier caught up with me for the walk, taking my hand in his.

'How's everything going? You looked miserable earlier.'

'The harvest is going well, and Chlöe is fine. That's the good news.'

I gave him a worried glance. 'And the bad?'

'I'm missing you so much, I'm finding it hard to think about anything else.' He gave me his cheeky grin, lifting my spirits immediately.

'I really miss you too. I wondered if I might try to get away early from my parents tonight, leaving them to catch up with Lottie. Perhaps you could do the same?'

'I'd like that.' He paused and from his face, I sensed there was more bad news to come. 'Unfortunately, I've heard from Isabelle's lawyers as well and I do need to talk to you about it.'

'That sounds serious.'

'I just want to get your advice. It's all the worst-case scenarios we'd thought of but we'll talk it over together. Don't go getting the wrong idea this afternoon, promise?'

'I promise,' I said solemnly, but I was already worried.

Fortunately, the afternoon passed quickly. I was soon on my way back to the cottage with Lottie and my parents, Ruby following at our heels. I'd missed her too, this past week, and I hoped to make more of a fuss of her over the weekend, although the harvest would still be continuing.

'What shall we do about dinner?' I asked. 'I have various things we could pick at but I haven't been able to get to the supermarket. I don't have anything I could turn into a meal.'

'Charles, would you go and get the cool bag from the car please, *chéri*?'

My dad jumped up and did as asked.

'What have you been up to, Mum?' I asked with a knowing smile.

'I knew you'd be exhausted so I did some cooking yesterday and brought it with me.'

I gave her a hug and so did Lottie, making my mum's face light up.

By the time we'd laid the table, my dad had returned with the bag of goodies. For the next twenty minutes we all mucked in, reheating vegetable dishes, slicing tarts and putting mouth-watering salads into bowls. Soon, the table was covered with food and we were all eyeing it hungrily.

'There's only one more thing we need,' said my dad.

'The wine!' we chorused.

'Yes indeed, but this time I have something very special.' He went back to the bag and pulled out a zip-up chiller jacket with a bottle hidden inside it. There was a little envelope attached to it, which my dad passed to me, indicating I should open it.

'*Santé* to our dear friends! Enjoy! With all best wishes, Didier and Thierry xx' I read the card out loud and my heart warmed as I did so. Lottie winked at me, making me giggle.

Dad poured the wine and we all clinked glasses.

'To our wonderful family!' my dad proclaimed.

As we talked over dinner, I relaxed, happy to be surrounded by my family.

'How are you enjoying life on the vineyard, Lottie?'

I narrowed my eyes at my dad's question. The last thing Lottie needed was an inquisition.

'It's been great thanks, Dad. And I'm feeling really good. Better than I have for a while, actually.'

'You definitely look better than when you first arrived,' I told her. 'I wonder why that is?' I was only teasing but she flushed bright red, laughing awkwardly.

'It's because life here is so much calmer. I have to confess I'm enjoying getting to know Thierry, as well.'

My mouth dropped open. I had really not expected Lottie to be so open.

'I'd like to stay here with Fran for the time being,' she went on, 'if that's all right with you both, and with Fran of course.' She looked at us all in turn.

'You know you're more than welcome to stay here,' I replied.

'Good, that's settled. Let's leave it at that,' said my mum. She paused for a moment before continuing. 'I would much rather talk about your lovely boyfriends.'

My dad covered his eyes, while Lottie and I both laughed at her honesty.

'Would you say Thierry is your boyfriend, Lottie?' I asked.

'No, of course not. We're just friends. I've only known him a few days but I do like him and he seems to like me. I would like to get to know him better. So, the burden falls to you, Fran, to tell us about you and Didier.'

I shrugged. 'What can I say? I love him and I'm so glad to have had this second chance with him. In fact, we were wondering if...'

'Yes, of course,' they cried in response.

'Do you think we haven't noticed how lovelorn you both look?' Lottie said.

'Oh God, does everyone else know?' I flushed at the thought of it.

'Not everyone, just those of us who know you really well.'

I finished eating and then made my excuses to send Didier a text.

'I'll meet you on the lawn by the courtyard xx' He replied at once, as if he had been waiting with bated breath.

Didier

Fran was approaching as I walked through the archway and her sweet smile made me instantly aroused. When she reached me, I took her in my arms and brushed her lips lightly with mine. She opened them in invitation and I didn't need asking twice. She tasted so good, I wasn't sure I'd be able to stop kissing her until she gently pushed me away, trying to catch her breath.

'God, how I've missed you.' I gazed down into her eyes, rubbing her now swollen lips gently with my finger. 'Come on, let's get home.'

'Lottie said we've looked lovelorn all week. It's so embarrassing to think everyone else was thinking that about us as well.'

'I don't care if they all know how much we love each other, Fran.'

She squeezed my hand as we hurried the last few metres to the kitchen door. I'd intended to take her to my bedroom and romance her a little but it had been too long and after we had kissed again, it was hard to contain the electricity flowing between us. My heart beat faster as the strength of my desire for her surged through me. I lowered her body gently to the rug in front of the stove and her hands slipped underneath my shirt to caress my back. The sensation of her fingertips on my bare skin was almost too much after a few days apart. A primal growl issued from deep within me and I sat up again to remove my jumper and shirt. I kept my eyes on her the whole time as she removed her outer layers and soon we were able to enjoy the sensual feel of skin on skin. I kissed my way down her neck, marvelling at the softness of her skin and continued until I reached the swell of her breasts. She arched against me and I savoured the fragrant smell of her skin as we came together. Her body was so warm as I covered it with mine. Soon we'd joined together, creating our own rhythm and enjoying the building sensation within our bodies.

'I love you so much,' she cried, shuddering from the sheer force of her release. My own followed shortly afterwards and was just as powerful. I lay down next to her, completely spent but feeling so much better than I had for several days.

'I love you too, Fran,' I whispered. We both panted gently, getting our breath back in the silence of my living room. Fran stood first, gathering her clothes to go to the bathroom. She emerged a short while later, looking just as breathtaking as before.

'Thank you so much for giving the wine to my dad earlier, that was really kind of you both. Thierry seems to be quite taken with my sister, and she didn't deny she felt the same, either.'

'It was our pleasure to give you a bottle of wine to share, after all you've done this week. I'm really pleased to see Thierry coming out of his shell. He's had a very hard time of it over the past year. It's been really good to see him getting on so well with Lottie.'

'Shall I make a drink and we can have a talk about what happened with Isabelle's lawyers?'

I nodded with a sigh, disappearing to get dressed myself before returning and taking a seat next to her on the sofa. I leaned forward to take a large gulp of the wine she'd poured out for me. My heart sank as I thought of the conversation ahead. When I didn't say anything, she turned towards me, looking deep into my eyes.

'Okay, I get the feeling it's not good news but you just need to come out with it. This delay is making me more and more nervous.'

And so I relayed my conversation with Alain. Fran's shoulders had slumped by the time I'd finished.

'Do you want me to go away? If you believe that's the answer, I will.'

I took her hand. 'Of course it's not the answer. Isabelle left me long before you were back in the country. I know we're not divorced yet but that shouldn't mean there's one set of rules for her and another for me. I want you here with me, Fran, by my side, as Isabelle and I work this out.'

'I understand that but Chlöe is your daughter and more important than anything else. You mustn't do anything that's going to put your relationship with her at risk.'

I stared at her and then put my head in my hands. Whatever decision we took, it was going to be difficult for both of us.

Fran

When I woke up, Didier was snoring gently next to me. I let out a sigh and turned onto my side to study his gorgeous features in the early morning light. His hair was all ruffled and he had grown a fine covering of stubble on his face overnight. I wanted to touch but I knew if I did, he would wake up and my secret study of him would be at an end. He had a smattering of dark hair on his chest - just the right amount - and his upper body was nicely developed without being overdone. His arms were folded across his chest and his muscles firmly defined. Sadly, the duvet was tucked underneath his arms, preventing me from seeing any more of his delectable body. I snuggled up next to him, spooning myself against him and enjoying his warmth. I breathed in his manly smell, mixed with a faint hint of citrus, and laid one hand on his hip, the other on his chest. His breathing changed almost imperceptibly as he stirred and became aware of what I was up to.

'You have a one-track mind, Miss Schell,' he said huskily. I smiled at the sleepy sound of his voice. I let my hand roam around under the duvet, tracing his ribs and wandering further. To my delight, we were thinking along the same lines. He turned lazily towards me and kissed me on the lips, awakening all my sensitive areas with just the one touch.

'How are you feeling today, *ma chérie*?' he asked me some time later.

'I've been awake for hours, thinking over everything, and I still don't know what we should do about Isabelle.'

'Nor me. It is a real dilemma.'

He kissed me gently before slipping out of bed and into the bathroom.

After a while my need for coffee grew too strong so I made my way downstairs. As the coffee pot gurgled in the kitchen and the logs crackled in the stove, I stood at the window looking out at the vineyard while I waited for Didier to finish in the shower. His arms curled round my waist a few minutes later and I relaxed back against his firm body.

'I asked Mum to supervise the breakfast this morning so I could spend more time with you, but I'd better get up there now. You take your time and I'll see you later. Try not to worry about things. We'll work out a way.'

'I'm going into the office this morning to ring the builders and to catch up on the paperwork. I probably won't see you till *casse-croûte* time.'

'That sounds like a good plan.'

After we'd kissed goodbye, I thought again about all Isabelle had said in the letter. My instinct was to go, to leave the way clear for Didier to gain custody of Chlöe, but my head told me I shouldn't really have to do that. I had done nothing wrong and neither had Didier; however, we didn't want to do anything to jeopardise Didier's custody claim. It didn't matter how many times I went round it in my head, I still came back to that. I continued to think about it as I had a shower and got dressed but even as I was walking up to the office, I still hadn't managed to reach a conclusion I was satisfied with.

I settled down to tackle the stack of letters on my desk, sorting the paperwork into two piles in order to deal with all the urgent matters first. Afterwards, I called the builders and arranged for them to come for their first meeting on Monday morning. They were delighted to get the job. I was so engrossed in my work that I was startled when the office door opened and Henri poked his head round.

'Hey, Fran, it's time for *casse-croûte*. Are you going to join us?'

Didier

'Morning, everyone. I just wanted to say a quick thank you for the wonderful work you have done this week on behalf of *Domaine des Montagnes*. I'm so grateful to you all for giving up your time. As we've done so well, we're going to take a day off tomorrow and start again on Monday.'

A light cheer followed my speech. Fran grinned at me from across the courtyard. They didn't know I would be working most of the day tomorrow in the winery with Thierry. We wanted to make sure everything was going according to plan with the pressing of the fruit we had picked so far. I'd been checking every day and Thierry was mostly pleased. Still, it would be good to make sure everything was going well before we went into the second week. I was also looking forward to spending more time with Chlöe over the weekend.

The afternoon passed quickly and soon I was on my way back with Thierry to collect Fran and her family for dinner at my mum's house.

'You're looking smart,' I told Thierry, as he appeared from the winery in a jacket, shirt and tailored trousers.

'I thought I'd make the effort for your mother,' he said.

I grinned knowingly at him. 'Your dressing up has nothing to do with my mother and everything to do with Lottie.'

He slapped me playfully on the arm. 'I really like her. I haven't felt like that about anyone, not since... since Nicole passed away. It feels really good and I think - I hope - she feels the same way about me.'

When we arrived at the cottage Fran came out first, followed by Lottie and her parents. We paired up to walk to the village. I took Fran's hand as we walked, enjoying the feel of her skin against mine.

'You look gorgeous. I love seeing your hair down like that,' I told her, leaning close enough to smell her floral scent.

'Thank you, and thanks for inviting Thierry. Lottie was delighted when I told her he was coming too.'

'He told me he really likes her and thinks she feels the same.'

'Oh, that's a given. I wish she could find a job here so she could stay. Otherwise, she'll have to go home and look for a job there.'

'We can mention it to Mum tonight and see if she knows of anyone who's hiring at the moment. She's always up-to-date on that sort of thing.'

We walked on in comfortable silence. Henri joined us at the village crossroads.

'Any news from Ellie?' I asked him.

'I've been calling her every day. She spoke to the police, as you know, and she's heard nothing more from Paul. Neither will we now, I hope. She's had some other news about work, though. Has she told you?' He glanced at Fran.

'No,' she said with a slight frown. 'I'll have to call her tomorrow. I haven't spoken to her for a while.'

When we entered the garden, delicious smells wafted our way on the breeze and my stomach rumbled in anticipation, making Fran laugh.

'Your mum is a truly wonderful cook, Didier. You really do get your cooking skills from her.'

I paused to give a little bow and looked up to find Chlöe barrelling towards me.

'Hey, sweetheart! How are you?' I picked her up looking deep into her eyes.

'I am fed up with this harvest,' she said with a sigh. 'It lasts far too long!'

She was growing up already and her vocabulary had improved greatly since starting at school.

'I am sorry, my little one. Still, we're going to eat a lovely dinner tonight with all our friends. What's grandma cooking? Do you know?' I set her down and she took my hand to lead me off to the kitchen.

CHAPTER TWENTY-FOUR

Fran

As our families and friends gathered together, I looked around at the familiar smiling faces, and wondered how I could ever have found life in Alsace dull and boring. Didier told Sylvie all about Isabelle's demands as we ate the delicious boeuf bourguignon she'd prepared for dinner. She listened intently before reaching out and patting my arm. That small gesture reinforced how much I already cared for her.

'So, what's your advice, *Maman*?' Didier asked.

'Fran belongs with you. You should fight this together. Don't give in to her by going away, Fran. That will only make you look guilty when you're not.'

'I agree, Sylvie. Deep down, I know it's right for me to stay and not to let her intimidate me into leaving.'

Didier's face brightened with relief at my decision to stay and a thrill of pleasure ran through me at the obvious love shining in his eyes.

'Changing the subject,' Sylvie continued, 'it is marvellous to see Thierry coming back to life. Will Lottie be around for a while longer, Fran?'

'I don't know. It depends on whether she can find a job. We did wonder if you knew of anyone in the village needing staff?'

She thought for a moment. 'Let me have a chat with a few people and see what I can find out. I'll let you know as soon as I can.'

The wine flowed and the food kept coming but soon it was time for Chlöe to go to bed. Even though she had been allowed to stay up a bit later, she still cried when Didier told her to say goodnight. She went round all the adults giving each one a tearful kiss as though she were going off on a long voyage and might not see them for years. When she reached Lottie, who she'd been chatting away merrily to all evening, she whispered something in her ear. Lottie smiled delightedly in response but raised her eyes to Didier.

'What is it?' he asked.

'Would it be all right if I read Chlöe a story tonight? She asked me if I would but I don't want to take away from your time with her.'

'Of course. We'll do bath time and then I'll read the first story and you can read the next one.'

Lottie nodded and smiled, pleased little Chlöe had taken an instant liking to her. We left the table and reassembled in the various comfy chairs in the living room. My mum came over to sit with me on a small sofa while my dad chatted to Sylvie and helped her to clear the table. He was asking for recipes and I had to smile at his dogged pursuit of new food ideas. He and Sylvie had a lot in common.

'We will have to go home tomorrow, Fran. I have work on Monday and I need to get the house sorted. I'm sorry we couldn't stay longer.'

I patted her hand. 'Mum, we're so grateful you could come at all. It's been good for you to be here and to meet everyone. I'm sorry I haven't seen much of you.'

'Don't worry. You're happy and that's the main thing. Thank you for looking after Lottie too. I can't tell you how relieved we are. Are you sure it's okay if she stays with you a bit longer?'

'Of course. We're trying to find her a job so she can stay indefinitely. She and Thierry have obviously hit it off.'

'And what about you and Didier? He seems lovely by the way.'

'Everything is wonderful between us but we still have the problem of his wife, Isabelle, to deal with.'

'He's still married?'

Her sharp intake of breath surprised me, even though I understood her reaction.

'He's trying to get a divorce, as well as full custody of his daughter, although Isabelle's fighting him, trying to say his lifestyle isn't suitable because he's going out with me.'

'Charming! So, what are you going to do?'

'I'm going to support Didier in his claim for custody. I know Isabelle is her mum but I honestly believe Chlöe will have a more settled life with her dad.'

'Look, I hope everything works out but you will let me know, won't you?'

'You know I will.'

Thankfully, Mum and Dad didn't want to get off too early so I was able to indulge myself with a bit of a lie-in the next day.

'Take care both of you and come and see us again soon,' my mum said as she climbed into the car after our leisurely breakfast. I put my arm round Lottie and she hugged me back as we waved them off.

'So, what shall we do today?' Lottie asked.

'As little as possible. The only thing I must do is call Ellie. What about you?'

'Thierry has asked me out on a lunch date. He said he'd pick me up at midday. Would you mind if I went?'

'Of course I don't mind, silly. I'm really pleased for both of you. Didier said he'd been through a really tough time this past year and you've brought him out of it. I think it's great.'

'Did Didier tell you what happened to Thierry?'

'No, and I didn't ask.'

'He still hasn't told me yet, either. I think he's nervous about sharing so much when we hardly know each other, and that's understandable. I haven't told him all about my past yet either, although I can't exactly hide my bump, can I?' She grinned before continuing, 'We need to take it slowly and get to know each other better.'

'That's a good plan. Didier asked his mum today if she could find out whether there are any jobs going in the village. If something does come up and you decide to stay, you can carry on living here with me in the cottage for the time being if you'd like to.'

'Oh, that's fantastic!' She threw her arms round me and I hugged her tight, glad we were together again and things were looking up for her.

'Right, I'm off for a shower,' I said. I spent a relaxing half an hour on my own in the bathroom before slipping on my easiest clothes and going back downstairs, just in time to hear Thierry knock on the door for Lottie.

'Hey, Fran, *ça va*?' He gave me a wicked grin, displaying at once what Lottie liked about him. He was very laid-back and almost film star gorgeous. His tall figure filled the doorway as he leaned his arm against the upper frame. I smiled back at him and did my best not to stare but he seemed to enjoy the attention.

Lottie threw on her coat. As I closed the door after them, I tried not to be disappointed to be spending the afternoon alone. Instead, I settled on the sofa, picked up my phone and dialled Ellie's number.

'I'd just about given up hope of hearing from you again,' she cried. 'How the hell are you?'

'I'm sorry it's been so long. I've been thinking about nothing but grapes all week.'

'It's good to hear your voice, especially after what happened with Paul. I've heard all about it from Henri.'

'I know. It was awful. I'm so sorry I haven't called you sooner, I just haven't had a chance. Everything was okay in the end. I hope that it's all over now, for us and for you.'

'How is the harvest going? Still as well as when I spoke to Henri the other day?'

'It's still going well and on schedule but it's so back-breaking. I had no idea. Mum and Dad have just left after spending a few days here, helping us with the picking. Lottie's living with me here now and has fallen head over heels for our winemaker.'

'Come on, I'm all ears.'

By the time I'd filled her in, I'd almost forgotten to ask her about the news Henri said she had to tell me.

'It's your turn to tell me your news now.'

'You won't believe it but I've been made redundant. As I've been there for so long, I'm going to get quite a good payout.'

'That's great news! Perhaps you can take some time now to think about what you'd really like to do. When will you finish?'

'Very soon. In fact, I was thinking about coming over again but this time to help with the harvest. I thought I could have a bit of a holiday while I consider my options.'

'Oh, Ellie, it would be wonderful to see you again and for longer this time.'

'Brilliant! That's settled then. Henri has said I can stay with him so you wouldn't have to worry about Lottie having somewhere to stay.'

'I hadn't even thought of that but that's even better.'

We carried on chatting until I glanced at my watch. We'd been on the phone for nearly an hour.

'I'd better go,' Ellie finally said reluctantly. 'Good luck with the harvest and with Isabelle, and I will see you very soon.'

Didier

Thierry and I had spent a productive morning in the winery, getting off to an early start because of his lunch plans with Lottie.

Once he'd gone, I set off for my mum's to spend some time with Chlöe, trying not to dwell on how much I missed Fran.

I had another enjoyable meal with my mum and Chlöe but it was quiet without all our other friends. After lunch, we went for a long walk around the village. The autumn trees were just beginning to shed their leaves and Chlöe enjoyed crunching them under her feet in her little wellies. Just as we started the walk back to the park, it began to rain. It was only a light shower but it was enough to spook me about the harvest.

'Do you know what the forecast is for tomorrow?' Mum asked me.

'It was just a bit of light rain today but clear again tomorrow.'

She placed her hand on my arm. 'Try not to worry.'

I gave her a tense smile.

It didn't rain again while we were out, but I slipped away shortly after we got back to my mother's house so I could go and check the grapes still on the vine. Rotting grapes were the last thing we needed and that was a very real danger when it rained at this time of year. I pulled on my woollen hat and hunched my shoulders against the cold as I rushed back to the vineyard to check for damage.

I walked straight past Fran's cottage, intent on what I needed to do, rather than giving in to what I wanted to do. It had started to rain again and I prayed it would be another light shower. At least it wasn't too cold. I reached the vines and bent down to inspect them. There was still enough foliage to protect the grapes for now, as long as the rain didn't get any heavier. I walked a few rows over to check a different batch of grapes and breathed a sigh of relief to find them just as healthy looking. The harvest would still be all right if the rain held off. I stood up straight and stretched my back. It was definitely getting harder to keep coming out in all weathers to do this work. I was looking after myself but if I was to continue doing this for the rest of my life, I'd need to do better than I was doing now.

I turned to head back up to the château only to see Fran coming down the hill towards me. My spirits lifted immediately to see her coming out in the rain to check on me.

'Didier! Is everything all right?'

Our eyes locked as she came closer and then she was in my arms, kissing me and holding me.

'Is everything okay?' she repeated.

'It will be, as long as the rain doesn't get any worse. Thanks for coming out to find me.'

'I was worried about you. I didn't want you to be down here on your own.'

Taking Fran's hand, I gave it a squeeze and led her up the hill towards the château.

We shrugged off our wet coats and boots and then I went to light the fire.

'Would you like a hot drink?' Fran asked me from the kitchen. As I turned round to accept her offer, I was struck by how perfectly she had fit back into my life.

'I wish we could be together like this all the time,' I told her as I sat down at the breakfast bar.

She looked up from stirring the drinks and smiled at me. 'I'd like that too.' She slid a cup of hot chocolate towards me and I picked it up to warm my hands.

'Let's move in together then,' I suggested.

'Do you really mean that?' she asked, wide-eyed.

'No, I was just joking.' I chuckled, as she came round the counter and sat down next to me.

'Where would we live, if we were going to move in together? In the cottage or here?' I reached out with my fingertips to smooth away her frown.

'Which would you prefer?' I asked, caressing her cheek and watching her eyes glow from my touch.

'It's not just up to me. There's Chlöe to think of too. She'd be better off here but I really do love the cottage. I don't mind it here but it's just not very homely.'

'I know what you mean but if you moved in, we could make it our home together.' I smiled and let my hand fall away, not wanting to distract her from this important conversation.

'Hmm, well, I'll give it some thought,' she said, picking up her cup to finish her drink.

'I know you love the cottage and I'm happy just to be with you. If you'd prefer to stay there, then that's what we'll do.'

'I need some time to think about it, Didier. I've only just regained my independence. I'm not sure I'm ready to give it all up again so quickly.'

'That sounds to me like you've already made up your mind.' I stood up to go and put our cups in the sink, trying very hard not to feel rejected by Fran's honest statement.

'No, I haven't. I'm just trying to explain my thoughts and obviously not doing it very well.'

I came back round the counter and pulled Fran into my arms. I held her to me, inhaling her intoxicating fragrance, never wanting to let her go. I bent my head and kissed her softly on the lips, hoping to convey all my love for her in that one touch before pulling apart. I waited for her to return to the conversation but she didn't say anything more. She needed some time alone to consider my proposal and I had to give her that space. It was definitely the next step for us but I didn't want to push her.

CHAPTER TWENTY-FIVE

Fran

Sylvie greeted me as I went to give her a hand with serving the breakfast to the team. 'Morning, Fran. You don't look good, if you don't mind me saying. Did you have a bad night?'

'I couldn't get to sleep for ages and then I fell asleep in the early hours just before it was time to get up.'

She groaned sympathetically. 'Is everything okay?'

'Yes, just a lot on my mind, that's all.' I'd left the château the night before in a daze. I was excited by Didier's proposal but also afraid of the leap we would be taking if we moved in together, as well as the commitment I would be making to this quiet country life.

'I wanted to let you know I'm going to Strasbourg today for some appointments,' Sylvie continued, 'so I won't be here for the *casse-croûte* or for lunch but all the food is ready. You'll just need to put the slow cookers on for the casserole, if you wouldn't mind. If you do that at break time, it will all be heated through by lunch.'

'That's fine,' I said, stifling a yawn. She patted my arm and continued serving. 'Will you be back in time for Chlöe or will Didier need to go and pick her up today?'

'Oh no, I'll be back in plenty of time for Chlöe.'

'I'm having the first meeting with the builders this morning, so that will be interesting.'

'I look forward to hearing about it. Would you and Lottie like to come over for dinner tonight? You could tell us all about it then.'

'I'd love to. I'll see if Lottie's free to come too.'

'Ah yes. She's been a bit busy lately.' She grinned and I returned her smile. Lottie still hadn't returned from her date with Thierry when I'd gone to bed the night before. I'd heard her come in some time in the early hours.

Didier called the pickers together and I followed on after helping Sylvie pack everything away. We'd been split into two teams, one picking the muscat white grapes, and the other the pinot noir. There were only a few vines for these grape varieties so picking them shouldn't take long. After that, we planned to move on to the noble grape varieties, like riesling and pinot gris. The weather was brighter today with no rain forecast and Didier was much more relaxed as a result. Even so, we had to get back to it with a vengeance while the weather was still on our side.

'Are you going to join me for the meeting with the builders after break?' I asked him as we walked back up to the courtyard a couple of hours later.

'I can at least be there for the start but then I'll need to go to the winery to make sure the grapes are getting there quickly enough for the pressing.' He smiled at me and took my hand. 'Have you thought any more about my proposal?' he asked, a gleam in his eye.

'You know I have but I need a bit more time.'

He nodded. 'Are you frightened of moving in with me?'

I hated the way he knew exactly what I was thinking sometimes.

'Truthfully, I am a bit, yes. But that doesn't mean I'm not committed to you.' I gave him a defiant look and he laughed.

We got out all the bread, ham and cheese that Sylvie had brought along that morning, and switched the urns on to high so hot drinks would be available in no time. Making sure everyone was fed and watered kept us busy for the next half an hour. While I was serving, a van pulled into the courtyard. The sign on the side told me it was the men from the building company. A few minutes later, father and son were approaching the table to introduce themselves.

'Would you like a drink before we get started?' I asked Dominic Hahn, shaking his hand. Dominic, a tall, wiry man, was the owner of the company and Tomas was his son. I passed them both a coffee and they stood and chatted to Didier while everyone finished their drinks and snacks. After all the workers had left to continue picking, I quickly cleared away with Didier's help, remembering to switch the slow cookers on for lunch. Finally, we led the builders off to the winery to discuss their plans for the Visitors' Centre.

Didier

After attending the start of the meeting with the builders, I checked in on the winery before rejoining the pickers for the rest of the day. After lunch, I sent my mum a text to check she was still able to collect Chlöe. When she confirmed, I carried on working. Around three, my phone buzzed in my pocket. I was tempted to ignore it but a sixth sense made me look.

'Didier, I've been involved in an accident on the autoroute. I'm okay but they're taking me to hospital. Cannot pick up Chlöe. Don't worry about me xx'

I straightened and started calling for Fran. When she stood up, I motioned for her to run with me. I was late for Chlöe and they hadn't brought her to me like they did before. Something wasn't right. We ran to the courtyard together.

'My mum...has had...accident...in car. She's okay...but hospital. Have to get...Chlöe. I'm late,' I panted, as we ran side by side. We both jumped in the van as soon as we reached the courtyard and we didn't say another word until we reached the nursery. I'd got my breath back by then but I was worried sick.

I walked into the nursery after they buzzed me in, looking all around for signs of Chlöe. I called out to a nursery assistant I recognised.

'*Mademoiselle, je m'excuse d'être en retard.* I'm looking for my daughter, Chlöe.'

She raised her eyebrows.

'She's in the office with her mother.'

'Her mother is here?'

'Yes, she is meeting with the supervisor. As Chlöe's grandmother had said she might be late today, we thought you had asked your wife to collect your daughter in the event of a delay. When she arrived, she asked to meet with the supervisor about the arrangements for Chlöe's care. Would you like me to take you to the office?'

'Yes please, I would.'

I took Fran's hand in mine and we followed her down the corridor but then I heard the sound of my daughter's voice. As we rounded the corner, I came face-to-face with my wife and the supervisor. From the satisfied look on Isabelle's face, their meeting had obviously gone well. Chlöe threw herself at me and I stooped down to pick her up, avoiding eye contact with Isabelle.

'*Ça va, ma chérie?*' I asked softly, pushing her curls back from her face and giving her what I hoped was a reassuring smile. She gave me a sloppy kiss in response and then reached for Fran. As I passed her over, I noticed the look of contempt that crossed Isabelle's face.

Turning to the supervisor, I said, '*Madame*, I would like to talk to you for a few minutes with my wife please.' She looked from me to Isabelle and seeing our thunderous faces, she quickly agreed, turning to lead the way back to her office. I glanced at Fran and she nodded back at me, confirming she would look after Chlöe.

'*Madame*, I apologise for being late to collect Chlöe today. My mother had an accident in Strasbourg, which is what caused the delay.' I paused to let her register that fact and then continued. 'It has made me realise we don't have a contingency plan in place for Chlöe to be collected in such situations.'

'I don't understand.' She frowned. 'Your wife told me you had asked her to collect Chlöe today.'

'My wife and I are getting a divorce, *madame*. At the moment, she isn't even permanently based in France.'

Madame raised her eyebrows. 'Well, this is all very unusual.'

'I apologise. We should have told you sooner what the situation was.' I looked over at Isabelle who was studying her nails. 'As I mentioned before, my wife is not based here at the moment. So, for the time being, if Isabelle agrees, I believe it would be best if only my mother or myself collect Chlöe. If that is not possible for some reason, I will always call and let you know.'

Isabelle didn't argue so the supervisor nodded and we all stood to leave. I strode back to Fran and Chlöe, scooping my daughter up again and going outside into the car park. I stopped and waited for Isabelle to follow, knowing she would want to say goodbye to Chlöe.

When she appeared, I put Chlöe down so she could go to her mother. I didn't say a word, I just waited patiently and as soon as Chlöe had finished, I picked her up again and walked away back towards the vineyard. Fran caught up with me after a few minutes as my pace slowed the further away I got from Isabelle. She reached out to touch my arm.

'Are you okay?' she asked softly.

'I will be. Let's not talk about it any more for now,' I said, nodding my head towards Chlöe.

By the time we got back to the vineyard, it was nearly five and I was desperate to check on my mum. I put Chlöe down in the courtyard where Ruby came to greet her, and called my mum's number again.

'Mum, what's happening?'

'I'm fine. How is Chlöe?' I thought about not telling her but she guessed at once that something was wrong. 'Didier?'

'Isabelle went to pick her up, Mum. They were about to let her go with her because we hadn't told them not to.'

'How did she know I wouldn't be there today?'

'I don't know. She just got lucky, I guess. She asked to see Chlöe when she came to see me last week and I asked for more notice. She obviously decided against that and has been hanging around since then, waiting for an opportunity to see Chlöe. Today, she got one.'

My mum made a strangled noise. 'Oh, Didier, I'm so sorry, I've let you down.'

'Don't be ridiculous, Mum. You had an accident. Do you need picking up?'

'No. They haven't said I can't drive but they have warned me about whiplash which can take some time to develop.'

'Mum, I don't want you to drive but I think it's best if I stay here with Chlöe. I'm going to ask Fran to take my car, and I'll get Henri to come with her and drive your car back, okay? Please stay there.'

'Okay darling. I'm at the CHU.'

Fran had already gone in search of Henri. Thank goodness I could rely on her calm support. She came back with Henri in no time. Henri's relaxed expression reassured me as we shook hands.

'Please stay in touch with me, won't you?' I said to her as I passed her the keys and pulled her in for a hug and a kiss.

'Of course I will,' she replied, and with that she was gone.

Fran

Henri and I were silent in the car for most of the journey to the hospital. I recognised the area as we crossed the River Ill for the second time and the university campus loomed ahead. We found the car park nearest to the emergency department and made our way to the entrance. The sign stated *Urgences* and that was how the whole day was turning out. Relief flooded through me when we found Sylvie sitting in the reception area. She was wearing a neck brace and was very pale. I understood then that she had kept the real extent of her pain from Didier.

She stood awkwardly when she saw us. I opened my arms and gently pulled her to me for a hug.

'Are you really all right, Sylvie?'

'I'm okay physically for the moment but I still feel a bit shaken up. The neck brace is just a precaution. I'm so worried about Chlöe. How was Didier when you left?'

Henri and I brought her up to speed as we walked slowly back to the car.

'Where is your car parked, Sylvie?' Henri asked as we reached Didier's car.

'I think the police took it to the station.' She frowned, confused.

'Don't worry,' I told her, with a glance at Henri, 'we'll pick it up tomorrow.'

Sylvie nodded, touching her forehead with her long fingers. She asked Henri to sit in the back with her, and he helped her to get in and get her seat belt done up so she didn't have to twist her neck. Henri rang Didier to let him know we were on our way and that Sylvie was safe.

We drove back to the vineyard in anxious silence and there was a collective sigh of relief when I pulled into the courtyard at the *Domaine*. Didier came out of the office at the sound of the car. He embraced his mum and Sylvie began to cry as he touched her face with the palm of his hand.

'Shhh, *Maman*. There was nothing any of us could have done to prevent this.'

The grape-pickers and carriers finished for the day. Many came up and offered their good wishes to us as they passed through the courtyard on their way home. Once everyone had gone, Didier, Chlöe and I started making our way down to the château, with Sylvie and Lottie following slowly behind, while Henri and Thierry walked off to the village to get us something for dinner. We'd just waved them off when Isabelle's car pulled into the courtyard.

Didier

At the sound of another car arriving, I spun round in surprise. My mouth dropped open. Why would Isabelle have come back here after all that had happened earlier? She climbed out of the car but didn't come towards me, remaining hesitantly by the driver's door instead. I glanced round to check that everyone else had left the courtyard before walking towards her.

'What are you doing here, Isabelle? I am in no mood for an argument with you.'

'I don't want to argue with you either, Didier. I...I just want to talk to you.'

'What else is there left for us to say to each other?'

She took a step towards me, the look on her face more vulnerable than I remembered seeing there for a long time. She swallowed nervously before speaking again.

'I've come to ask you to consider taking me back, Didier. After what happened today, I realised that Chlöe is the only one who matters in all this. I know that I have been selfish, putting my interests before hers, but I do love her and I think we could rebuild our marriage.'

I was stunned into silence by this change of heart. I dragged in a long breath as I worked out what to say next. Isabelle came closer and I studied her face for signs of sincerity. Despite everything that had happened between us, I still wanted to believe what she was saying, if only for Chlöe's sake. I shook my head a little, trying to clear my thoughts.

'I know you love Chlöe, Isabelle, and you're right, she is the only one who matters here. We have to do what's best for her now but I don't think us getting back together is in her best interest.' Tears sprang to Isabelle's eyes and I reached for her hand, giving it a squeeze of reassurance. 'I've been angry with you for so long that I've lost sight of a few things myself but my love for Chlöe is just as strong as it ever was. You and I have both made mistakes and I'm truly sorry for that. We owe it to Chlöe to forgive each other now and move on.'

She put her arms round me and instead of pulling away, I embraced her warmly, knowing that it would be the last time we would be this close.

'I'm sorry, Didier. It's just that when you asked for full custody, I feared you wouldn't let me see Chlöe if I agreed to that and I realised that I would never want that to happen.'

I pulled away so I could look her in the eyes.

'I would never stop you from seeing Chlöe. You're her mother and she loves you. You have a busy life with your job, and you need to travel at short notice. It just makes sense for Chlöe to live with me most of the time because, even with the vineyard to run, my life is a bit more stable than yours. That's not meant to be a criticism at all and I would definitely want you to see Chlöe whenever you could.'

'And there's really no chance for us?' she asked again.

'I love Fran, Isabelle. I want to build a new life with her, and take the chance I should have taken several years ago. I'm sorry.'

Isabelle gave me a final quick hug before returning to her car. A moment later, she pulled away and I turned to go and rejoin the others.

Fran

Once I'd made sure that Lottie would be all right looking after Sylvie and Chlöe for a while, I dashed back towards the courtyard to give Didier my support. As I approached the archway leading to the courtyard, I heard voices and I slowed down in an effort to catch my breath. The sight of Didier holding Isabelle in his arms as I passed through the arch was more than I could take and I ducked back out of sight at the last minute, confused by what could have happened between them during my brief absence. Instead of going back to the château, I made my way to the cottage, desperate to avoid having to explain what I'd seen to anyone else.

I shut the door quietly behind me and collapsed onto the sofa.

My mind was a mess of irrational questions and my heart was pounding. Why had Didier been holding Isabelle in his arms when just a few hours earlier, he had been furious with her? Were they getting back together? How could that be when he'd told me he loved me? But what other explanation was there? I stood suddenly, my mind clear. I had to go before Didier found me. I rushed upstairs to my bedroom and dragged my battered suitcase down from the top of the wardrobe. I flung an assortment of clothes and underwear into the case, as well as a few other knick-knacks from my bedside table before going back downstairs again. I'd just picked up my purse when Didier burst through the front door.

'Fran, what are you doing? I've been looking for you everywhere.' He was out of breath and his hair was all over the place. Then he saw my suitcase and his face fell. 'Fran? Talk to me please.'

'There's nothing to say. Just that I hope you and Isabelle manage to work things out this time.'

I took a step towards the door but Didier blocked the way.

'Are you leaving me, Fran?'

'Please, Didier, just let me go. Don't make this any harder for me.' My voice cracked as I finished speaking and my eyes filled with tears.

'I love you, Fran.'

My head snapped up at that.

'How can you say that to me when I've just seen you hugging Isabelle? You can't love both of us.' I let my suitcase fall to the floor, struggling to contain my anger.

'I don't love both of you,' he said, taking another step closer and stretching his hand out towards me.

I folded my arms protectively across my chest, willing myself not to take his hand. I lifted my chin and looked him straight in the eye. 'Can you just tell me the truth please?'

'Isabelle and I have worked things out, but not in the way you think. She wanted me to take her back so we could try and rebuild our marriage for Chlöe's sake. I hugged her just after telling her that I couldn't do that because I am in love with you, and I want to build a life with you. That will probably be the last time I give her a hug.'

He closed the final gap between us and slipped his arms round my waist. I relaxed into his arms and lifted my hands to his face, pulling him close enough to kiss. As our lips met, I poured all my emotion into that caress, desperate to show my relief at his words. When we parted at last, he rested his forehead against mine.

'I'm so sorry,' I said, 'for jumping to the wrong conclusion.'

'As long as you know how much I love you, that's all that matters.'

I nodded but didn't say anything. He left shortly after that, needing to get back to Chlöe but for the first time, I wished he could have stayed to reassure me that I was doing the right thing by not leaving.

CHAPTER TWENTY-SIX

I hardly saw Didier the next day. He had decided to resume taking Chlöe to nursery so that Sylvie could rest, and we were kept busy all day with the harvest. He disappeared again before the end of the day's picking to go and collect Chlöe, and Lottie told me she was going home with Thierry. The walk back to the cottage left me feeling lonely and down after the events of the past couple of days. After some dinner, I stretched out on the sofa with my phone and gave Ellie a call.

'Hi, how's everything?' she said.

'Oh, Ellie, I don't even know where to start.'

'God, what's happened in just a few days? Come on, I have wine, tell me everything.'

And that was why I'd called her of course. She always understood my jumbled feelings. I explained everything that had happened.

'And now Didier has retreated back to the château with Chlöe. He took her to and from nursery himself today, which is understandable because he's trying to ease the burden for Sylvie, but it's still bound to make her feel guilty. I'm worried she's in pain after her accident too.'

'Why don't you go and see her? I'm sure she'd appreciate it.'

'I might do that. I just don't want anyone to think I'm interfering. Anyway, the other thing is that before all this happened with Isabelle, Didier asked me to move in with him. But now I don't know if he still wants me to after all.'

'What was your reply going to be before Isabelle intervened?'

'I hadn't made up my mind. I love this little cottage and as much as I love Didier, I'm worried it's all too soon after Paul, especially after the way I reacted yesterday. Do you know what I mean or am I just being silly?'

'Listen, if this is how you feel, it's never stupid. Moving in with someone is a big decision and you have to trust each other to do it. I'm still worried I'm doing the right thing by moving in with Henri.'

'I'm sure you and Henri will be fine. At least you only have each other to think about. Maybe Didier and I just need more time. In my heart, I know I trust him but everything feels so fragile still. He needs to deal with his divorce, and to settle down with Chlöe if the courts decide to give him full custody. Then when everything is calmer, we could talk again about moving in together.'

'Hmm. Well you'll need to talk to him about it in a few days. What about Lottie? What's she doing now?'

'That's another thing I need to speak to Sylvie about - whether she has found a job for Lottie. She needs to have something to do once the harvest is finished or she really will have to go home.'

'How's it going with her and the winemaker? What did you say his name was again?'

'Thierry. She's out with him now. She's not said much about it, just that she likes him. Anyway, have you got a date yet for coming over? I'm desperate to see you now.'

'I have got a date, yes.' She paused dramatically.

'When is it?'

'I'm going to come on Sunday!'

'Brilliant! I can't wait. Does Henri know?'

'No. I've only just confirmed it finally with the landlord today but I'm pretty much packed up. I'm just going to take Saturday to do last minute bits and set off early on Sunday.'

'I am so pleased you'll be here at last.'

We rang off shortly after that. I gathered my coat and keys while I was still motivated to do so, and left the cottage to go and see Sylvie.

I pulled my coat tight around me as I walked along the path to the village. The nights were still quite light but it was definitely getting colder. I approached Sylvie's house from the front, not wanting to frighten her by suddenly appearing in the back garden. I knocked lightly and waited for her to answer.

'Sylvie, *c'est moi*, Fran.'

'Oh, Fran, I'll meet you in the garden.'

I walked to the back garden, entering through the gate. Sylvie was waiting just inside the doors. She still had her neck brace on and from the stiff way she was holding herself, she didn't look back to normal as yet. She let me in and we exchanged kisses gently.

'Would you like a drink?' she asked. 'I have a bottle of wine open if you'd like a glass.'

'Yes please but let me get it. You go and sit down.' I brought two glasses and the bottle in and sat down opposite her.

'It's lovely to see you,' she said. I poured her a small glass until she gestured to me to stop, and then a larger one for myself. 'I was worried when you didn't come back last night. Didier didn't really explain why Isabelle had come back again either.' She looked pointedly at me but I didn't take the bait.

'I'm fine,' I replied, trying not to give anything away. 'I was just tired out after everything that had happened with Isabelle. Seeing her again was a shock to us all but she just wanted to check up on Chlöe.' I consoled myself with the fact that I was telling the truth about most of that at least. 'I was worried about you, though,' I continued. 'It's been a tough couple of days for us all. So how are you feeling? Are you in pain?'

'I do feel better. I probably ought to leave the brace off tomorrow, just to see how I get on.'

'You'd have to be extra careful but if you feel strong enough to try it, that has to be good.' I took a sip of my wine and relaxed a little, hoping we could move away from the topic of Isabelle now.

'I am very sad about everything that has happened. I can't believe Isabelle would just plan to take Chlöe like that. And now I'm worried Didier is blaming himself for it all. I don't like that one little bit.'

'We don't know for sure that Isabelle was trying to take Chlöe, to be fair. It's possible that she just wanted to be involved in her care.' I said it gently, trying not to take sides. 'Didier's just trying to make it up to Chlöe now. He's not upset with you.'

'I know but I hate it when he shuts himself away. He did it when his father died as well, and when he split up with Isabelle originally. There have been other times too.'

'Like when I left, you mean?' She nodded, looking pained. 'He needs to sort things out for himself in his own time,' I went on, 'but he'll come back round.'

'You're right,' she said with a sigh.

'Changing the subject, I wondered if you had managed to ask around about a job for my sister before all this happened?'

'I did ask but no-one had anything. Something will turn up but you might have to be patient for a while longer.'

'Thank you for trying.'

'Will she go home to your parents' house if nothing else comes up?'

'Yes, she'll have to.'

'Would you miss her if she went?'

'Oh, definitely. It's been lovely having her here with me and it's been good for both of us too.'

'And Thierry would definitely miss her. She's been good therapy for him after what happened before.'

'I'm sure you're right, Sylvie, although I don't know what happened to Thierry before. I'm not sure whether Lottie does yet either.'

'If Thierry hasn't said anything, that's because he isn't ready. It was a terrible tragedy, Fran, and it's not my place to talk about it. I'm sorry.'

'No, don't be. I didn't mean to make you feel awkward but I think Lottie should know everything if there's going to be a future for them together. Maybe he has told her now and she just hasn't had the chance to tell me.'

'Anyway, we've talked about your sister but what about you? How's everything going with you and Didier?'

I took a deep breath before answering. I definitely didn't want to reveal my trust issues of the previous day but I would have to say something in reply to her question. 'Didier asked me to move into the château with him.'

'And what was your reply?'

'I said I needed some time to think about it.'

I was uncomfortable discussing this with Sylvie when I hadn't had the chance to talk to Didier about it again.

'I see,' she said but I wasn't sure she did. It was all still very complicated in my own mind, let alone hers.

Didier

After dropping Chlöe off at the nursery the next morning, I went to the office to call Alain and fill him in on what had happened. He listened carefully as I explained the situation and then came straight to the point.

'Have you had any thoughts about where you want to go from here?'

'I still want to push for full custody, but I do want Isabelle to see Chlöe as regularly as she wants to. I don't want to fight with her any more and I hope she feels the same way, although I do want you to emphasise that Fran is not to blame for our marriage falling apart.'

'Yes, of course. I'll send them a reminder by email today and ask for quick processing if possible.'

I rang off and made my way to the vineyard, thoughts swirling round my head. With any luck, my divorce would come through fairly quickly, with all my assets from before my marriage intact, and I would have Chlöe with me most of the time. And Fran's name shouldn't even come up again. I half hoped Fran would come down and see us later in the day but she didn't appear. I wanted to talk to her about moving in as we hadn't had the chance to talk about it since I'd first mentioned it to her. She hadn't seemed very enthusiastic about the idea and I was plagued with doubts about her commitment to me all over again. Seeing her on the brink of leaving me again the other day had only increased my fears.

Before falling asleep that night, I decided to ask my mum to pick Chlöe up for me the next day if she was feeling up to it. Perhaps if we shared responsibility for the rest of the week, I would begin to feel more relaxed about releasing control again, as well.

After dropping Chlöe at school in the morning, I was back in time for breakfast at the courtyard. My mum was busy serving but she glanced at me as I approached.

'*Bonjour, Maman,*' I said gently, as I came and stood beside her to help. She only nodded in reply and I knew then I had upset her. 'I hope I didn't upset you yesterday. I was worried about how you were feeling but I was still spooked after what happened with Isabelle too. That was nothing to do with you. I just wanted to be in control of things myself.'

'I understand,' she said, her rigid frame relaxing a little.

'How are you feeling now? I guess you feel better now you've taken the brace off?'

'A bit better, yes, but I'm trying not to overdo it.'

'Mum, if you're sure you're feeling better, I wanted to ask you if you would pick Chlöe up today for me, please. I thought perhaps we could share taking and collecting her this week, just until things settle down again.'

I waited patiently for her reply, knowing she'd say yes because she loved Chlöe so much.

'All right. Do you want me to take her home with me or bring her here?'

'Would you bring her here, please? Maybe I could make you dinner for a change?' That merited a smile.

'That would be lovely, thank you.' She reached out and patted my hand, and I knew we were all right again. Now all I had to do was speak to Fran.

I caught sight of Fran as everyone walked across the courtyard to go back down to the vineyard after break. I didn't call out to her, not wanting to draw too much attention to us. Instead, I weaved my way in and out of the pickers, saying hellos as I went and smiling to encourage them to let me pass.

'Hey,' I said as I finally came up alongside her, puffing from the effort of getting through the crowd.

'Hello.' She gave me a tentative smile.

'I'm sorry I didn't see much of you yesterday. I wanted to give my mum a break until she felt better and to reassure Chlöe that everything was okay.' I pushed my hand through my hair.

'I understand,' she said, slipping her hand into mine. 'I appreciated how you were feeling after what happened...and I don't think I helped by the way I reacted.'

'I didn't mean to shut you out. I do have a bit of a habit of doing that. I'm sorry.' I gave her hand a squeeze.

'Have you sorted things out with your mum?'

'I think so. I've asked her to collect Chlöe this afternoon and then come round for dinner. I wondered if you'd like to join us.'

'That would be lovely.'

'I know we still need to talk about everything,' I said after a slight pause. 'But I don't want you to feel under any pressure.' I wished I could have stayed and spent the night with her when she was having doubts.

'We need to be on our own to have that conversation. Let's not talk about it tonight.'

'Is everything okay between us now though? No more thoughts of leaving?'

She was biting her lip. I tugged gently on her hand to get her to stop walking and look at me. I reached out and touched her cheek, trying to reassure her but only reminding myself how much I'd missed touching her these past few days. Her breath caught, and all of a sudden I wished we were somewhere far more private. I dropped my hand and looked down at my feet, forgetting the question I'd just asked her.

'No, honestly, I'm fine,' she said, bringing me back to what we'd been talking about.

'Will you stay with me tonight?' I whispered in her ear. My voice sounded husky even to my own ears and I imagined my desire for her written all over my face. Her throat bobbed.

'Didier...'

I pulled her to me, needing to feel her body against mine. She nodded and I pulled away from her to kiss her lightly on the lips. I didn't trust myself with anything more. I let her go but we stood staring at each other for a few minutes longer, both of us overwhelmed by our need for each other. For my part, I wanted with all my heart to take her home with me right now and to show her just how much I loved her. As it was, I had work to deal with. Our passion would have to wait until later.

Fran

Didier gave me one last rueful smile and walked away, leaving me feeling like my body was on fire and in no doubt of how he felt about me. How was I supposed to get through the rest of the day? I craved his touch and his look. Surely it would make sense to move in together, despite my need for independence pushing me to stay in the cottage? Deep down, I was just afraid to take the final step of giving myself to him completely.

I wasn't ready to go down to the vineyard so I turned round to go back to the office to check on the post and any messages. I'd forgotten it would be so cold within the brick walls of the office and I shivered as I opened the door. I flicked the switch on the manual heater, turning the dial as high as it would go.

I put the pile of post on my desk and switched on my computer, intending to check my emails. There weren't many new ones, thank goodness, but there was one from the builder to say they would like to start work on the Visitors' Centre the next Monday, if we were in agreement. They estimated it would take twelve weeks to complete the centre. They also suggested that a smaller team get started on the château at the same time, if we had the funds. I was going to have a lot to talk to Didier about at lunchtime.

I started sorting through the post, which was made up of bills for the most part, then I noticed a large brown A4 envelope with the name of Isabelle's solicitors stamped on it. I turned it over in my hands, aware of its importance. I didn't really think I should wait till lunchtime to tell Didier about this one.

'There's a letter in the post today from Isabelle's lawyers. It looks official.' Once the text was sent, I continued sorting through the remaining post.

Didier burst through the door a few minutes later, making me gasp.

'God, you must have run at real speed to get here that quickly!' He couldn't reply because he was so puffed out. I passed him the envelope and studied his face while he opened it and examined the contents. He got to the end of both sheets of paper and went back to the beginning to read it more carefully.

'What does it say?' I asked, when I could stand the suspense no longer.

'It's Isabelle's reply following my request for a divorce and custody. She will not be pursuing any of my assets, after all. She agrees to a divorce, citing irreconcilable differences between us, with the blame only being between ourselves. She also accepts my suggestion that Chlöe should live with me, as long as she has "reasonable" visitation rights.' He looked up at me, his handsome face etched with concern.

'That sounds like it's fair, doesn't it?' I asked, unsure as to why he still seemed so worried.

'It would seem so at first glance. What I'd like is to talk to Alain, just to make sure she really is agreeing to everything I've requested.' He heaved a sigh. 'If it is really is true then I'm very happy about it all - especially the divorce and the custody, of course.'

He came towards me and pulled me up from my chair and into his arms for a kiss. He touched my lips lightly and then the kiss deepened.

'Now we are free to be together.'

CHAPTER TWENTY-SEVEN

Didier

Waking up next to Fran's beautiful, lithe body stretched out in my bed was the best feeling. I reached out to touch her soft skin, and memories of the wonderful night we'd spent together came flooding back. Before I knew it, my body was heating up in all the right places but there was no time to explore those feelings now. I jumped in the shower instead, to help me cool off.

By the time I went downstairs, Chlöe and Fran were chatting away as normal, as though everything was...well, normal. We would both have to be sensitive in the way we explained things to Chlöe but she already knew we cared for each other, and so this was the next step. I gave them both a hug and a kiss, noticing Chlöe was already dressed and eating her breakfast.

'*Papa*, can Fran take me to nursery today?' Her little face was absolutely serious, while Fran was wide-eyed at the precious gift she was being given.

'Of course, if you'd like that.' Fran would look after her as if she were her own and she needed to know I trusted her. I kept the smile pasted to my face, despite my inner turmoil. Fran mouthed 'thank you' at me and gave me a warm smile.

They set off not long afterwards, leaving me alone in the house to ponder a few things. Fran had told me honestly the previous evening that she wanted to be with me, but she was also frightened of taking the leap and moving in with me. The incident with Isabelle had also unsettled her, even though I'd reassured her there was nothing between the two of us any more. I didn't know what else I could do to convince Fran how much I wanted to take that next step with her and that it was the right thing for both of us.

I pulled on my coat, scarf and hat and left the house for the office to try and get some work done there before everyone arrived for breakfast. I switched on the heater, followed by my computer and then the coffee machine. Finally, I prepared an email for Alain, explaining that I wanted him to move ahead with the divorce, and seeking his advice about how to approach the issue of custody. As Isabelle moved around so much, it wouldn't be easy to come up with a regular arrangement that would suit us all.

Hearing voices outside, I went out to greet everyone and to give my mum a hand with serving. We were making better progress with the harvest than I would have expected after just a couple of weeks, which I put down to a mostly experienced group of pickers helping us this time. After breakfast, I announced that we would be able to take Sunday off again because we were doing so well. There were grinning faces all around at this news and I couldn't resist a grin of my own. Fran came and joined me after my little speech.

'Chlöe was absolutely fine, chatting all the way. She asked me if I'd enjoyed sleeping over at your house.' I let out a roar of laughter, causing one or two people to turn and look at me. I raised my hand in apology, wiping my eyes.

'What did you say?'

'What do you think? I said yes of course! I don't think we need to say any more to her about it now. If that's how she sees it, that's fine.'

'You're right. Come on then, shall we get going?'

Fran

Henri and I set off after lunch on Sunday to pick Ellie up from the station, neither one of us able to contain our excitement at seeing her again. I desperately wanted to sit and have a long chat with her but understood I would have to share her with Henri from now on. It made me nostalgic for the times when we would sit and talk for hours at her flat in London. So much had changed in such a short space of time. Still, we would be seeing much more of one another now she would be living in the village, as well as helping out with the harvest.

I waved and yelled in her direction as soon as she stepped off the train. She broke into an enormous grin. She had two big suitcases with her so we made our way to her as quickly as we could through all the crowds of people.

'Hey! I made it,' she cried, throwing her arms round us both for a hug.

'It's so good to see you,' I said, stepping back so she and Henri could share a more intimate moment. She winked at me over his shoulder and I had to laugh as I picked up one of her discarded bags. She was her own woman and always would be, and that was one of the many things I loved about her.

Henri took her hand and pulled her other suitcase alongside him as we progressed slowly along the platform towards the exit.

'So, how is everyone? Has everything calmed down a bit now?'

'Didier was very stressed immediately after what happened but he's much calmer about it all now.'

'Yes, it was tough on him but Isabelle has agreed to the divorce now and they're negotiating custody terms,' Henri added.

I glanced at Henri, wondering how he knew as much as I did. He and Didier obviously found time to talk regularly. I hoped Didier hadn't told him that I'd almost left him after seeing him hugging Isabelle.

'Oh, that's excellent news, Fran. You must be pleased.'

'I am.' There was a "but" I could have added but I didn't want to say anything about my inner feelings in front of Henri, given his friendship with Didier. Ellie gave me a quizzical look so I knew she would ask me about it later.

We reached the car and Ellie climbed in the back with me so we could chat more easily.

'How much longer will the harvest be going on?' she asked.

'Didier estimates we need another couple of weeks to finish everything.'

'I'm looking forward to getting stuck in and doing my bit,' she said. Henri glanced in the mirror at us, a little frown on his face.

'*Elle attend participer dans le vendange avec impatience,*' I translated for him.

'Oops,' she giggled, covering her mouth with her hand. 'I will have to be more careful about using slang. Poor old Henri, what are you going to do with me?' An intimate look passed between them in the mirror and I had the feeling Henri had a very good idea what he was going to do with her. My face flushed at being the gooseberry and I hastily looked out of the window.

Henri pulled the car into the courtyard shortly afterwards and I got out after kissing Ellie goodbye.

'Good luck with moving in and I'll see you later, okay? Seven o'clock at Didier's.'

'We'll be there,' she replied, hopping out of the back and moving into the passenger seat next to Henri.

Didier

Chlöe loved cooking and so we'd spent all morning preparing food for the party. First of all, we made little cakes with chocolate fondant on top and then she helped me prepare an onion tart and some potato salad.

'You're an expert at rolling out pastry now,' I told her, as we washed up after cooking.

'I can't wait to show Fran what we've made,' she said with a smile. It was reassuring to know she loved Fran as much as I did.

We took Ruby on a tour of the estate afterwards, arriving back at the courtyard just as Fran was coming through the archway. Her long brown hair was blowing gently in the breeze as she appeared, and I found her beauty breathtaking once again. Chlöe ran up to her and she bent down straight away to give her a hug and a kiss, and to listen to her tales of what we'd been up to that morning.

'Hey, Fran, how was Ellie?' I asked, kissing her softly on the cheek.

'She was her usual, outgoing self,' she laughed. Her face lit up as she thought about her friend.

'Well, we're all ready for the welcome party tonight, aren't we, Chlöe? Why don't you tell Fran what we've made?'

We listened to Chlöe all the way back to the cottage, hardly able to get a word in edgeways while she chattered on.

'Are you going home for lunch now?' Fran asked.

'Yes, would you like to join us?'

'I thought you'd never ask,' she teased. 'Your house is the place to be if I want to get fed today. I never seem to get round to going food shopping.'

'If you ever need anything, you must tell me,' I chided. '*Maman* and I take turns to shop, and we can easily add things in for you too.' I paused for a moment, considering the possibilities for this conversation. 'Of course, if we lived together, you wouldn't even have to think about food shopping.' She rolled her eyes lovingly.

'You, Monsieur Le Roy, are very persistent,' she said, prodding my chest gently with her finger.

'*Qu'est-ce que cela veut dire* - per-sis-tent?' Chlöe interrupted.

'It means *déterminé*!' we cried together.

'*Ah, oui, c'est vrai*!' Chlöe agreed and ran off across the lawn with Ruby.

'I've had an idea about the whole living together debate,' Fran said, catching my attention.

'I'm listening,' I said, slowing down.

'We decided the builders should start on the château rather than the Visitors' Centre while the harvest is still going on because of the dust,' she began. I nodded, remembering our discussion from Friday. 'Well, the château would get dusty too, when they start work there, which might make it a bit uncomfortable for you both.' She stopped, waiting for me to get her point.

'For me and Chlöe, you mean?' I replied, trying to process what she was saying.

'So, maybe it's not me that should be thinking about moving in with you but...'

It suddenly clicked and my mouth fell open. 'We should move back into the cottage with you!'

I picked her up and whirled her around, bringing her face to mine for a kiss.

'I take it you like the idea?'

'I love it, and Chlöe will too. Are you sure you wouldn't mind us being there?'

'I've given it a lot of thought,' she said, shaking her head. 'I love the cottage and I've put my stamp on it a little now, but it would feel more like a real home with you and Chlöe in it too.'

'You've made my day. I love you, you know.'

'I know,' she said, stroking the hair away from my face.

Fran

The party for Ellie was in full swing by the time Lottie arrived on her own. She'd gone out first thing to spend the day with Thierry, so I thought they would come along together some time in the evening. As soon as she found me, she pulled me to one side.

'Thierry and I have had an awful row,' she said, keeping her voice low. I heard the wobble in it though.

'What!'

'Shhh,' she hissed, frowning at me. 'I don't want everyone else to get involved.'

'What happened? And where is he?'

'I don't think he'll be coming.' She stopped, struggling to find the words to tell me. 'We were just talking about where things might be going between us and I told him if there isn't a job for me after the harvest ends, which isn't looking likely, I'm going to have to go home. He just came right out and said maybe we should stop seeing each other now, seeing as I was only going to leave anyway.'

'What did you say then?'

'Nothing. I just stood up and stormed out.'

I groaned and covered my face with my hands. She pulled them away gently. 'You know you should have stayed and talked it through together?' I said, looking her straight in the eye, ignoring the fact that I didn't exactly always follow my own advice.

'What's the point? He made it very clear he didn't want to try and get over the issue, so why should I make the effort?' I recognised that defiant tone at once. I'd seen it so many times when she really cared about something or someone but was trying hard not to let it show.

The French doors opened and I glanced up.

'Don't look now but he just walked in and he's scanning the room, probably looking for you.'

She raised her eyes to the ceiling and suddenly my heart was in my mouth as Thierry spotted us and started walking our way.

'*Salut,* Fran,' he said softly before turning to speak to my sister. 'Lottie, we need to talk. Please. I'm sorry for what I said before.' He blew out a deep breath, waves of frustration radiating off him. Years of living with my sister had made me more than aware of how trying she could be.

Lottie didn't reply. She just turned on her heel and went back outside, with Thierry following close behind. It was only once they'd gone that I realised the room had fallen silent. Suddenly, everyone started talking again. Didier found me and led me into the kitchen.

'What was all that about?'

I told him what Lottie had told me. He blew out a big breath, as sad as I was that Lottie and Thierry had argued when they seemed to be so good for each other.

'Had you thought about where Lottie would go if Chlöe and I moved back in?'

'To be honest, I was thinking she'd either go home or move in with Thierry.' I pulled a face, knowing how bad that sounded and Didier raised his eyebrows.

'We'll just have to wait and see what happens. We should let them work it out for themselves, no matter how much we might want it all to end happily.' He gave me a little smile before pouring out two new glasses of wine for us. He refilled a plate with food for everyone and, passing me a glass, he moved out to mingle.

The room was full of our friends, old and new, including many of the grape-pickers and carriers who had worked so hard for the *Domaine* over the last couple of weeks. It was good to thank them in this way in the middle of the harvest. There would be lots of parties in the region when the harvest was over but for now, this smaller, intimate gathering was more our style.

Ellie and Henri had been at each other's side all evening and so I was surprised to see her come into the kitchen on her own.

'Hey you, is everything okay?' she asked. 'I saw Lottie come in briefly and then go again.'

'I'm okay. She's just had a bit of an argument with Thierry because she still doesn't have a job to go to when the harvest ends.'

'And he wants her to stay, is that it?'

'I think he does but he just hasn't quite worked out the right way to tell her that yet.'

'Ah, I see,' she said.

'Anyway, how have you settled in at Henri's?'

'It's been fine so far but it's going to take some getting used to, living with someone else. Have you thought any more about that issue?'

'Yes I have, and I've even come up with a solution that Didier likes too, but it all kind of depends on what happens with Lottie now.' I looked away, embarrassed to tell her what else had happened.

'What is it? I had the feeling there was more to this in the car.'

'I can't talk about it now but honestly, everything's fine.' I gave her a quick smile and she didn't push any further.

CHAPTER TWENTY-EIGHT

Didier

Two weeks later

A great cry rang out across the vineyard as we finally downed tools. I called out goodbyes to everyone as we walked up the hill for the last time during this harvest. Despite the constant ache in my muscles, I was satisfied that it had gone well. I would be concentrating on the new, young wines in the winery now, with Thierry's advice. I had every hope the resulting wines would be as good as the grapes suggested. That work would continue on Monday, though. For now, I wanted a good night's sleep and a lie-in before I thought about it all again.

I reached the courtyard just as Fran was going into the office. There wasn't anything that couldn't wait till Monday and I wanted her to have a rest too.

'What are you up to?' I asked, following her inside.

'Just checking there's nothing urgent to be dealt with.'

'Come on. There won't be anything important now. Let's leave it all till Monday and enjoy our weekend.'

'Let me just check today's post at least. I'll feel better if I do.' She gave me that special smile of hers, making it hard for me to deny her whatever it was she wanted.

'I'm giving you five minutes, that's all.'

I stood in front of her, arms folded, watching her sort the envelopes into two piles.

'I told you there'd be something important,' she declared, handing me another manila envelope, with the all-too-familiar name of my law firm printed on the outside.

'I'm going to have an irrational fear of these envelopes soon. I've had enough these past few weeks to last me my whole life.'

I opened it, as Fran finished sorting her piles.

'Okay, let's see,' I said. I read it through quickly, trying to focus on the highlights but I got no further than the first line. I read it again to make sure before I told Fran. 'Isabelle has accepted I have no more assets or money to give her and she accepts my request for full custody of our daughter.' I looked up at Fran who was watching me very closely for my reaction. I swallowed before studying the rest of the letter. 'She agrees that her itinerant lifestyle would be unsuitable for a young child. She wants to go with my suggestion that she should see Chlöe for a minimum of one week per month during term-time but spend longer with her during the holidays. She also agrees that we should negotiate this as we go along.' I sank down into a chair, feeling suddenly weak now that everything I had wanted for so long was finally coming true.

'And the divorce papers?' Fran whispered.

I lifted the letter summarising everything and looked underneath it at the other papers.

'*Mon dieu*! She's signed the divorce papers too. I just have to wait for the official paperwork to come through now.' I glanced back at Alain's letter. 'There's a final note saying Isabelle would like to take Chlöe for a week during the next school holidays, which I have no issue with. I hope this will pave the way for a good relationship between us in the future.'

'I can't quite believe it's all over,' Fran said. 'This is really the end of it all. How do you feel about it?'

'Pretty good. Relieved mostly.' I stood up and she came towards me for a hug. I closed my eyes as I held her tight, relishing the feeling of finally being able to move on from the past.

'Shall we go and see how everything's going in the château before we go to your mum's?'

The builders had been working through the upstairs rooms at the château for the past two weeks, re-plastering the walls where necessary, and would soon be moving onto the downstairs to do the same job. I'd asked them to give me a couple of weeks to get the first wine pressing safely closed up in the tanks before they started work on the Visitors' Centre. I'd have a better idea of the finances by then, as well.

We'd crossed the courtyard and passed through the archway on our way towards the château when I had a change of plan.

'I'm fairly sure the builders can wait to talk to us until next week, you know. I have a much better idea of what we could do now.' I looked sideways at her and she laughed before changing direction to turn towards the cottage instead.

Fran

The door of the cottage banged shut as Didier left with Chlöe for the nursery. Now they had moved in with me, everything seemed to be right in the world. I closed my eyes again and snuggled back under the duvet savouring the novelty of my Monday morning lie-in for just a few minutes longer. As I stood under the water in the shower not long afterwards, I thought about my conversation with my mum and dad the previous day.

'Hello sweetheart, how are you?' my mum had asked.

I'd filled her in on the news about the harvest and how well it had all gone.

'There's going to be a festival in the village next weekend to celebrate the end of the harvest and I wanted to invite you and Dad to come.'

'That would be lovely. And what's the news on Lottie? I haven't spoken to her for a few days.'

'We think there may be a job coming up in the village. It's as a nursery assistant at the place Chlöe attends. She'd have to train up so it wouldn't pay much to start with but if she likes it, it wouldn't take her long.'

'That sounds great. Is she happy with the idea? I never really had her down as someone who'd like to work with children.'

'She's volunteered a couple of times and got on quite well with both the children and the other staff. I think she's going to give it a shot.'

'And you're okay about her staying with you?'

'Actually, she's moved in with Sylvie for the time being.'

'Really? Whose idea was that?'

'It was Sylvie's. It has resolved a lot of potential issues. Anyway, I'll let her tell you more about her situation but she's very pleased she can stay here and continue seeing Thierry.'

'So, are you on your own in the cottage now?'

'Well, not quite, sorry. Didier and Chlöe have moved in with me.'

There was a pause.

'Does that mean Didier's divorce is now sorted out?'

'Pretty much, yes, and he more or less has full custody of Chlöe.' I'd gone on to give her all the details.

'I'm so pleased for you, I really am. Look, I'll pass you over to your dad and we'll see you next weekend. Take care, love.'

I got dressed and had a quick breakfast before heading out towards the office. Didier was just arriving back as I walked through the archway.

'Did you see Lottie?' I asked.

'I did and she was fine. She was a little nervous, but once the children came in and started chattering, she seemed much more at ease. Chlöe went straight up to her and took her hand in hers.'

'Oh, that was sweet of her. I bet Lottie will have a wonderful day and won't even notice the time passing.'

I unlocked the door to the office and shivered at once from the cold. Didier went to reset the storage heater since we would be here all the time now the harvest was over. Henri arrived a few minutes later, followed by Ellie, and I had to stop myself from squealing in pleasure to have my friend with me once again. Today was Ellie's first proper day with us after the harvest. She was going to help me go over the whole Visitors' Centre project and work out a detailed timeline of events before the spring opening we had planned. I was so pleased Ellie was with me to help me think it all through. After a quick hug, she helped me sort the post and then I went through my emails.

'Right,' I announced around ten, standing up from my desk. 'Ellie and I are going to have a conference at the cottage about the building project. We'll probably be there for the rest of the day.'

The two men saluted me and with a little smile, I turned on my heel and walked to the door with Ellie right behind me.

Didier

The bedroom door creaked open in the semi-darkness.

'*Papa, quelle heure est-il?*' Chlöe's little voice whispered right by my ear. I strained to see the clock and groaned when I saw that it was only six o'clock.

'It's very early, little one,' I whispered back, trying not to wake Fran.

I pushed the duvet back gently and swung my legs out of bed. I would go downstairs with my daughter and keep her quietly busy until her mum came to collect her for the week's holiday they were going to spend together at Isabelle's new apartment in Strasbourg. Chlöe was excited to see her mum and I was very glad about that.

'*Qu'est-ce qu'il y a?*' Fran murmured from the bed as I stood up.

'Shh, go back to sleep, it's still early.'

I turned to leave the room with Chlöe, putting my finger to my lips to encourage her to stay quiet, but it was too late. Fran sat up in bed and rubbed her eyes before smiling at the sight of both of us trying to creep out.

'Is it time for breakfast?' she asked.

'Yay!' cried Chlöe.

We threw on our clothes and went downstairs to go and get breakfast from the *boulangerie*. Chlöe ran ahead down the path, while Fran and I followed at a more leisurely pace. With her hand swinging gently in mine, I felt like the luckiest man on earth. I thought about telling her my plans at that very moment but I didn't want to spoil the surprise. I wanted to keep it for the festival celebrations in the evening, even though it was going to require superhuman control not to reveal the secret ahead of schedule.

At the *boulangerie*, we decided to buy extra pastries and take them round to my mother's so she and Chlöe could see each other before she went off on her holidays. We'd just rounded the corner of the high street, ready to make our way round the back of Mum's house, when we almost bumped into her hurrying the other way.

'*Maman*!'

Her face lit up when she saw us but I noticed the slight stiffness in her shoulders.

'*Ah, ma petite*!' she cried as Chlöe ran towards her for a hug. She bent down awkwardly and I exchanged a worried look with Fran. For the first time, I wondered whether my mum needed to slow down a bit.

'Where are you off to this early?' I asked as we accompanied her along the street.

'Why, to the *Salle* of course! We're already setting up for this evening and there's always so much to do.'

'Have you had any breakfast, Sylvie?' Fran asked.

'No time for that!'

'Well, we've got some lovely pastries from the *boulangerie*,' I told her. 'Why don't we come along and give you a hand and then perhaps you'll find time to eat something, as well?'

Her shoulders sagged with relief. We carried on along to the *Salle* which was filled with people moving tables and chairs and decorating them for the celebrations. I threw my hand in with the furniture moving while Fran and Chlöe followed my mum into the kitchen. Before I knew it, two hours had passed and Isabelle was texting me to say she was nearly at the vineyard. I went in search of Chlöe, saying my goodbyes along the way. My mum had tears in her eyes as she hugged her grand-daughter goodbye, making my own emotions rise to the surface too. I didn't want Chlöe to see any tears, though, so I put on my brightest voice and took her by the hand.

'Come on sweetheart, we don't want to be late for *Maman*.' As I was helping Chlöe into her coat, the door to the *Salle* opened and Lottie came in, looking flushed and happy, Thierry close on her heels.

'Oh, I'm glad you two are here. Can you give Sylvie a hand so I can go back with Didier?' Fran asked. When they nodded, she joined us for the walk back to the *Domaine*.

Fran

Even though things were much better between Didier and Isabelle now, he still seemed anxious about meeting her again. I gave his hand a gentle squeeze as we left the *Salle* to take Chlöe to meet her mum for her week's holiday. We reached the courtyard to find Isabelle already there. She put out her arms to her daughter, who ran straight into them. I nodded at Isabelle and made to walk round them all to go back to the cottage. They needed their privacy as a family.

'Please don't leave on my account, Fran,' she called.

I stopped beside her. 'No, no, it's fine,' I replied with a smile, 'I have things to do anyway. I hope you have a great week together.'

'I just wanted to say I'm sorry for what I said about you. I overstepped the mark and I had no right to.' She blushed and looked tentatively between me and Didier.

Didier's eyebrows shot up at her apology and I swallowed, not knowing quite what to say.

'That's all behind us now,' Didier replied, 'but thank you. Take care, won't you? And if you need anything, anything at all, please call me.'

I left then, passing through the archway and away from them, their voices fading on the breeze. My mind returned to Didier's mum, Sylvie. She'd seemed so fragile that morning. Perhaps she was overdoing things. The problem was how to make her slow down without offending her sense of independence. I was so glad we'd helped her this morning, though. At least that was a start.

I reached the cottage and stood looking out across the landscape. There was an autumnal look to the trees in the distance, like a sunset of yellows, oranges and browns in the middle of the day. I thought about all the changes that had happened to me between the summer's end and the start of autumn and I felt lucky. My love for Didier was all-consuming and I longed for us to be together forever. He'd confirmed his feelings for me when he'd chosen me over getting back together with Isabelle. Now, I hoped we could share our feelings about our long-term future soon so we could move forward together. I heard a crackle of leaves behind me and turned to see Didier arrive.

'Everything okay?' I asked.

'Fine, yes. Isabelle seemed like a changed woman, didn't she?'

'Yes. It was nice of her to say what she did.'

'She owed you that, at the very least,' he said, putting his arms round my waist and pulling me towards him. He lowered his head and moved his face closer to mine. My lips parted in anticipation of the kiss I knew was about to come but he waited, his hot breath caressing my lips and his warm smile enveloping me. I licked my lips, and his eyes darkened. I lifted my hands to his face, enjoying the feel of his newly-shaved skin under my fingers. He bent his head to mine and kissed me. When we came up again for air, I was overwhelmed by the depth of my feelings once again.

'I hope you know how much I love you,' he whispered, his voice husky after our kiss.

'If it's anywhere near as much as I love you, then yes, I do.'

CHAPTER TWENTY-NINE

Didier

We spent the afternoon back at the hall, helping to set everything up for the evening. We even managed to persuade my mum to go home for a rest. At five, we left to get ready for the party. Normally, for me, that would just mean a quick shower and a change of clothes from one shirt and one pair of jeans to another but this evening was going to be special for me and for Fran - I hoped - and so I planned to take extra care of my appearance.

Nothing could have prepared me for how beautiful Fran looked when she descended the staircase.

'You look wonderful,' I said, standing up to kiss her softly on the cheek. Her long, wavy hair curled softly round her shoulders, caressing her skin, and her eyes glowed. She was wearing a long, figure-hugging dark blue dress and I had to stop myself from thinking about the luscious body underneath it.

'You too,' she said. 'I don't think I've seen you so dressed up since Amandine's wedding. Very smart.' She grabbed the lapels of my dinner jacket and pulled me gently towards her. As our bodies pressed against each other, I had to work really hard not to let my feelings for her show too obviously. There would be plenty of time for that later. Our lips touched and it was electrifying. The effect rippled through my whole body and Fran shuddered.

'Shall we go?' I asked, taking her hand in mine.

The moon was bright as we walked out into the night, and lit up the sky.

'The stars are shining especially brightly tonight, wouldn't you say?' Fran asked.

'I definitely would say,' I replied with a grin. I put my hand in my pocket just to check my surprise was safely there for later and put my other arm round Fran's shoulders as we walked down into the village.

When we arrived at the *Salle*, it was already full of people bustling around making last-minute touches to the tables for the dinner and ball. First of all, there would be a wine tasting, mainly of the *vin nouveau* but also of the wines of the region. I was pleased to see Thierry was already here. Fran removed her coat and went in the direction of the kitchen to look for my mum.

'*Salut, Thierry, ça va*?' I greeted him, shaking his hand firmly. I surveyed the small display of wines he had chosen to bring along. It was a great selection of both old and new.

'Do you agree with this selection?' He was confident he had made the right choice - I knew him well enough for that - but he wanted my confirmation too.

'I couldn't have chosen any better myself.' We exchanged smiles and I noted his relief. 'What time is the tasting supposed to start?'

'In about twenty minutes. I brought along some of the leaflets Fran had printed too. Hopefully, this will bring visitors our way.'

'Excellent, thank you for remembering.'

Lottie made her way over and after exchanging kisses with her, I went to find Fran.

Fran

I found Sylvie in the kitchen, looking much calmer than she was when we had left her earlier. She was wearing a stunning emerald-green dress, which shimmered as she moved.

'Fran, you look beautiful, *chérie*,' she said, looking over my outfit.

'You do too.' I gave her a warm smile. 'Is there anything else you need a hand with?' I asked, glancing round at all the food laid out on the worktops.

'No, everything is ready, so we can go and enjoy the wine tasting now.'

Didier smiled broadly when he spotted us leaving the kitchen.

'Everything all right?' he asked his mum, taking my hand once again.

'Absolutely fine,' she confirmed. 'What I need now is a glass of our wine.'

'The tasting is just about to start,' he replied.

I accompanied Didier as he worked his way along the tables laden down with wines for guests to try. He studiously tried them all but he didn't swallow. He used the spittoons professionally and didn't seem to look any the worse for wear as he consumed each new one. I had to pace myself, though, taking small sips of each wine only so that I could try a good selection. You could tell with a quick glance which people were pros, like Didier, and those who were simply tasting the wines for the love of it, like me. I noticed Didier making some notes and I realised he was constantly evaluating each and every wine he tasted. About halfway through, I took a quick break to keep Lottie company, leaving Thierry and Didier to it while we caught up.

'How's the job going after your first week?' I asked her.

'It's been good but I had no idea how much hard work it would be looking after little children all day!' She frowned.

'Well, I suppose it's good practice.' I smiled at her. 'Are you going to stick it out do you think?'

'Yes, I want to keep at it. It's impossible to tell after only a week whether it will be good for me in the long term but I want to try and give it a proper go.'

'And how are things with you and Thierry after the party?' I asked tentatively.

'I'm still here, aren't I?' A flash of annoyance crossed her face. I didn't say anything more, heeding Didier's advice to let her sort her own life out. 'Listen,' she continued after a moment, 'did you invite Mum and Dad tonight?'

'Mmm,' I replied swallowing a sip of a very dry riesling. 'They should be here by now.'

I glanced round the room, searching for them, and found them near the main entrance taking off their coats. They didn't see us for a few minutes, as they were so intent on getting started on the wine tasting but my mum soon came over.

'It's so lovely to see you both!' she cried, giving each of us a hug in turn. 'Isn't it wonderful to see all the wines on display and to taste them, as well?'

'It is but I don't think I can taste many more,' I complained. 'I'm already a bit drunk.' They both laughed. It was good to see Lottie's smile back again. I left her and my mum to talk and went to find my dad. He wouldn't have any trouble tasting all the wines.

'Hey, Dad,' I tapped him on the shoulder when I found him, right in the middle of the wines.

'What a wonderful event this is, Fran. I hope you'll invite me every year from now on.'

'I will Dad, don't you worry. So, which has been your favourite so far?' We walked together along the line as he tasted more and more, giving me his opinion on each one. After Didier joined us, I left them both to carry on without me while I went to see if Sylvie had found us a table. Dinner was about to be served and I was really ready for some food to soak up all the alcohol. I spotted her sitting at a table in the middle of the room, with my mum and Lottie alongside her.

'Ooh, it feels good to sit down,' I said, sinking into a chair. The tasting had been in full flow for over an hour. The chatter in the room was silenced by the master of ceremonies chinking his glass and announcing dinner. The men joined us, and shortly afterwards Ellie and Henri came up too, followed by a smartly dressed older, silver-haired man I'd not met before who went to join Sylvie. He greeted her with a hug as well as the usual kisses. He held her in his arms for a long moment and from the intimate look they shared, it was clear they knew each other very well. He pulled out Sylvie's chair for her before sitting down himself and greeting others around the table.

The first course was a delicious *salade* with ham, gruyère and potatoes all combined together with a sharp vinaigrette and served with one of the region's *pinot blancs*. Each course was accompanied by a different wine and one of ours was to be served next. I'd noticed there were leaflets on each table advertising different wineries so I'd run round putting some of ours out, as well. The next course was a rich *flammekueche* and Thierry had matched it with one of our older Gewurztraminers. It was a fantastic pairing and there were lots of appreciative noises from the tables around us, as well as from our own. By the time we were served dessert, I was almost full to bursting but I managed to squeeze in a little of Didier's *Kugelhopf* sponge, and a sip of his *vendange tardive* wine too, before I had to give up.

As I looked round the table at my family and friends, I marvelled at how everything had worked out so well for us all, even Lottie. She still had a way to go to sort out her new life as a single mother but I was hopeful she would get there in the end. It was a real joy to see everyone smiling at each other as we celebrated not only the successful harvest but all our relationships, as well. The band began setting up as we finished eating, and I looked forward to the dancing that would follow.

Didier

Fran's calm, beautiful face captivated me every time and tonight was the night to show her just how much I loved her. I dipped my hand into my jacket pocket for at least the tenth time that evening to check the velvet box was still there.

The first songs were all catchy numbers, designed to get everyone up on the dance floor as tradition dictated, but we were all a bit jaded after so much food and wine. Once the music got going, though, and the bottles of *Crémant d'Alsace* were served, people's spirits seemed to pick up and many of our friends and family started to dance. My mum's companion, Frédéric, asked her to dance and they walked hand in hand to the dance floor, looking for all the world as though they were meant to be together. This was the first time she had been bold enough to ask him to come to a public event with her, despite me encouraging her to do so for many months now.

'I just don't want you to think I have forgotten your father,' she said when she told me she wanted to ask Frédéric to come with her to the *Fête du Nouveau Vin*.

'I know that will never happen,' I reassured her. 'All I want is for you to be happy and if Frédéric makes you happy, then that's all that matters.'

'Let's dance, Fran,' I said, standing up and reaching out to take her hand as the first slow dance started to play.

I led her out onto the floor and as we started to dance, everyone else faded away and it was as though the music was playing for the two of us alone. I pulled Fran closer, feeling her head on my shoulder and her soft hair brushing my cheek.

'Have you had a good time this evening?' I asked.

She looked up at me, her eyes bright. 'It's been a fabulous evening. More than anything, I've just enjoyed seeing our friends and family all settled and happy.' She sighed and my heart beat a little faster.

'And what about you? Are you settled and happy?'

'This is the happiest I have ever been,' she replied. 'How about you?'

'There's only one more thing I need to make me really happy,' I said. Suddenly, my throat felt dry.

'What's that?' Her eyes met mine, filled with concern and my love for her grew even stronger.

'If you would marry me.' I said it quietly, but I knew she'd heard me because she stopped dancing right in the middle of the dance floor and her hands flew to her mouth. She swayed and I had to catch her to stop her from falling.

'Did you really just say that or did I dream it?' she whispered. I laughed softly, taking the box from my pocket and opening it to show her the ring. It had been my grandmother's engagement ring and I'd been into Strasbourg to have it cleaned up earlier in the week.

'I want you to be my wife, Fran, and I want us to be together for always. Please say yes.'

She was staring at me intently, as if she could see deep into my heart and soul.

'I'd like nothing more than to be your wife, Didier.'

She threw her arms round my neck and I pulled her in tight for a tender kiss. Suddenly, a great big cheer went up from our family and friends, who must have been waiting with bated breath to find out what Fran's answer was going to be.

When we'd finished kissing, I took out the ring and slipped it on to her waiting finger, leading to yet another round of cheering in the background. She studied the gleaming sapphire and diamond ring for a moment.

'This looks really old, it's beautiful.'

'It belonged to my grandmother. Do you like it?'

'It's stunning, and a perfect fit too. Thank you.'

We danced again and again, as the rest of the evening flew by. When we finally left, we were guided along the path by the same wonderful array of shining stars in the dark, moonlit sky.

'I'm so glad we had a second chance at being together,' Fran told me.

'Me too. I think we're really ready for it now.'

'Everyone was in such high spirits tonight. It actually felt like a night full of second chances.'

I smiled at that and drew Fran in tighter to me, knowing I would never let her escape from me again.

Fran

A few days later, I was sitting at the table in the cottage with Ellie once again, poring over the latest update to the plans from the builders. Didier was working with Thierry on the new wines every day, so it was just as well I had Ellie to help me with the building projects. Didier had confirmed to me that the new vintage was a great success and that financially the vineyard estate would do very well out of it - well enough to pay for all the building work and more, thank goodness.

'How are things with you and Henri, now you've been living together for a while?' I asked as we broke for a cup of coffee mid-morning.

'Well, it's taken some adjusting to, living with someone else, I mean. And not just anyone, but a man. A French man, at that!' She pulled a face and I didn't know if she was concealing her true feelings.

'Yes, I know what you mean. We're both quite independent, you and I, and it does take time but I'm sure you'll get there. You're not changing your mind about coming here after all, are you?' I studied her face while she composed her reply.

'No. I am glad I came here. I still like Henri just as much. It's just that it's all different, that's all. I'm so pleased you're here too, and that we're working together. I think I might have gone mad if I hadn't had this to do each day.'

'I wanted to talk to you about that, actually.' I bit my lip before going on, nervous about how she might take my proposal. She was staring at me with obvious interest.

'Go on.'

'You know by now that there's a lot of work involved in these two projects, the Visitors' Centre and the château.' She nodded as I gestured at the paperwork covering the table. 'And to be honest, I don't think I can manage it all on my own.'

'That's why I'm helping you, isn't it? I don't mind helping out for as long as you need me, Fran, really.'

'I know that, Ellie, but I don't want to take advantage of your kindness on that front. This is going to be a long-term job and if you're going to help me over months, I want you to be paid.'

Her eyes widened. 'But you really don't need to! I have my redundancy money and I'm glad to help.' She laid her hand on my arm.

'You are such a wonderful friend for saying that but it still wouldn't be right. Anyway, Didier knows the harvest has been a success now and the vineyard's finances are secure for the foreseeable future. If we get the Visitors' Centre finished and the château restored, we can start welcoming more guests and improving our profits even further, so this would be an important investment.'

'Are you offering me a job?'

'I am. I spoke to Didier and explained I'd like to put you in charge of the restoration of the château, and longer term the running of the château as accommodation for paying guests. You'd report to me and we'd continue working together, just like we are now.'

'It sounds great, and I know we're friends but are you really sure about this?'

'Yes, I've given it a lot of thought over the weekend. Eventually, I'm going to need a team of people to help me run both the Visitors' Centre and the château when we open and you'd be perfect for the château. I'd also really appreciate your help with getting everything up and running beforehand. So, what do you say?' I blew out a big breath. Ellie jumped up without speaking and flung her arms round me. She sat back down again a few minutes later, her eyes sparkling.

'This is perfect. I just can't believe my luck!'

'And there's one other thing you'll be able to help me with, as well.'

'What's that?'

'Planning the wedding, of course, as my maid of honour!'

'Oh God, this is going to be wonderful.'

I smiled at her and let my mind wander over the past couple of months as we got back to studying the plans once more. Coming back to Alsace had been a risk but now it felt more like home than ever. I had made the right decision to take the job here. This is where my heart belonged all the time and I was so glad I had been given a second chance to realise it.

THE END

Because reviews are vital in spreading the word, please leave a brief review on **Amazon** if you enjoyed reading *The Vineyard in Alsace*. Thank You!

READ AN EXCERPT FROM STARTING OVER AT THE VINEYARD IN ALSACE

BOOK 2, DOMAINE DES MONTAGNES

Chapter One

Lottie

Lottie Schell gazed out of her bedroom window at the dormant vineyard estate of Domaine des Montagnes on the hillside in the distance. At last winter was coming to an end and soon the vines would be coming to life again as the new season got underway. The vineyard had been in the Le Roy family for generations and was now run by Didier, together with Lottie's sister, Fran. Lottie smiled as she thought how close she and her sister had become since she'd found out she was unexpectedly pregnant. When she'd had to return home to Alsace from her travels, Fran had taken her in.

Lottie glanced down at her stomach in the mirror, still unable to believe it had grown quite this big, even though she'd had eight months to get used to it. She turned from side to side, amazed at how taut and shiny her skin was. Her baby was due in about four weeks' time, according to the dates her doctor and midwife had given her, and she was impatient to meet him or her after all these months. At the same time, the thought of moving the baby from the relative safety of her body to face the dangers of the outside world scared her half to death.

As if to confirm agreement with her on that thought, the baby kicked, and Lottie touched her hand gently to the spot.

'I know you're ready to come out, little one. You're in the driving seat on that, I'm afraid.'

She slipped her clothes on before negotiating the twisty staircase of Sylvie's old cottage and emerging into the living room. Sylvie Le Roy was tucking away the knitting she'd been busy with for the past few months since Lottie had moved in with her. Lottie kept up the pretence of not knowing what she was up to so it would be a surprise when Sylvie finally gave her the gift she'd been making. This was sure to be at the upcoming baby shower, which the whole village seemed to have been invited to, despite Lottie's request not to make a fuss.

'*Bonjour*, Lottie. *Ça va ce matin*?'

'Yes, I'm fine, thanks. How are you today?'

Didier's mum was only just fully straightening up after pushing herself gently out of her chair, and Lottie caught the grimace that passed across her face as she did so. Not for the first time, she worried about the added pressure she was bringing to Sylvie's life by staying with her.

'I'm absolutely fine. Now, what can I get you for breakfast, before you go to the doctor for your check-up? You need to keep your strength up.'

Lottie willed herself not to roll her eyes at the older woman's mantra. Sylvie was always quick to deflect the conversation away from her aches and pains in favour of fussing over Lottie's wellbeing and, by association, that of the baby.

'Fran will be here to take me in a minute, Sylvie, and we're going to get breakfast on the way, I promise.' She didn't want to impose on Sylvie any more than she already felt she was doing by staying in her house.

Sylvie looked sceptical, but she didn't say anything else, and luckily Fran chose that moment to appear through the back door from the garden.

'*Salut, tout le monde*,' she said with a smile as she kissed them both. 'The garden's looking beautiful, Sylvie. It's ready for spring.' She touched Sylvie affectionately on the arm and was rewarded with a pat on the cheek.

'It's my favourite time of the year, but it's always hard work keeping the garden looking so lovely during spring. Thank goodness Frédéric is helping me now, which is making a huge difference. I don't think I could manage it on my own any more.'

Sylvie missed the glance that Lottie exchanged with her sister at the mention of the man who was now openly sharing Sylvie's life, having been kept a secret for quite a long while. Lottie was glad Sylvie had a companion in her older age, especially since she'd been without her husband for several years.

'Anyway, how's my Didier and little Chlöe?' Sylvie asked Fran. 'Will I be able to come over and see my granddaughter again soon for a sleepover?'

'Yes, of course, she'd love that. We'll sort something out later today, shall we?'

Lottie envied Fran for the easy way she had with Didier's mum, and she was glad they got on so well. She only hoped that things would work out as well for her one day, but whereas Fran was about to get married to the love of her life, Lottie was on her own and facing an uncertain future. With a great effort, she hauled herself back from her negative thoughts. Right now, all she needed was to give birth safely to her baby and to make a success of her new life as a single mum, and she was determined to do it.

Once she was safely in the car with Fran and they were on their way to the doctor's in Strasbourg, Lottie blew out a sigh of relief.

'Is everything okay?' Fran asked as she drove.

'Yes, I'm nervous about this check-up, that's all. I want to be sure everything's all right with the baby, with the due date being so close. Thanks for taking me, Fran.' Lottie didn't admit she was nervous about the impending birth, too. There was no way out of it now.

'You don't need to thank me. That's what sisters are for. I'm sure everything will be fine. How did it go with Thierry when you told him I was taking you today?'

'He wasn't very pleased about it.' Lottie shrugged. Although she'd been seeing Thierry for several months, it was still early days for them. 'He's so protective of me, which is great when it's not even his baby, but sometimes he can be so bossy.' She laughed despite her frustration.

'It shows he cares for you, even if he overdoes it a bit at times.'

Lottie chose to change the subject. 'How are things with you and Didier? Any more news about your wedding plans?' Since leaving her job in London and returning home to Alsace to work at the vineyard, everything in Fran's life had finally fallen into place.

Fran's face fell. 'No. We're too busy with the vineyard at the moment. It's not only all the work that needs doing in the vineyard itself, it's all the building work in the new Visitors' Centre and the restoration of the château. There's hardly time for me and Didier, with all that going on. And then, of course, we want to spend time with Chlöe.'

Fran bit her lip, and Lottie waited for her older sister to reveal what the real source of her worry was.

'The thing is, Lottie, Didier and I have been trying for a baby of our own for a good few months now, but I'm still not pregnant.'

'Oh, Fran, I'm sorry. There's me, having fallen pregnant with no trouble at all. It hardly seems fair for you to be struggling, when you and Didier are so in love and settled together.'

'That's the way it is, I suppose, but it's hard to keep on hoping month after month. I can't even think about a wedding when this is so much on my mind.'

'What does Didier think about it all?'

'Didier definitely wants more children, but as he already has Chlöe, he's not too worried about it. But I want us to have a child of our own, even though I love Chlöe as if she were my own daughter. Right now, it feels like it might never happen for me.'

Lottie's heart ached for her sister. Just when she'd got back together with Didier and everything seemed perfect, something else was stopping her from being happy.

Thierry

As he strode up the slope from his house on the other side of the estate, Thierry Bernard cast his critical winemaker's eye over the vineyard. Spring was his favourite time of the year, and he was looking forward to seeing the vines coming out of their resting phase after the harsh winter months. Buds would soon be appearing and the vines would start spreading along their canes, looking for the sunlight to help them grow. There was even some sunshine today, at the beginning of March, and although it was feeble by summer standards, he appreciated the warmth on his face.

He pushed his mop of dark hair out of his eyes and squinted against the sun. When he reached the top of the hill, he glanced across to the cottage to see if Fran's car was there. He wanted to catch up with Lottie after her appointment at the doctor's to see how things had gone for her. She'd not told him in so many words – when did she ever tell him what was on her mind? – but now that her due date was so near, her anxiety about the baby's health was increasing.

Fran's car wasn't there, so he continued towards the courtyard where the estate office was, planning to go and ask Didier when he expected them to be back. As he emerged through the archway that led to the courtyard, Fran was pulling in, and he was glad to see Lottie smiling in the front seat.

'*Bonjour*, Fran, Lottie. How did it go?'

'Everything's fine, thank goodness.' Lottie beamed at him and he sensed her relief.

'Are you walking back to Sylvie's now?' he asked. 'I can come with you if you like. I have some things I need to get in the village.'

'Okay. Thanks again for taking me, Fran. See you soon. Take care, won't you?' They kissed each other goodbye, and Lottie turned to Thierry to follow the path back to the village.

'How are you feeling in yourself?' he asked, taking her hand as they walked at Lottie's waddling pace along the path.

'I'm relieved after speaking to the doctor, but he said it could be even more than four weeks before the baby actually comes. I'm not sure I can wait that much longer.' She rolled her eyes and Thierry chuckled. 'It's all right for you,' she said. 'You're not the one having to carry all this extra weight around.'

'I know it must be hard for you, but it's not so long to go now, and then you will have your baby with you.' He paused for a moment and then continued, 'Have you thought any more about my suggestion?'

'I have, but I'm happy at Sylvie's for the time being. And as I've said before, I can look after myself, and the baby, when it comes. I wish you could accept this and not keep asking me to move in with you.'

Lottie blushed as she finished speaking, which confirmed Thierry's thoughts. It was his turn to roll his eyes before cutting straight to the point she was trying to hide. 'I want to help, and I have plenty of room in my house for you and the baby, whereas at Sylvie's cottage it must be a squash, even with only the two of you living there. And I'm sure it's awkward for you knowing that, because you're there, Chlöe and Frédéric can't stay over.' He paused to let his words sink in. 'I don't understand why you keep fighting me on this when it makes perfect sense to me. It's as if you don't trust me.'

Lottie stopped on the path and turned to face him. 'Look, Thierry, we've discussed this. It's nothing to do with me not trusting you. After I had to move out of Fran's last year, I went to live at Sylvie's rather than moving in with you because I don't think it's fair for you to take on the responsibility for someone else's child, especially when you and I have only been seeing each other for a few months. It is a squash, that's true, but we've managed so far.'

Lottie started walking again, rubbing her lower back with one hand as they continued on their way into the village.

'But in that time, six months nearly, we've... we've developed feelings for each other, so there's no reason for us not to be together. We'll get to know each other more over time, and especially if you move in with me.' He wanted so much to tell her he loved her, but he was afraid he'd scare her off if he did, so he kept quiet.

'We don't need to rush this, Thierry. I want us to take our time getting to know each other before we take this next big step. I still know very little about you or your past, or about Nicole's death, for example. All that makes me feel you're still holding on to so many emotions you're not ready to share yet.'

Thierry turned the wrought-iron handle to open the back-garden gate and stood back to let Lottie go through first. She sat down on one of the wooden benches in Sylvie's beautifully tended garden, and Thierry took his place next to her. He rubbed his temple, his dark brows drawing into a frown as he wrestled with what he was trying to say.

'Why would you want me to talk to you about my wife? You didn't know her, so it would feel weird for me to talk about what happened between us with you.'

'I think the fact you don't understand why says everything. You still have a lot of pent-up emotion and grief to deal with,' she said softly. She reached out and stroked his stubbled cheek with the palm of her hand, and his body lit up at her touch.

'I still don't understand why any of this would stop you from moving in with me,' he retorted, turning reluctantly away from her and folding his arms as he stretched out his long legs on the still dewy grass.

Lottie laughed at his exasperation. 'I'm independent, I know that, but I have a right to do what I want to do, for me and the baby. After everything that's happened to me, and finding myself on my own now, I need to feel sure before making any more decisions.' She paused and he glanced at her to show her he was listening.

'Please will you think about it?' He took her hands in his. 'I want to be with you, and this arrangement with you living here doesn't make our relationship any easier. I can only see that getting worse when the baby comes, and there'll be even less room for you all at Sylvie's.'

Lottie opened her mouth to reply.

'No, don't say anything now,' Thierry interrupted. 'Just promise me you'll give it some thought.' He leaned forward and kissed her gently on the lips. 'I'll leave you to get on.' With that, he slipped back through the gate, shutting it firmly behind him, and disappeared away down the street.

ALSO BY JULIE STOCK

From Here to You series

Before You - Prequel - From Here to You

From Here to Nashville - Book 1 - From Here to You

Over You - Book 2 - From Here to You

Finding You - Book 3 - From Here to You

From Here to You series

Domaine des Montagnes series

First Chance - Prequel - Domaine des Montagnes

Starting Over at the Vineyard in Alsace - Book 2 - Domaine des Montagnes

A Leap of Faith at the Vineyard in Alsace - Book 3 - Domaine des Montagnes

Standalone

The Bistro by Watersmeet Bridge

Bittersweet - 12 Short Stories for Modern Life

ABOUT THE AUTHOR

Julie Stock writes contemporary feel-good romance from around the world: novels, novellas and short stories.

She published her début novel, *From Here to Nashville*, in 2015, after starting to write as an escape from the demands of her day job as a teacher. *A Leap of Faith at the Vineyard in Alsace* is her latest book, and the third in the Domaine des Montagnes series set on a vineyard.

Julie is now a full-time author, and loves every minute of her writing life. When not writing, she can be found reading, her favourite past-time, running, a new hobby, or cooking up a storm in the kitchen, glass of wine in hand.

Julie is a member of The Society of Authors.

Julie is married and lives with her family in Cambridgeshire in the UK.

Sign up for Julie's free author newsletter at **www.julie-stock.co.uk.**

ACKNOWLEDGMENTS

It was a long journey to publication for my debut novel, *From Here to Nashville,* and it's been an equally long one for this second book! In between the two, I have spent a lot of time wondering what it is I want to get out of my writing. In finally deciding to self-publish this book, I realised that at last, I know what that is.

I would like to thank my writing friends, Kate and Ros, for their unwavering friendship and support over these past few years. I count myself very lucky to be making new friends at this time in my life.

I have been a member of the Romantic Novelists' Association since January 2014 now and I have been lucky enough to have so much help and support from many RNA writers on my writing and publishing journey. Thank you to all the RNA members I have met and come to know over the past few years for your generosity of spirit. It really is wonderful to be part of such a professional and fabulous organisation.

Thank you also to everyone who continues to follow me on Twitter, on my Facebook page and on my blog. I 'meet' new people all the time and sometimes, I get to meet them in real life too!

Made in the USA
Monee, IL
07 June 2022